GRIFFIN HAYES

HIVE
THE COMPLETE COLLECTION

Trebor Books

Trebor Books

ISBN: 978-0-9918881-8-4
eISBN: 978-0-9918881-9-1

Cover design by Conzpiracy Digital Arts
Edited by Andrea Harding

Also by Griffin Hayes

Malice
Dark Passage
Primal Shift Volume 1
Primal Shift Volume 2
Hive: The Complete Collection
Night Terror
Nightfall

Author Note

The Hive series was conceived at the end of 2011 as I sat on a beach in Thailand, braving hundred and ten degree heat, and trying to imagine what a fresh take on the zombie apocalypse would look like. I set out to write a story unlike anything I'd ever seen, told in the distinctive, and I hope endearing, voice of your narrator Azina. She doesn't put up with crap from anyone and yet her wit only masks a sensitive side at odds with the post-apocalyptic world around her.

I want to send out a quick thank you to everyone who read through those early drafts. To my editor Andrea for her eagle eyes and lightning fast turn-around time. To Conzpiracy for the awesome cover and as always to you, the readers, for taking a chance on a little known writer.

Now that that's over with, it's time to buckle up. Remember to keep your arms and legs inside the vehicle at all times. It's gonna be a bumpy ride!

Griffin Hayes

-1-

"Whoever sealed this opening did it in one hell of a hurry," I say, planting my hand firmly on the curve of my waist. My repeater's slung over my right shoulder, its weight digging into my back. That's good, because I know it's right where it should be. I can have it in my hands in well under a second if I need to.

Bron steps forward. Nearly three hundred pounds of raw muscle, but it's the robotic implants that usually draw most of the attention. Especially his arms, two polished chrome killing machines. "Looks more like a barricade to me."

The others stir uncomfortably and I know it doesn't have a damn thing to do with his thick Norse accent.

Pennies is fiddling with the cuff of his tunic. His eyes keep dropping to my breasts and I'm a second away from knocking his teeth straight into his nasal cavity. "What do you think they were trying to keep out?" he asks.

Ret, my second in command, is sitting on a nearby rock, watching a dark patch of clouds roll in. He's wiry and handsome, and more than one fellow Mercenary has taken those traits as a sign of weakness. A mistake they'll never have the chance of repeating.

"Have a look at the way those metal beams are welded together," he says coolly, still watching those clouds, low and heavy on the horizon. "They weren't trying to keep anything out. Whoever did this wanted to keep something inside, and badly."

There's a narrow opening below the tangle of beams, no more than few feet high. Keeper Oleg braces a hand on his knee and bends down to study the hole. "This was where the Prospectors entered from," he proclaims. "I'm sure of it."

1

Yeah, no shit it is. That's the thought running through my head, right along with a savage thirst that's been building from the moment we left Sotercity. But as long as The Keepers are footing the bill, I don't have much choice but to keep a lid on it.

Keepers of Knowledge. They've been around since long before I was born. Formed during the end times – an era beyond memory, now – when an advanced civilization slowly self-destructed. They are tasked with gathering whatever scraps of knowledge and technology they can get their hands on.

As a child, I remember the Keepers telling stories about cities swarming with hordes of monsters. They'd swept across the planet like a plague of locusts with an insatiable appetite. A single bite was enough to kill you or turn you into one of them. The Keepers said it had been a chemical in the water, supposed to calm the people down. But something had gone terribly wrong. It had taken years to destroy the monsters, and by then there wasn't much left to save.

Civilizations rose and fell, and great ones usually died by their own hands. That's about all I know of history. All that really matters, I suppose.

Oleg stands watching me, then waves his hand dismissively at my men: Bron, Ret, Jinx –my temperamental explosives expert – and Sneak, my tunnel rat. "Hiring Mercenaries was Prior Skuld's idea, not mine. Look around you. We're surrounded by ruins just waiting to fall on people's heads. A rescue mission requires the proper tools."

Oleg is name-dropping now. He thinks that because the Prior runs The Keepers and The Keepers run Sotercity, we're supposed to be scared.

Bron clasps a massive beam in the jaws of one of his gleaming, metallic arms and lifts it with ease. "Is this tool good enough?"

2

I put a hand on Bron's firm shoulder and he lowers the beam. Tact is in order, not quick tempers.

"Four Prospectors are missing," I say, scanning the tiny hole that had been cut into the barricade, "and this is their last known location. Doesn't look like much more than your run-of-the-mill, shake-and-bake operation. We do 'em all the time. Head in, locate your boys and then hightail it out. One thousand USC each, ten for me since I'm leading this crew, and we all go our merry way."

USC. Units of sodium chloride. Fancy talk for tiny pouches of salt. Just don't get caught out in the rain with it or you're liable to lose a fortune.

I pause to let this sink in, even though I'm sure he knows most of this already. "Besides," I say. "Prior Skuld already signed the papers. If you think our fee is high now, just wait till you see what it costs to cancel. Now, as far as your partner goes, if you wanna bring Pennies along so he can keep an eye out for anything valuable, fine by me. But my team works fast and we work alone, so you all better keep up 'cause Bron's not gonna carry you."

Bron flashes a mouthful of brown teeth.

Oleg is spearing me with his icy stare, and we hear a voice shouting in the distance.

"Wait for me! Please! Please, wait!"

Ret lifts a pair of binoculars. "Azina, we got company. Grinder from Sotercity, by the looks of it."

I grit my teeth. "Perfect."

A Grinder is a term of endearment Ret coined for the hundreds of maintenance men laboring day in and day out to keep Sotercity from drowning in its own shit and dying of dehydration.

Apparently, since the world went sliding down the crapper, things have become much simpler. At least that's what the billboards say.

Come to Sotercity for a Taste of the Good Old Days.

3

There's something here for everyone. You got yourself a big brain? Join The Keepers of Knowledge. What's that, you say? You're a greedy bastard? Become a Trader like Pennies. You got a fetish for squeezing into tiny holes looking for artifacts? I understand The Keepers are always looking for new Prospectors. Oh I get it. You like to work with your hands. Grunt work for little or no pay. Got it, not a problem, Public Works goes through Grinders like some people go through dirty tunics. But no, you want it all, don't you? Then find yourself a trusty weapon – they're lying around all over the place – and start freelancing as a hired gun.

Sounds like one of those damn brochures they're handing out on every corner, I know. But it's true.

Ret's still got the binoculars to his eyes. "It's Glave," Ret says, snarling. "Rosaline's husband."

I snatch the binoculars and watch the man stumble over a boulder and fall flat on his face. I turn to Oleg. "A panicked husband searching for his Prospector wife is the last thing we need. Send him home."

Oleg chuckles. "Worry doesn't suit you, Azina. You said so yourself; this job is a cake walk. The Keepers are paying you a lot of money. I'm afraid you'll just have to roll with the punches."

I sigh. So much for tact. I wanna spit so bad, but my mouth is too dry.

-2-

We squeeze through the tiny hole. Oleg curses under his breath as he snags and tears his long, crimson robe on a nail. I'm behind him, cursing myself at what an unwieldy group we are. Sightseers and tourists mean this is turning into a babysitting job, not a rescue mission, and I'm tempted to call the whole thing off; but the truth is I need the money more than I care to admit. I duck under a cracking concrete slab and I'm hit right away by the silence.

The place is quiet. Too quiet.

"Gimme a light!" I shout, hoping to drive away the ominous feeling that's creeping into my bones.

Sneak scurries up and hands me a florescent glow stick. I bend it back and forth until it snaps. The room fills with glowing green light. We're in a sewer system; I can tell by the concrete walls and rusted metal pipes overhead. Relics from a bygone era. Murky, brown water sloshes about our feet. The smell is too foul for Pennies, and he buries his nose into the neck of his tunic.

Bron lets out a bellowing laugh. "Maybe you'd prefer to be back home, counting your money. To me this smells like breakfast."

Just then Bron stumbles over a dead rat and lets out a noise that sounds like a whimper. Now Pennies is the one laughing. "Looks like you found your breakfast after all," the Trader says.

Bron throws Pennies a menacing look. The big man doesn't like it nearly as much when the joke is on him.

I stop in front of the dead rat. *Or is it a cat?*

Whatever this once was, it isn't just dead, something has turned it inside out.

"Do you think one of the Prospectors might've done

this?" Oleg asks.

Ret shakes his head. "Not unless they've taken to eating the uncooked flesh of sewer rats."

We don't get more than a few yards before we find more mangled corpses. None are larger than small dogs and all have been ripped apart. A few are little more than mounds of bones peeking out from the putrid water.

Jinx wipes the sweat from his brow. He's got enough explosives in his pack to drop and seal this tunnel for the next thousand years, and from here it looks like he's fighting the urge to do just that. "These floating meat bags were caught and killed before the Prospectors cut their way in here," Jinx says.

For once, I have to admit he doesn't sound so sure of himself. "Why's that?" I ask.

"Well, for one, we ain't found nothin' bigger than a house cat. Which is strange considering there's no shortage of wolves and cougars roaming through No Man's Land. Surely some of 'em would've wandered in."

Bron cracks his own glow stick. "But some of these are half-eaten."

"Maybe there's something wrong with the meat," I say, diverting my eyes from the pulverized flesh. "Look at where these rats are living. Drinking this shit-water all day, I can guarantee they don't taste like the chicken we're used to in Sotercity."

"Did you have to mention chicken?" Ret asks. "I can hear Bron's stomach rumbling from here. How many full chickens was it you ate at the fair last year? Twelve?"

"Twenty-six," Bron mumbles. "I was in bed with a bellyache for a week. That Dehlia, I swear she rubs some kind of drug into those little chicken bodies."

I pull to a stop. A clump of what looks like hair rests on a dry patch of concrete. Strapped to my back is a twenty-eight-inch Katana, and I nudge it from its sheath and use the tip to scoop up the mound. I hold it up high

6

and the others look on in disgust. There's some kind of netting underneath and the hair is stuck to it. I look at Ret, and he moves in beside me. "What do you make of this?"

He shakes his head. "I'd say someone was scalped, but I don't see any flesh or any knife marks."

Oleg snickers behind us. "It's a wig."

"A what?"

Oleg sighs. In his world, Mercenaries are nothing more than barbarians, and it's starting to show. I pretend not to notice.

"Before the end times, wealthy citizens bought hair if they didn't have any of their own or if they wanted to change the way they looked."

Bron erupts into thunderous laughter and rubs the smooth top of Pennies' head. "Why don't we give it to Pennies? His head's as bald as a baby's bare ass."

Pennies swats Bron's thick hand away.

"Could it have belonged to one of the Prospectors?" I ask.

Oleg snickers and now I really want to kick his head in. "You're looking at a museum piece. Judging by the cut, it probably belonged to an upper-class woman."

"A wealthy woman who liked to hang around in sewers?" Ret asks. "Makes perfect sense. Anybody else wondering what we've got ourselves into?"

Something catches Pennies' eye. He reaches down and comes up with two twinkling stones, each hanging from a tiny hook.

"Earrings," Oleg proclaims. "And by the looks of them, they're quite expensive."

Pennies' eyes are shining. He slips the jewels into the pocket of his tunic.

"Leave it to Pennies to sniff out the valuable stuff. You're lucky we're on a rescue mission, or I'd have to confiscate those."

7

"Don't be bitter, Bron," Ret warns. "You'll get yours. Maybe hanging out in sewers was a favorite pastime for rich people back before the world sent itself to hell."

"Yeah, or maybe Pennies just found the only good stuff in the whole stinkin' place."

I trudge through the muck and the bickering fades behind me, while an uneasy feeling that I can't quite shake builds inside me. Mutilated rats, killed for the sake of killing. Rich people running around in putrid sewer systems, leaving artifacts behind. It isn't making a whole lot of sense. A little voice is telling me to turn around. It's low and muted, but it's there and I usually listen to that voice; but then another chimes in, and this new voice is talking about a large sum of money I owe and the cost of forfeiting payment. In the silence, the second voice is louder.

-3-

I raise my hand and the group halts. The tunnel breaks off in two different directions up ahead. Ret comes and crouches by the foul-smelling water. He's the best Tracker I've ever worked with, but in a watery cesspool, I don't hold high hopes he'll come up with much of a trail.

Sneak's looking at me and I sign to her with the fingers of my right hand. She races off down the tunnel and disappears.

Chained to a Trader's cart. That's where I found Sneak. She was mute and had the body of a child, though her eyes told me she was at least twice as old as she looked. The Trader, a prick named Lars, had been in the throes of beating her for snatching a handful of bread from his duffel bag. She was quick and agile, and by all accounts she didn't deserve to spend the rest of her life tied to a cart, especially one owned by a Trader who was too dimwitted to see the girl's true talents.

Somewhere, a rumor had started that I'd shoved that Trader's prick into his gaping mouth right before I'd put a round between his eyes. Maybe I'd told the story that way myself, a time or two. Hard to keep track, sometimes. This new world that had emerged wasn't exactly kind to us women, if you know what I mean. Regardless, earning your right to lead a motley band of Mercs always starts with rule number one: Never show your soft side.

The far less heroic truth is that I'd bought Sneak's freedom for fifteen thousand USC. Which is why I desperately need the ten thousand I'm getting from this job. For a reason that never made much sense to me, a purchased slave has the same rights as an earthworm. A slave freed in a bankruptcy sale, on the other hand, has all the rights in the world. There's logic in there somewhere, I guess. I'm just never able to find it.

"They went right," Pennies says, pointing, and you can see it in his face he's still glowing from the bejeweled earrings he found earlier.

"What makes you so sure?" Ret asks, looking skeptical.

Pennies points to a white hash mark on the dirty tunnel wall. "A good Prospector always marks his route. Just common sense."

I slide two fingers into my mouth and let out a sharp whistle for Sneak. We continue down the sewer tunnel on the right.

Glave is pulling up the rear, pointing into the darkness behind us. "What about–"

"Sneak?" I finish.

Glave lets out a skittish cry as Sneak runs a hand up his back. Bron's bellowing laugh nudges a smile onto my face.

"Lucky for you, Sneak don't have a mind for thievin'," Bron says, "or she'd have your wallet before you knew it was gone."

In the distance, broken patches of green light dance around an archway. Twisted remnants of an old, metal door are lying askew on the ground. Across the front, letters are inscribed in the old tongue.

Jinx is fingering the pin on one of the concussion grenades tied to his belt. "That dead language always spooks me," he says.

"Oleg, what does it say?"
He studies the letters. They're peeling and frayed with time. "Boiler Room. Leads to an old boiler room." He must see our blank stares. With as much patience as a cranky old school master, he explains. "Pipes and large machinery that were used for heating. The larger the

10

building, the larger the boiler room. Electronic computing devices were doing most of the work by the end."

"Thanks for the history lesson," Bron says. "But what does it mean?"

I step inside to the suffocating odor of oil and grease. "It means we're heading in the right direction."

-4-

We find the body lying face down beside what looks like a giant, black water heater. Glave pushes through us and collapses before the body, sobbing.

"Bron," I snap.

The big man scoops Glave up by his tunic. Glave's arms and legs cycle wildly as he's lifted out of the way. Oleg is beside the body, and Jinx and a reluctant Pennies help turn it over.

"Calm yourself, Glave," Oleg says. "It's not your wife. Guy's face is covered in blood, but even I can tell this Prospector's male."

"His legs!" Pennies shouts. "Where are they?"

Jinx nods. "Must've been blown off."

Strips had been torn from the man's tunic and tied around the stumps to stem the bleeding. White shards of bone protrude from each stump. His legs, or what's left of them, are hard to look at.

"Damn fools," Jinx spits. "Must've happened when they blew the door."

Ret kneels down next to the man. "Hold on! He's not dead."

"What nonsense is this?" Oleg asks.

Ret might not be as learned and knowledgeable as Oleg, but he's the medic for our group. There's no one's judgment I trust more, but right now I have to seem impartial. "Can we save him?" I ask.

"Hard to say." He's looking up at me and it's clear as day he knows I'm playing the politician. "Guy's got a pulse. It's faint as hell, but it's there."

Oleg has an indignant look on his face. It's obvious he's not a big fan of being shown up, especially by his inferiors.

Ret pulls the six-inch knife from the sheath on his vest and holds it under the Prospector's nose. The blade fogs. Oleg storms off. The old man's pride isn't sitting well with me. That sort of thinking down here can get people hurt or killed.

Ret gets to work tending to the man's wounded legs. It isn't long before he waves me over. "I've never seen anything like this before." His voice is low, and I lean in, and he must see the puzzled look on my face. "Jinx was dead wrong," he continues. "His legs weren't blown off in an explosion. They were eaten."

-5-

"Oh, come now," Oleg starts. "The Prospector stepped on an explosive. Didn't your own man say that?"

"He did." I concede. "But the bones sticking out from his legs have obvious teeth marks."

Ret stands. "And that's not all." He's holding the twelve-shot pistol that Prospectors use to fend off thieves and wild dogs. "His gun is empty."

Pennies looks shaken. "Bullets aren't cheap," says the Trader. "No self-respecting Prospector I know would fire a shot unless he had to."

"Spoken like a true cheapskate," Bron adds, flashing those rotting chompers of his.

Oleg looks hesitant. "Let's not draw any hasty conclusions. For all we know, this man could have been shooting at the rats gnawing on his legs."

"You mean the same rats turned inside out not fifty yards back?" Jinx replies.

There's a look on Oleg's face that says he doesn't care one bit for Jinx's sarcasm.

This bickering is really pissing me off. "Is he stable enough to move? Yes or no?"

Ret hesitates and then nods.

"Bron, stop bothering Pennies and carry this guy."

Bron grumbles and scoops up the Prospector, as if he were a sack filled with goose down.

I realize I'm about to err on the side of caution, and I signal to Ret and Jinx. They draw their weapons: a multi-barreled grenade launcher for Jinx, and a hundred-round automatic shotgun for Ret.

Ret says he came upon the shotgun in a camouflaged bunker in the desert. It was lying in the skeletonized hands of a man dead more than a hundred years. The bastard was sitting on more ammo than he'd ever need, and perhaps out of despair or loneliness, he'd used it on himself.

It's hard to say what drives men in desperate times, and harder still to judge the decisions they make. In his day, the world outside was swarming with the worst kind of bloodthirsty monsters. Those must have been bleak times indeed, and thinking about it now, I'm still not entirely sure how humanity managed to pull through.

The man in Bron's arms starts to moan, and I can't tell if he's about to keel over or wake up from whatever Ret gave him to ease the pain. "Can someone tell this guy to shut up?" Bron pleads.

Ret smirks. "I doubt those arms of yours make a comfortable bed."

The Prospector's cheeks are dark and sunken. His body begins to convulse. "I don't think our friend here's going to make it," Bron says.

There's a dusty control panel up ahead, and Ret points to it. "Take him over there and I'll have another look at him."

I wipe off a deep layer of dirt and grime with my sleeve, and Bron plops the Prospector on a bed of old buttons and levers. His body is flopping about like a fish out of water. With one hand, Bron holds him down.

"I don't understand," Ret says. There's a disturbed look on his face I've never seen before. "His legs, they're healing."

I look and see that he's right. Since we'd examined him, the loose flaps of shredded flesh around the man's severed legs had fused together. Only the tiniest hint of bone is still showing. I look at Oleg. "What do you make of this?"

Oleg comes so close his nose is almost buried in the man's festering stump. "I need more light," he demands.

I bring the glow stick closer. He stands there for a moment, transfixed. "Magnificent!" he exclaims. "I didn't think it was possible. The wounds are closing before my eyes."

Jinx is shaking his head. "I find that hard to believe."

"See for yourself," Oleg says, a defensive look on his

face.

Jinx turns to survey the perimeter. He's not crazy about blood, and is too proud to tell Oleg anything of the sort. An odd sort of affliction, given that his chosen profession centers around blowing people apart.

I snap myself back into the moment. "So he'll live, then."

Ret and Oleg both nod.

Bron groans.

"We need to take him back to Sotercity right away." There's a fire in Oleg's eyes, and for a moment, he almost looks younger.

"What about the others?" I protest.

"We'll come back."

"Rosaline can't wait that long." It's Glave, and he has an almost feral glint in his eye. "Look at the one guy we've found so far. His legs were eaten off, and you want me to believe my wife can just wait?"

"Glave's right," I say. "No one's leaving. For all we know, there are three other Prospectors in much worse shape."

Oleg's face sharpens into a scowl. He's about to raise another objection when the wounded Prospector's eyes snap open. Two glowing, white orbs cut streamers of light through the darkness. There's a gurgling or a growling sound coming from the back of his throat. His mouth stretches open and reveals a foul, blackened gullet. In a flash, his hands swing wildly to grab the first thing in reach. It's my luck that thing just happens to be my head. The Prospector's vise-like grip is ripping my skull from the rest of my body. Thunderbolts of pain fire through my neck and head.

My arms hammer down into the soft bends of his elbows, but nothing happens. I see what he's trying to do. He's pulling my face toward his festering jaws. They smell like rancid meat. Bron closes his metal hands around the Prospector's neck and squeezes. The sound of snapping bone is sharp and brutal. Blood bursts through his mechanical fingers. A thick and syrupy blood-soup pours from the Prospector's mouth, but he's not letting go.

I pull the Katana off my back and swing it down on the man's head in a single, graceful arc. The blade slices through bone and brain, and stops when it makes contact with Bron's hand. Twisting the blade, I split the Prospector's head in two and it falls to the floor.

I stagger backwards, fighting the urge to rub the sides of my head. I don't want to let on how much it really hurts. For a moment, everything looks like a shadowy blur.

Ret rushes to my side. He's checking to see if I'm okay. "Bron, what took you so goddamn long?"

Bron's looking down at his blood-soaked hand in disbelief. "They usually drop when I hear that crunch." A second later, Ret's barbed comment seems to register. "I didn't see you do much of anything, pretty boy."

"Because I didn't have a shot."

"Well how about next time a guy with glowing eyes tries to—"

"Stop it!" I shout. "Both of you!"

The two men silence at once.

"Can anyone tell me what the hell just happened?" I eyeball each of them. "Ret, did you give him an adrenaline shot?"

Ret throws his arms in the air. "Don't look at me. All

I did was tie off some tourniquets."

Bron is flicking a lump of flesh off his hand. "I don't get it either. I was sure I felt his neck snap."

I sheath my Katana. "Oleg?"

The old man looks shaken. He's mumbling to himself, and I'm sure he's praying to Newton or Copernicus or one of the other gods they're always blabbing on about.

Pennies has wedged himself behind some old heating pipes about fifteen feet away. He holds out a hand to Sneak, and she slaps his hand away.

Jinx grabs the Trader by the arm and pulls him to his feet. "She doesn't like your kind," he says with a wink. "Don't take it too personal. And if I were you, I'd keep my eye on those jewels of yours."

Pennies pats himself furiously and checks for the earrings. It's only when he plucks them from his pocket a second later that a look of calm settles over him.

I spear Oleg with my eyes. "Those old stories The Keepers are always so eager to tell about cities swarming with monsters. What did they call them?"

"The Volgoroth." Oleg's voice sounds grim.

As a young girl, I remember playing Monsters and Keepers with the other kids. My father used to call them shitsacks, and I was never quite sure why. You didn't need to hear more than a few stories to realize these things had been soulless killers, and zombie – or Zee for short – seemed as good a name as any.

I see a light go on in Ret's eyes. "Volgoroth. You make 'em sound like a race of people when all they were was a disease."

Oleg opens his mouth to say something, but I cut him off. "A disease that was wiped out. I mean, that's what I'd been taught as a child, that the hordes of Volgoroth had been driven back and exterminated."

There's a rusted chair beside a row of old pipes and

Oleg settles into it. "Driven back yes, and untold numbers of them were destroyed."

"But not all of 'em," Jinx adds.

"The cities." Oleg's eyes look tired, as if he wants nothing more than to sleep for a hundred years. "That was where they came from, and in the end, that was where many of them were driven. Our ancestors believed that the people infected by the tainted water would eventually die off. As far as I'm concerned, they have." Oleg's head sinks into his hands, and it's clear that he's not nearly as convinced as he lets on.

-8-

Even in the dim light of the control room, I can see Glave's hands trembling.

"I don't know why we're wasting time on this," he complains. "My wife could be just around the next corner. Isn't this supposed to be a rescue mission, or do I have to go it alone?"

"Be my guest," Bron says, sweeping his arm to show Glave the way.

Glave mutters under his breath and storms ahead.

"We should follow him," Ret whispers in my ear. "We can't let him wander off, even if he is just an idiot Grinder."

I agree.

As we make ready to leave, Bron flings the Prospector's corpse into the corner. What just happened has affected us all. I can see the fear on Pennies' face, and Oleg is showing signs of fatigue. I'd bet the old man hasn't walked this much in his whole life. I motion forward and we press on. There's an access tunnel ahead.

Glave's there, standing in the damp passage, crying. I want to reach out and comfort him. I know what it's like to lose someone you love. Inside, he's still soft. Hasn't built up a hard shell yet. He will, eventually. Emotional pain and heartache in large enough doses act like anesthesia for the soul. I try to tell myself the men that follow me aren't my family, that Sneak means nothing to me, but I'm not having much luck believing it.

The access tunnel seems to go on forever. Framed light fixtures are built into the wall, but it's clear they stopped working years ago. Jinx is saying something behind me.

"We need to protect our rear."

21

I agree. "What do you propose?"

He holds a proximity mine over my shoulder. "But we'll only use a few of 'em," he promises. "That way, anything tries to sneak up on us will have one hell of a surprise."

Jinx has been itching to play with his toys since we arrived, but he has a point. I'm not sure what drove that Prospector mad, but the eerie glow from his eyes is still fresh in my mind, along with the throbbing headache that's accompanying my thirst. I should have brought more than a flask of whiskey. I got cocky. Again.

Up ahead I see something. The others are close behind and I can hear Bron grunting. He's about to start complaining again, which is good because I only worry about him when he's quiet.

The tunnel comes to an end, and from here it looks like it opens into a much larger space. We haven't seen a sign of anyone since the boiler room, and I'm getting worried we won't be finding much more than a pile of corpses.

Ret, Bron and I draw our weapons. Even Pennies is clutching his little semi-automatic pistol. Jinx is behind us, setting his proximity mines. I take a second to make sure everyone's accounted for and we move on.

We enter an open area with high ceilings, once covered with paintings, now blackened and crumbling. Just ahead is a thick, wooden railing which overlooks several lower levels. On either side of us are abandoned shops. Mounds of dirty and rotting clothes lay fallen near each entrance. Used to be some kind of indoor market, is my guess.

"Hey get a load of this," Bron calls out. He's holding what looks like a matted coat made from animal fur. "This whole place is full of 'em."

"Bron, quite messing around," I say, "and keep your eyes peeled for those Prospectors. Where are we, Oleg?"

Oleg tears his eyes way from Bron's windfall and scans our surroundings. "Looks like we've entered a shopping mall."

Ret and the others throw him puzzled looks. Oleg points above one of the shops to a series of damaged signs with missing letters. "Louis Vuitton." And then others. "Ralph Lauren... Chanel. These were places women of society and the well-to-do shopped for clothing and goods. During certain times of the year, thousands of people would be here at the same time, rushing around and fighting each other to buy gifts."

"Touching," I say, "but it still doesn't explain why Prospectors were snooping around in here. Traders, like Pennies, I get, 'cause they're only interested in turning a profit. But Prospectors work for Keepers, and Keepers gather knowledge and technology. So, why would a group of Prospectors risk their lives to find a bunch of old stores?"

"I'm not sure," he says, and I can smell the lie from here.

I look at Glave. His wife was one of them, and maybe he knows something, but he's got a beaten look on his face and that tells me he's not gonna be much help.

Bron is pointing to a shop with glass cases flanking the doorway. "What's the name of that one?"

Oleg squints. "Cartier. Why?"

"Cause Pennies just ran inside."

Crap! I knew this was gonna happen. Another reason I hate Traders, they're always running off to fill their pockets. "Dammit, wait here," I bark, and take off running. I can see my hands wrapping around Pennies' scrawny neck, shaking him senseless. I sure as hell didn't sign up for this.

Broken glass crunches under my feet as I clear the doorway. I'm not sure what Cartier used to sell, but it must have been worth a ton for Pennies to run off on his own.

Rows and rows of display cases. That's what I see. Most of them are intact, but there's too much dust and debris to tell what I'm looking at. Ten feet away, I catch Pennies' head pop up from behind one of the cases. He's trying to shatter the display glass with the butt of his pistol and I can tell he's afraid of getting a shard in his eye. Pussy.

"Pennies, are you a damned idiot?" He knows straight away I'm pissed as hell, and he looks up at me like a frightened animal. "You already got your loot, greedy bastard. I oughta leave you behind."

He points at his stash. "Do you see what this is?" There's an intense lust in his eyes. "Enough gems in here to buy every square inch of Sotercity."

With my light, I catch something blue twinkling at

24

me. Maybe Pennies has a point. But owning all of Sotercity isn't on my to-do list. Only thing I care about is paying Lars back and having a little left over. Looking at Pennies, I raise my repeater, stock over the glass case and that's when I hear Ret. He's peering into the doorway and the look on his face spells one thing. Trouble.

-10-

By the time we reach the others it's too late. Bron's got both of his 20mm cannons aiming down that black tunnel we came through moments before, ready to unleash holy hell. Something's coming at us in a dead run, and I can hear it hissing and shrieking and the hairs on the back of my neck stand on end. I can't see a thing, but I can tell there's more than one; a lot more. Whatever comes out of that darkness, Ret and Jinx are ready to blow it away. Pennies is next to me, grasping his pea shooter like it'll do him any good, his face full of fear and determination.

I remember Jinx's proximity mines and realize our blunder. A hissing shape nearly makes it into the light when the mines go off. All of them at once. Knowing Jinx, he's stacked way more than he should have. Fire, smoke, and ancient concrete dust come billowing out. The tunnel acts as a rifle barrel, firing chunks of rock and concrete. I hear a deafening clanging sound as a rock bounces off one of Bron's arms. Savage grunts are coming from inside the tunnel. Some of them aren't quite dead.

Then the ground begins to shake as the tunnel collapses in on itself. Dust is flying everywhere. It's hard to breathe, and I grab Sneak and pull her away from the growing cloud. Ret is waving his hands in front of his face to clear the air. We all retreat a few yards to let everything settle, including our minds.

A minute later we assemble inside the Cartier shop. I notice Pennies' eyes darting back and forth. Bron doesn't know there are jewels worth a fortune right under his nose and you can tell Pennies wants to keep it that way.

Glave keeps running his hands through his hair like

he's looking for something he lost.

"We're trapped," he says. "You went and blew up our only way out, and now we're trapped."

"Glave relax," I say. "You're not doing anyone any good right now."

"The noise coming from that tunnel," he says. "Did anyone else hear that?"

I feel my temperature rise.

"That awful sound they were making! Oh my wife. My poor, poor wife."

I can't take it anymore.

I stand in his face and point away from the group. "If you're not going to help, stay out of our way."

Glave disappears into a corner of the shop.

These people want to act like children, I have no problem treating them like children.

Part of me wants to lay into Jinx real bad, but the truth of it is he ran that mine idea by me, and I okayed it. This was my fault. I look at Ret and the others. "Did anyone see what they were?"

"It was too dark," Ret answers. "But we heard 'em, and call me crazy, but they sounded an awful lot like our Prospector friend who tried to take your head off."

I can still feel where the fleshy parts of his fingers had buried into my skull.

"This place might be crawling with them." Bron says and he almost sounds excited by the idea.

I shrug. "There's no way of knowing, but one thing's for sure. We're not alone."

There's a noise from the back of the store and every weapon snaps to attention. It's Glave, and he looks like he's just seen a ghost, and something inside tells me it has nothing to do with the arsenal pointing at his face.

-11-

Glave's gesturing behind him, his face as pale as the concrete dust still swirling around outside. I signal to Bron and Ret, and we move to the back of the shop. Jinx stays with Sneak and the others. We come to a desk and behind that is a curtain. Glave's still pointing and I push him out of the way.

I'm sure Jinx is itching to join us, but close quarters is no place for big bangs. We snake behind the counter and I inch the curtain back with the barrel of my repeater. My glow stick fills a room that looks like it might have been a rest area for the shop workers. Four figures stand huddled together. From here it looks like they're asleep. Their clothes are torn, but expensive looking, and it reminds me of those old pictures the Keepers always show us of rich people decked out for balls and fancy dinner parties. Not a care in the world. The two men are in black suits they used to call tuxedos, and the women are in silk dresses. Their skin looks brown and wrinkled like a rotting piece of meat and a word pops into my head:

Shitbag.

The dress on the woman closest to me is clinging to her body, caked in blood, and I can't tell if it's her blood or someone else's. I see her lips and I have my answer. A thick trail of gore, or something that looks like it, is all over the lower half of their faces and dripping down their chins. By their feet is what looks like a rat, and there isn't much of it left, except some bones and even those have been picked clean.

I raise my hand to give the signal to back away and the woman's eyes snap open. I can see them glowing, and the light they're emitting is pointed straight at us. She hisses, and when her mouth opens I can see that it's black. We back away and the curtain swings closed, but I can hear them coming and I see the lights from their eyes dancing around the edges of the fabric wall between us.

The woman runs into the curtain and tears it off the wall. I pull the trigger on my repeater and watch thumbnail-sized holes riddle her body through the curtain. She drops at my feet.

Then Bron opens up with his 20mm cannons, and I'm nearly deafened by the noise. Huge chunks of plaster and splinters of wood go flying. I see one zombie's face explode. Another's head is severed at the neck by a shell. The head rolls to the ground, its teeth still gnashing at dead air.

I feel a hand on me and look down to see the woman I dropped a second ago. She's clawing at my leg, and her dress has come off, and now all she's wearing is a diamond necklace. There isn't any room for the Katana, but I have a six-inch blade tucked into my boot and I shove it in her eye. She stops moving for good after that.

A second later, Bron stops shooting. I can see his chest heaving, and his eyes are filled with bloodlust. Ret, standing behind him, never got a chance to fire a single shot.

"The head," I say to Bron. "You can do whatever you want to the rest of 'em, but they don't die till you shoot 'em in the brain."

The room is calm except for the severed head, which is gnashing wildly at empty air. This time I use the Katana.

When I turn back toward the front of the shop I see Sneak, and I know by the look on her face that something bad is about to happen. We make it back to Jinx and the others. Glave looks like he just wants to go home, wife or no wife. I don't blame him. The rescuers are now the ones who need rescuing. That's when I discover what it is that's got Sneak so spooked.

-12-

Hissing. And bare feet. Dozens, maybe hundreds, crunching through the rot and debris that's littering the entire shopping plaza. I rush to the door and shine my light. There's nothing to see, but there's at least one level below us, and from where I'm standing it sounds like they're coming from there. "We're about to have company," I say. "And lots of it."

The barrels of Bron's 20mm guns are glowing red hot. "I say we stay and fight."

"Noble," I say. "But I'm not interested in being anyone's lunch. Besides, we came here to find lost Prospectors and I intend to do just that."

Ret pipes up. "Azina, I hate to be the bearer of bad news, but those Prospectors are probably all dead."

Sneak's banging on the wall by the doorway and signing madly with one hand. She's telling me she can see them and we don't have any more time to argue.

"There must be another door," Ret says, scanning our surroundings for some sort of way out.

I head toward the back of the shop. "Oleg, you're the historian. Do these shops have a back exit?"

Oleg's face is blank; I know he can hear the noises outside and it's preventing him from thinking clearly.

I head to the room at the back of the shop. One of Bron's shells has punched a hole the size of my fist in the back wall, and I can feel a trickle of air coming through it.

"Azina," I hear someone calling. "Whatever you're doing, make it fast."

I follow the vent up toward the ceiling, and overhead is a metal grate. I put one foot on a shelf and climb up. I use my knife like a pry bar and the grate falls to the floor. It's big enough to hold a man. I just hope it's enough to

31

hold Bron.

"Up here!" I shout, but the words are drowned out by gunfire. I climb down. The others are using the shop counter as a firing platform. A handful of dark-faced Zees are streaming into the store, and I can see more close behind.

I grab Sneak and motion to the vent. Glave is next, then Pennies and Oleg. Now it's only me, Jinx, Ret and Bron left. The stream of Zees goes from a trickle to a flood and they jam the doorway. The few who managed to make it inside are either dead or headless.

"Wait here till Jinx and Ret are up," I tell Bron. "Then it's your turn."

"What about you?" he asks.

"I'm last, as always."

Ret slides in, and Jinx winks and throws me a grenade. I catch it and slide it into my pocket. "Bron, you're up."

He rolls out of position and I take his place. He gets about halfway up the shelf when the glass at the front of the shop shatters, and a tsunami of hissing gray-faced Zees comes pouring in. There are too many of them for my repeater to be much use. I glance back. Bron's nearly through, and I can see the vent dipping under his weight. If it comes down on top of this horde, it's all over.

I pull out the grenade, pop the pin, and toss it in front of me. The Zees don't care one bit and keep charging. I duck into the back room and feel the ground shake as it goes off. Shrapnel flies in all directions, even at the vent leading out over the shop. I hear a scream from inside. Someone's been hit, but there's no time to worry about that now. Screaming's good. Means they're still alive.

I grab onto the vent opening and start pulling myself in. I'm dangling in mid-air when I see the room fill with Zees. They look like they're dressed for a cocktail party.

One man has what looks like a monocle dangling from his jacket. They're grabbing at my feet with their hands. I'm kicking them off as best I can and trying to find something to hold onto when I feel the bite. One of those fuckers has my ankle in his mouth and the pain is excruciating. I look down and can't believe what I see. The bastard who has my leg is a Warden – a member of the Prior's personal bodyguard. What the hell?

I kick him off and struggle the rest of the way into the shaft. Up ahead, it sounds like aluminum sheet metal bending back and forth. Everyone's inching forward through some sort of air duct, and none of us have the slightest idea where we're heading.

-13-

We make slow progress and I can't help but feel the tiny walls closing in around me. Below us, the Zees are hissing and moaning something awful. My only hope is that they're too stupid to clamber up into the vent after us.

Then another thought occurs to me. What on Earth sent that horde swarming toward us in the first place? Was it the sound of Bron's heavy guns? Maybe, but the mine detonation and tunnel cave-in had been so much louder. This job was supposed to be a cake walk. That's the way Prior Skuld had pitched it. "Should be run-of-the-mill, for an experienced crew like yours." He was smiling at the time, too, and I thought the expression on his weathered face was betraying a secret admiration. If we make it out of this alive, Prospectors or not, this job's gonna cost double.

Without warning, the vent takes a forty-five degree dip and I can hear them sliding down. This isn't good. Down isn't where we want to go. I hear a thud, and someone cries out, and I'm sure I know what's happened. "One at a time!" I shout ahead. "Or you'll get your head rammed up someone's ass."

Bron's in front of me, laughing, and the vent starts wobbling even more.

Now it's my turn to slide, and there's so much debris the trip down's not nearly as fun as I thought it would be.

It doesn't take us long to reach the end of the air duct. Everyone's touching ground and dusting themselves off. Oleg's robe has gone from mostly red to mostly black. Even his face looks like someone powdered it with crushed coal.

By the looks of it, we've gone down at least two

levels. I scan the surroundings. Open space. Low ceilings. More shops on both sides. On the dirty floor, mixed in with the debris, is a sign that looks like it once hung from a pair of hooks on the wall. I point at it, and Oleg wipes off the dirt with a bare hand.

"Food Court," he says. "Where in heaven's name have you led us, Azina?"

I'm not feeling nearly as diplomatic as I was before. "Led you? I didn't lead you anywhere. You were more than welcome to stay behind with those things."

Then the burning pain in my ankle makes me think of that dark-faced Keeper zombie. "How long have you known about this place?"

He gives me a blank stare.

"This complex. How long has the Order known about it?"

"We didn't. Those four Prospectors had been the first to discover it, and that couldn't have been more than a handful of days ago."

I don't believe him. The others are watching us and I can see the worried look on Ret's face. "That horde that charged the store. Mixed in with 'em was what looked like a Warden Captain. He was one of 'em. Shit-colored face and all."

Oleg laughs. "I highly doubt that," the old man says. "Everything was chaos. How can you be sure?"

"Because he tried to bite my leg off." I leave out the part where he succeeded.

"I don't understand," Bron says.

"You're not the only one," says Oleg. "What are you implying, Azina? That The Keepers have known about this place for a while?"

"I never said that, but if you're asking me to risk the lives of my people, I'd like to know what we're getting involved in."

Oleg crosses his arms over his chest and I can tell

35

he's shutting down. "I know as much as you do," he says. "If The Keepers had any knowledge of this place, don't you think they would've told me?"

I decide to let it go for now. Besides, we have a job to do.

-14-

The second Prospector is easy to find and nearly impossible to identify. The body looks like it's been mauled by wild animals. Most of the flesh has been stripped to the bone.

Glave is about to do his crying routine again and I stop him cold. "This isn't your wife."

"How on Earth do you know that?" His eyes are wide and frantic.

I point to the slight bulge at the crotch, the one area left intact. Glave sighs with relief. I don't want to tell him his chances of finding Rosaline alive are slim, but he's probably thinking that already.

The Prospector's pistol is still in its holster.

"Looks like they at least finished him quick," Ret says.

Even in the dark I can see the blood drain from Pennies' face.

Glave collects the pistol, grabs a handful of clips, and wedges the gun under his waistband.

Personally, I'd prefer that he leave it alone. Popular thinking always says the more guns the merrier. I beg to differ. A gun in the hands of someone who doesn't know how to use it usually creates more problems than it solves. One of the few bits of history I can remember has to do with a huge war that engulfed the entire world. At one point, these guys called the Germans armed old men and young boys to defend their capital. Problem was, the raw recruits had a nasty habit of either getting in the way or shooting their own guys by mistake. I couldn't say if the stories were one hundred percent true, but it doesn't take more than one or two experiences in the real world to figure it probably was.

Sneak goes ahead a few yards and I can see by the tilt of her head she's listening for the sound of those things. The blinding urge to pull up my pant leg and check the wound is almost unbearable. Not to mention my head's starting to swim and I can't tell if it's because of the intense pain or the thirst that's still kicking my ass.

I don't dare check the wound in front of the group though, not before I find out what it might mean. I can still see that ghoulish Keeper's face, his skin like tree bark, and that single-minded, feral glare in his glowing eyes. He'd looked vaguely human, but there wasn't a shred of humanity left. It's becoming clear now that something had turned both the Keeper and that first Prospector from men into monsters, and I need to know if I'm at risk.

Ret covers the body with a jacket he's taken from a nearby shop while the others sit down on the cold, hard floor. Oleg is staring off into thin air, and he has a look on his face like he's not so sure he's gonna make it out of this. Maybe he's praying.

Oh Newton, God of weight and movement, grant me the speed to outrun these lowly Mercenary barbarians or the courage to end it all with a single bullet...

I sidle up next to him. "These things are what nearly killed the human race, aren't they?" I whisper.

Oleg's eyes are still on the jacket and the form underneath it. The jacket isn't quite long enough, and one of the man's skeletonized toes is sticking out. "It seems that way."

"If we want any chance of getting home," I say, trying to keep my voice down, "then I need to know what we're up against. I get that The Order insisted you accompany the rescue mission, but if you're not going to open up and be honest, then frankly, you're no good to us."

This seems to make a dent. "What is it you need to know?"

"For starters, what are they? And how long have they been down here?"

Oleg shakes his head and I worry that I'm gonna get another load of bullshit.

"It's taken us years to piece together what happened in those final days," he starts. "Nearly two centuries ago, our forefathers felt the need to start pumping a psychotropic substance into the water supply in the hopes that it would calm a people who were growing dangerously... shall we say... restless. Only years before, they had introduced a compound called fluoride into the water designed to prevent tooth decay. To them, this next step hardly seemed like a huge leap."

"And they ended up killing people." I jump ahead.

"Not exactly. You see, everything dies eventually. It's just a matter of when. For the human cell, death comes after fifty divisions. Cellular replication and death are part of the ageing process. Whatever they dumped into the water created a series of genetic mutations in the population. One of those mutations halted cell growth once it hit that fiftieth division. They were locked into an indefinite holding pattern. But, without new cells, the skin darkens and begins to wrinkle. The chemicals in the water also seem to have disconnected the brain's higher functions. The human race began to regress."

Cells. Genetics. Evolution. Most of this goes over my head except for one thing. Their infinite lifespan. "How long have they been down here?"

"That's hard to say. If they've been locked away all these years, I'd say upwards of two centuries."

"So let me get this straight. These things have been trapped down here, starving to death, for over two hundred years."

Oleg nods, and I'm shocked he can be so casual about all of this.

"And is it catching?" I ask, trying to keep my voice as

neutral as possible. "Like a disease?"

"Almost. The chemical that mutated their genes festers in their saliva. That was how it circled the globe. Once the chemicals were introduced into the bloodstream, the changes started almost at once."

I swallow hard and suddenly I'm feeling a surge of anger, most of it directed at him. "You seem to know a hell of a lot for a guy who didn't know anything a few minutes ago." He's looking at me strangely and I try to relax. "So, is there a cure?"

His eyes darken and somehow I know exactly what he's about to say.

"The only cure I know is death."

-15-

Oleg turns his gaze in my direction and I'm not crazy about the way he's looking at me. He'd seen me favoring my leg earlier and he knows. Knows I've been bitten; knows I'm changing. I'm sure of it. I take a deep breath and try to calm myself down. I'm just being paranoid. The old man isn't suspicious at all. Why should he be? I just saved his ass from being a zombie hors d'oeuvre.

We need to get moving again. I order a sweep of the Food Court, and we learn that anything and everything edible has been consumed long ago. It's unnerving and reinforces the idea that these freaks have been starving for centuries. And what's worse, they're desperately looking for a way out.

My mind returns to the two Prospectors we've found, scattered at different places in the complex. I'm starting to wonder if they'd been running away when they died. If so, then the first one we found in the boiler room was probably the last one alive. Damn bugger nearly made it out, too. And then I'm struck by a thought that chills me to the core. If he *had* gotten out, imagine what would have followed him home.

Before long, the Food Court falls behind and we come to what looks like a blast door, hanging half way open. According to Oleg, the sign above reads 'Living Quarters.'
"The name is just strange," Oleg says. "Living Quarters is a military term."

"Maybe we're on some type of military base," Jinx says.

Deep lines crease Oleg's brow. "There's a good chance the horde that attacked us earlier once called these living quarters home."

41

Ret chimes in. "Maybe this place was built special for the stinkin' rich. Their own private hideaway while the world around them went to hell in a hand basket. I wouldn't put it past 'em."

"It was built into the base of a mountain," Pennies says. He's holstered his gun and he looks calmer. "Fact, this very spot is probably right under Mount Kepler."

Bron is looking impatient with all this talking. "Is there anything in there the Prospectors might've been after, or is this another dead-end?"

"Maybe it's not the living quarters they were interested in," Oleg says, "but something on the other side."

We press on. I clear the doorway, hoping that as we climb deeper inside this hellhole, we're moving one step closer to home.

-16-

The living quarters are anything but. Skeletons everywhere, frozen in a gruesome tableau of death. The dead are decked out in their finest clothes, awash with jewels. I see piles of worthless money, scattered about like confetti. Even Pennies is too sickened to care.

"They locked themselves away from a dying world," Ret says. "And once the Zees got in, all their money and shiny jewels couldn't save 'em."

We pass a room with yet another body and I don't think anything of it. It isn't until I hear the gurgling behind us that I remember thinking the corpse lying on that bed somehow seemed fuller than the others. But the truth is, there's more to it than that. Somehow, I knew she was there.

I spin around in time to see her stumbling out of the room. The glow from her eyes fills the entire hallway. Her movements are stiff and awkward and, because of that, I'm sure she's only recently been turned. Her head hits the wall, and the sound of bones breaking is unmistakable. She rights herself, her head snapping back into place with a grotesque series of cracks, and I know without a doubt she's a Zee. Judging by the outfit she's wearing, I can also tell she's Glave's wife.

I try to push through, but the corridor is far too narrow. Glave sees the Zee and jumps with fright. Then I see him freeze. His face is turned from me, but I know he's just recognized his wife and he can't help the urge to run to her. I shout, but he takes a step toward her. That's when she lunges.

A shot rings out.

But not from Glave. It's Pennies. He's right behind Glave and a trail of smoke snakes up from the barrel of his pistol. The bullet grazes Rosaline's neck and a thin stream of blood paints the wall. Her eyes release Glave and lock onto Pennies. Pennies tries to move, but there's nowhere to go. Ret raises his shotgun, but I can already tell he doesn't have a clear shot. She lunges at Pennies, knocking him to the ground, her teeth tearing at the flesh on his face. I'm almost there but he's screaming. She's bitten his lower lip off and the eerie quality of his lipless yell echoes in my ears.

Ret takes the shot anyway and Glave's wife flies back five feet. She tries to prop herself up but Ret keeps firing. The buckshot turns her head into a bloody soup. She collapses in a heap.

I become aware of an invisible hand pushing me forward. I look behind me and wonder if I'm just in shock.

Pennies is shrieking now. Ret and the others move him onto the bed where I'd first seen Glave's zombified wife. Pennies must've gotten a dose right in the mouth because his body starts shaking. And I feel it again, like being shoved, only no one's there. A thought forms in my mind and it's as clear and bright like a sun-filled day. They know we're here. I'm not sure how they could possibly know, but they do and a big group is heading our way.

-17-

Every muscle in Pennies' body is bunching up like taught cords. There aren't any clean bandages, so Ret's using the bed sheet to soak up the blood from his wound. Pennies' lower lip is gone and the upper one is dangling by a small piece of flesh. The inside of his mouth is starting to darken, and I know he's turning. There isn't much time left for Pennies - or for us.

"We need to get out of here," I say urgently.

The shock on Ret's face is clear. "And just leave him?"

Sneak's watching all of this, and I can tell that, in spite of her burning hatred for Traders, she knows this is no way for someone to go.

Pennies is kicking harder and Jinx is having trouble holding him down.

I have no idea which way the Zees are coming from, but somehow I know they're getting closer. There's a bend in the corridor not far from where we are, and I'm taking a chance the Zees won't come from the other direction. I send Sneak into the hall to act as lookout. She darts past Glave, who's on the ground, holding the shredded body of his dead wife and for a moment the sight makes me want to cry.

I duck back into the room and look at Pennies. His face is already about three shades darker.

"There isn't much we can do for him," Ret says.

I thought my conversations with Oleg had been quiet and inconspicuous, but it's clear everyone knows what's happening. "We'll take him with us," I say.

Jinx glares at me. "You heard Ret, he's gone. The best he can hope for at this point is a bullet in the brain. Fast and easy."

45

"I'm afraid he's right." This time it's Oleg, but the prospect of losing someone I'm responsible for is a tough pill to swallow. I also know we don't have more than a few more minutes before we're overrun.

"It might not be fatal," I say.

Jinx slams the wall with the palm of his hand and it makes a hollow, booming sound. "Azina, you saw what happened to that Prospector who tried to rip your face off."

"We don't know what the fatality rate is, all I'm sayin'. He could have a fever and pull out of it."

"I can do it quick and painless," Ret whispers. He reaches into his vest, pulls out a morphine injector, and shows it to me.

Pennies suddenly springs forward, gnashing with a mouthful of blackened teeth. He's going for the exposed flesh on Ret's arm. Bron snatches Pennies' head, less than an inch from his target. One of Bron's titanium fingers slips inside Pennies' mouth and the Trader chomps down. I recoil at the sight and sound of Pennies' shattering teeth. A ten-inch, spring-loaded blade whips out from the palm of Bron's right hand and pierces Pennies' right temple. The glow in Pennies' eyes dims and goes out. Bron retracts the blade and Pennies' body falls back onto the bed.

Bron's hand is covered in dark blood and shards of broken teeth. He uses Pennies' tunic to wipe it off and inspects his gleaming index finger. "Not even a dent," he boasts.

And this time I don't find Bron's little crack one bit funny.

-18-

I feel them coming a few seconds before I hear Sneak running toward us, banging on the wall. Glave looks like he's ready to sit this one out and accept a quick death, and I know he's fooling himself. There's no such thing as a quick death when you're being eaten alive. He'd be better off using that pistol on himself.

"Glave! Get on your feet." I slap him across the face. He doesn't respond, not even a flinch. I grab him by the collar and the crotch of his pants and haul him to his feet. He doesn't seem to appreciate that I'm saving his life.

"If you want to kill yourself, do it when we get home. Right now, I need you to move your ass!" This seems to do the trick.

The entire exchange lasts less than sixty seconds, but any delay is bad when a bunch of Zees are after you. The first one ambles into the hallway and spots us right away. The stilted walk seems strange at first until I realize how many years they've been standing around.

I aim my repeater and squeeze off a three-round burst. He's just outside of my weapon's effective range, but a shot catches him square in the forehead, his body goes limp, and he skids a half dozen feet before he stops.

The others are behind me. I signal for Ret and Jinx to hold them off while we retreat.

The hallway is filling with dark, half-dressed shapes, surging forward with pure, unfiltered rage. Jinx lobs a grenade and the whole building shudders, and all but a handful of them drop. Entrails and clumps of flesh ooze down the walls like some macabre painting. Ret picks the crawlers off one-by-one. But no sooner are a dozen killed than two dozen take their place.

The rest of us race ahead to a sign with faded letters

47

and an arrow pointing forward, but there's no time for Oleg to decipher its exact meaning. We come to a pair of rusted doors. I'm up front and Bron is watching our rear. I give each handle a healthy pull but neither budges an inch. Even a kick with my good leg doesn't rattle them loose.

"Bron," I call out. I can hear Ret and Jinx down the hall, around the corner, out of breath and cursing. They're running this way, and by the sounds of it they have a massive swarm of Zees right behind them.

Bron yanks the doors and nothing happens. He pulls with everything he's got and the veins in his neck bulge. I hear the sound of twisting metal, and I hope it isn't one of his arms giving way.

Ret and Jinx come scrambling around the corner. Just a few feet behind them are the Zees. They sound like a basket full of snakes, but their faces are contorted with rage and caked in that tarry, blood-like substance. Running at full tilt, Ret raises his automatic shotgun behind him and pulls the trigger. The gun kicks wildly. The buckshot fans out and cuts down a handful of Zees. The rest are unfazed as they trample over the fallen.

Ret and Jinx are ten yards away when Bron finally pries open the doors. A terrifying thought flashes through my mind: that we'll run inside this new sanctuary and find it filled with Zees. I hope to hell I'm wrong, or we'll all be dead in a matter of seconds.

-19-

Oleg, Glave and Sneak run in and gather behind us. Bron's holding one of the doors open. Jinx and Ret are hightailing it down the hallway. There's a Zee reaching for Ret, barely an arm's length behind him. Jinx is the first one in, followed by Ret. Bron slams the door shut, but that Zee is too fast, and the next thing we know he's inside. Ret doesn't have a chance to turn around when the Zee crashes into him, sending them both tumbling.

I know right then and there that if I'm not fast enough, Ret's going to die. I leap over a row of seats and come down with the Katana. If I put too much into the swing, the blade will slice right through the Zee's flesh and into Ret. I pull up at the last moment. The sword's edge enters the back of the Zee's brain box and kisses the front of his skull. A millisecond from closing down on the back of Ret's neck, it dies with its jaws wrenched open.

That's the second time in less than ten minutes he's nearly become Zee-steak, and I almost thank one of Oleg's gods that nothing but a set of old chairs was in my way. I don't know what I'd do without him. Ret takes my hand and I help him up. He's heavier than I am, and my leg starts burning like I'm being branded with a hot iron poker. I grit my teeth and try not to let on I'm having trouble.

"Thank you." He smiles, and I feel my cheeks flush. I'd lie to myself and say it's because I feel like crap, but I suck at lying and I know the truth anyway. And besides, I can't help thinking about rule number two: Mercs don't date Mercs. Especially when you're a woman in charge of a bunch of reprobates.

I turn away and slide the Katana into the sheath on

my back. "If the tables were turned, you'd do the same."

He nods, and he quickly turns and shoves the tip of his boot into the Zee's prone torso, and it goes skidding into darkness.

I finally get a good look around us and my jaw nearly drops. The room we're in is impressive. Rectangular. Hundred-foot ceiling. Rows of seats facing a screen that I'm willing to bet was once white, but is now torn and coated with grime. The seats are plush, and far more inviting than anything in my dump back in Sotercity.

Bron's still holding the set of double doors closed. "Ret, you ungrateful bastard," he says. "Pennies would have eaten you for dinner if Bron hadn't saved your scrawny ass."

Oh boy. Bron's talking in the third person again. He needs a lot of reassurance, and maybe under different circumstances I'd be happy to give it to him. But now is not the time.

Outside, the Zees are kicking up a racket throwing themselves against the doors. We're lucky those doors open outward, or we'd have a hell of a time keeping them shut. I find a closet with cleaning supplies, and bring back an armful of mops and brooms to shove between the door handles. "That won't last forever," I say.

I can tell Bron is miffed about Ret's lack of acknowledgement because the big man is ripping out rows of seats and stacking them against the door. After a few minutes, he claps the dirt off his hands. "That should hold 'em."

I nudge Ret. "Good work, Bron," he says, with all the grace of a newborn calf.

The subtle frown on Bron's face morphs into a childlike smile. "Maybe you're not such an asshole after all, Ret."

"Listen," I say, looking for any obvious exits. "We need to find out where this assembly hall leads to."

Oleg reclines in one of the dusty seats and half-turns to look back at us. "This isn't an assembly hall, I'm afraid. It was called a movie theater." He pauses. I can tell he's disgusted with us. "Have none of you heard of a movie theater before? Moving images projected onto a blank screen? They were all the rage."

For a moment, I wonder if Oleg really thinks we're idiots. What he's forgetting is that The Order keeps most of the technology they've recovered in their own greedy, little hands. Then I see Bron's gleaming, metal arms and realize I'm looking at the exception to the rule. There's probably only one person on the planet who can replicate those. Bron's father was a wealthy Trader who pulled an enormous amount of strings to have his son outfitted that way. I've seen the prototypes, and they were sleek and utilitarian. At least utilitarian, if loading and unloading carts all day long sounds like a promising career path. It was Bron who convinced the engineer to alter his initial plans into something far more deadly. Bron's father somehow got his head stuck on the idea that his son would carry on the family business, not become a hired gun.

My mind snaps back to Oleg in the middle of his history lesson. "I dare say, at one time, this dead civilization you see around you had inventions that would make the very idea of this movie theater seem like child's play."

The Zees aren't banging on the door nearly as much and the thought of what that might mean is making me nervous. I'm also starting to hear things. It began as a low, ringing noise after Bron decided to fire his 20mm cannons a foot from my head. But since about the time we entered Oleg's movie theater, I've started to realize the noise isn't a ringing at all. It's a voice I'm hearing, low and muffled, like someone talking into the sleeve of their tunic, but every once in a while I can almost make out what it's saying, and I swear it's calling my name.

The sound gets louder, and I feel an overwhelming and inexplicable urge to tear down Bron's makeshift barricade and let the doors swing open. Not so much to let the Zees in, but it's more like I'm being... summoned.

Behind me, Oleg is still blabbing away.

"The wondrous, ancient Romans and Greeks. Yes, both long gone, I know, but each in their own time built empires that spanned the known world. They were masters of art and engineering. They were the light of the civilized world."

While the others are distracted by Oleg's oration, I hike up my pant leg and survey the damage. I crack a new glow stick and hold it over the wound. It's almost impossible to make out any of the details, but I can tell that the skin around the bite is bubbling. If that weren't bad enough, most of my leg below the knee has become a dark patchwork of intersecting lines. I run my finger along the flesh, and it feels rough and leathery, like deer hide.

"In the fifth century, hordes of barbarians overran an empire already weakened by decadence and laziness. After the collapse, centuries of learning were lost. Western Europe was thrust into darkness for a thousand years. During the Dark Ages–"

"These are the dark ages." Ret jokes.

Oleg laughs.

"Azina, you okay?"

It's Ret. I shove my pant leg down and hope to hell he didn't see anything. I mean, I'm not a danger to the group. Not like Pennies. He hadn't been able to fight the chemicals surging through his body. They had started changing him immediately. During the end times, there must have been others exposed to the chemical who managed to pull through. The death rate couldn't have been one hundred percent, could it? My hands begin to shake and I shove them under my armpits.

"You don't look so good."

I brush past Ret and address the others. The noise outside is completely gone, and I'm hoping to high hell those things aren't smart enough to circle around and box us in.

"History class is over," I say. "We're leaving."

-20-

We creep through a second set of doors and find ourselves in a room where the walls are covered in mirrors. Before them are dozens of iron weights.

"We've entered a gymnasium." Oleg informs us. "An exercise room. Most Dusters didn't do much manual labor. So to keep themselves in shape they'd lift heavy weights and run on machines."

I'm surprised to hear Oleg use a street term like Duster to refer to those living before the end times.

Jinx snickers. "Computing machines that did their thinking, mechanical doors that opened and closed on their own, all the food they could eat. I'm surprised they weren't all eight hundred pounds."

"Some of them were." Oleg furrows his brow.

My foot snags on something and I nearly fall flat on my ass. Ret reaches down and comes up with a weapon. "Warden's rifle."

Everyone knows the Prior's personal bodyguard are tough sons-of-bitches. There isn't a damn thing that'll frighten them. Oleg hardly looks at it.

We find the gymnasium reception area and an access door leading to the rest of the complex. The exit is blocked by a hastily erected barricade made from weightlifting equipment, tables turned on their sides, and even the body of a dead horse.

"How the hell did that get in here?" Jinx asks.

Sneak's face blanches.

It's a perfect choke point. The bodies of dead Zees are piled at the door like cords of firewood, blown away as they tried to surge through. I can see the mound stirring slightly. Some of the Zees are alive, pinned beneath the wave of bodies.

54

We enter the reception area and I feel my attention being drawn behind a desk opposite the barricade. That drone in my ear is getting so loud that it sounds like the buzzing of an insect.

Zees are piled around the desk, and most of their skulls have been cracked open with blunt weapons. I peer over the edge and make another gruesome find – half a dozen Wardens, huddled together in death. Most of their flesh has been ripped off. Except for one of them.

"Azina."

I turn around, annoyed. "What is it?"Everyone's eyeing me like I'm the town drunk.

"We didn't say anything," Ret says.

He has that 'are you okay' look on his face again, and I'm not liking it one bit. I hear my name again, but this time I know it's coming from the pile. That one Keeper whose face hasn't quite been completely eaten. His eyes are open and glowing and it looks like he's trying to climb out. He'd make it if his arms and legs weren't trapped. "Azina..."

But what I hear in my head is, "*Asssseeeenaaaahhhhh.*"

The edge of the Katana hits him right between the eyes before he has a chance to say anything else. All I see are the dim confines of his mangled features as I hack his face off. Contaminated blood sprays close to my mouth before I can stop myself.

Ret rushes over to me. The Keeper's head looks like a bowl filled with gore, and Ret curses under his breath. He's seen the Wardens. He turns to Oleg, his eyes ablaze. "You knew about this all along, didn't you?"

"I don't know what you're talking about."

Ret grabs him by the collar of his robe and drags him over to the barricade. Oleg peers over and his eyes close with resignation.

"Don't insult my intelligence by trying to tell me The Keepers sent in an elite hit squad and you knew nothing

55

about it."

Jinx removes a shiny blade from his vest. "I say we feed him to a pack of Zees."

"And what will that accomplish?" Oleg asks, the fear in his voice unmistakable. To him, we're looking more and more like a bunch of savages.

"Accomplish?" Bron says. "Not much, but it'll feel damn good."

I'm worried that if this crew gets their way we'll prove him right. "Back off, all of you! Get back!" I turn to Oleg, who's fixing his robe. "You've been bullshitting us from the start. Now start talking or I won't stop Bron from ripping your arms and legs off."

Oleg's eyes are flitting between me and Bron.

Bron has a twisted little grin on his face as he stares the Keeper down, making tearing sounds.

I collect myself for a moment. "This mission has nothing to do with rescuing a team of lost Prospectors, does it?"

Oleg doesn't answer. Bron comes forward and I signal for him to back off. "You've got the next ten seconds to start talking, or so help me, I'll feed you to the first pack of Zees we find."

"You wouldn't dare." His frantic eyes reach out to Glave for support. Glave is still wearing the same half-dead expression he's had since his wife came shambling out from that apartment.

"Glave's not going to help you, Oleg. Start talking." I see in his eyes that no one's ever spoken to him like this. There's hatred there, plain as day. But he knows he doesn't have a choice and I'm about to break his face a bit to get his lips warmed up when he begins.

"The Order has been searching for this complex for decades. We told you that a small group of our Prospectors stumbled upon it, and that was the truth. What we neglected to mention was that there weren't four Prospectors. There were five, and the fifth made it out alive, but barely. At least, that was the story he gave. He told us they located the complex, but that they were overrun by swarms of Volgoroth.

"We didn't believe much of what he said, of course. After all, The Order exterminated them over a hundred years ago. We assumed that the few remaining creatures died of starvation not long after. That was before we discovered what the chemical really did to its victims."

"So you sent in an elite squad to finish the job," Jinx adds.

Oleg nods. "We sent in our very best. Not to battle any Volgoroth. I already told you we thought the Prospector was lying. He wouldn't be the first to stumble onto a cache of hidden wealth and let his greed get the better of him. What better way to throw off suspicion than to invoke the name 'Volgoroth'?"

"And what was it they were looking for?" I ask.

Oleg's eyes sparkle. "An immense storehouse of information, unparalleled since the Library of Alexandria. This complex was one of the last known refuges during those final days. It became an ark of sorts, built to prevent thousands of years of knowledge from disappearing forever. Somewhere here is a reinforced chamber with the answers to all of our questions. The moment we lost contact with our elite team, we knew that the Prospector's story must be true."

"So if that Prospector knows the way, why the hell isn't he here with us?"

Oleg's eyes flicker and suddenly I know.

"You killed him, didn't you?"

"Not I."

"Prior Skuld."

Oleg nods.

"To protect your secret."

"Yes, but don't be naïve. This isn't only about the

library. Maintaining a level of order and security is our second mandate. We could not allow people to know that a Hive had been located a half day's journey from Sotercity. There are rules that forbid such a disclosure."

"Hive? You make these Zees sound like insects."

"In a way, they are. Their minds are connected in ways we have yet to understand. If one of them sees you, they all see you."

"Oh great," says Ret. "Something we should have known earlier, don't you think?"

"To do what with? It wouldn't have done you any good."

Bron crosses his arms. "Well, I hate to burst your bubble, but we don't have enough ammo to kill them all. Hell, look at what happened to your Warden friends. They were left using their rifle butts as glorified clubs."

Oleg won't look at the dead Wardens, and I can't blame him.

"Somebody doesn't like you very much to send you on a suicide mission with a bunch of Mercs," I say.

"The Order and Prior Skuld don't like to be questioned. I openly objected to the Prospector's... silencing, as well as the foolhardiness of the current operation. My reward for speaking out was an ultimatum. Return with proof that the library is real, or be cast along with my family into No Man's Land, condemned for the rest of our days to wander the desolation."

"Why should we believe you when you've lied to us all along?"

"Because it's the truth."

As much as I hate to admit it, Oleg's story makes sense. How the Zees were able to show up so soon after we took out their friends in the Cartier shop. Their strange, ant-like behavior. Not to mention that muffled voice that's been yapping in my ear.

Ret isn't impressed. "This is bullshit. We got

thousands of bloodthirsty Zees running around out there and you want us to find you a library."

"I'll give you this," Jinx says. "You've got balls, expecting us to help you."

"It might not be that easy," I say. "This library may be the only bargaining chip we have."

The muscles in Bron's face tense. "How do you figure?"

"Think about it. The Order sends us on a suicide mission. As far as they're concerned, we're already dead. Any of us lucky enough to make it back will end up just like that fifth Prospector. Unless we find that library. Then, we have leverage."

Everyone seems to be thinking it over, including Oleg.

"Or maybe we just don't go back," Ret offers.

"And wander through No Man's Land for the rest of our lives?" Bron replies. "No thanks. And if you're talking yourself into traveling to one of those rotting cities you can just forget it. No one's ever come back from there."

Jinx is eyeing the mangled Warden bodies. "It'd sure beat living under The Order's steel-toed boot."

"Then by all means," Bron says, snorting with laughter. "Just remember to send us a postcard."

I feel Sneak tapping my leg. She has something in her hand. It's a beaten-up sign, and it's riddled with bullet holes and covered in blood. There's a clean spot on the wall from where she's taken it and it looks like some sort of emergency exit plan. A large arrow points to a small room, and I assume that's where we are. Below it is another level and a picture of something I've seen before in an old book that was printed before the fall.

I turn to Oleg. "If you were a Duster and wanted to move large quantities in and out of this complex... Say, enough stuff to fill up that library of yours, and you knew that crowds of Zees were topside running ape-shit, how would you do it?"

Oleg pauses. "I'm not sure."

It's the first time I hear him admit there's something he doesn't know. I hold the sign up. "Sneak may have just found our ticket out of here."

Oleg studies it for a moment and his face brightens. "I'll be damned."

-21-

We're still in the gymnasium reception. The exit is clogged with the bodies of dead Zees, and it takes us almost twenty minutes to cut a path to freedom. Our plan is simple, really. According to the sign in my hand, there's an underground railway system two levels below us. Problem is, once we find it, none of us have a clue where those tracks will lead. Or worse, whether those old tunnels will be clear enough of debris and Zees to be passable. Some kind of transportation hub makes sense for a complex like this, given the amount of material that had been sent here for safekeeping. I'm also willing to bet Oleg's library will be somewhere near that depot.

There's an old, weathered picture, hanging in a saloon in Sotercity, of a colossal machine belching great plumes of smoke and squatting on a pair of metal tracks like some kind of metallic caterpillar. Trains are what they called them, and I wonder if we'll find anything so magnificent.

I'm also thinking back to Oleg's comment about the Zees being part of a Hive. *If one of them sees you, they all see you.*

That's what he'd said. The Warden I'd found buried under that pile of corpses. He'd already turned by then and was trying his damndest to get free, and I'd used the Katana to turn his skull into a serving bowl. The question nagging away at me was clear, though. How come the swarm didn't show up on the heels of that little incident?

In the Cartier shop, the Zees had clamored over their fallen comrades as if they weren't even there. I'm wondering if they're sometimes blind to their own kind, the way Dusters might have become immune to each other after living in cities teeming with millions of people.

61

Was that why the Warden hadn't raised the alarm? Because all he saw was one of his own?

We walk two-by-two. My light is fading and I crack another glow stick. The space opens up and thick pockets of shadow cling to the walls. We're heading down a set of metal stairs. The grip feels soft and corroded. I bring my fingers to my nose and recoil at the smell of rotting rubber. Oleg sees me.

"Escalator." He says this as if the word should mean something to me. "A set of stairs that moved on their own. Quite popular at the time. In fact–"

I hear something below us and shove the light into my pocket. The room goes from dark to black. Oleg's getting the hang of this and stops flapping his fish-lips. We're halfway down the escalator, and I can distinctly hear something shuffling around on the level below us.

Could it be a Zee, somehow cut off from the others? Hard to say. So far they don't like doing things on their own. If I can sneak up and drop it silently, maybe we can avoid signaling the others.

I make it to the bottom and my eyes have already started to adjust to the darkness. In fact, I'm surprised by how well I can see. I can even make out Oleg, Bron, Ret and the others crouching in place on the escalator, waiting for me to finish. They're staring off into the blackness, completely blind. The broken bits of wood, glass and concrete on the floor make it difficult to stay quiet.

The Zee is just ahead. I can see it standing in a corner. Its eyes are emitting a dull glow which tells me one thing; he doesn't know I'm here. I can see this Zee is a man because he's wearing a pair of short pants that are ripped on one side. I also catch a tattered sweater draped over his shoulders. He almost looks human.

His back is still turned and I slip to within three feet of him. The Katana is halfway out when he turns and walks directly at me. I try backing away, but I'm crouched so low I'm not nearly fast enough. The Zee stumbles and raises one of his legs, and I can see the skin there is scabrous and covered in coarse hairs. He's going to walk over me like I'm some inanimate obstacle. I'm hoping this Zee has a serious malfunction, because the other possibility – that he thinks he's climbing over one of his own – is far less appealing. I stand and shove him away with both hands. He goes spilling onto the ground and is back on his feet in a second as though nothing happened.

The others must've heard him hit the floor because I hear them coming, and Oleg is filling the silence with more useless information. That's when the Zee's eyes light up and nearly blind me. His head snaps in their direction and he takes off at a lumbering run. I swing the Katana at his head, but I'm not even close.

"Whoa!" Someone shouts, and I think it's Glave.

The Zee is at full gallop and out of range. I can't take the shot because the others are in my line of fire. Ret raises his shotgun, pulls the trigger, and chops him in half. He falls to the ground. A final shot to the head stops the hissing. I rush forward.

"I thought you took care of it," Bron snaps at me.

Ret's shaken and I'm sure it's because he knows we've just rung a giant dinner bell. "I missed him," I lie, wondering how I'll ever be able to explain the horrible certainty growing within me – Zees don't bother their own kind.

Almost on cue, I feel a pain on my side. I slide a hand inside my shirt and down to my waist to find a patch of rough, leathery skin. It's climbing toward my armpit, and I desperately want to tell Ret. He and Sneak are the only ones who'll understand; the only ones able to keep a level head about this. Something's different with me. For some reason, I'm not like Pennies, that Prospector, or any of those dead Wardens. They were exposed and the chemical consumed their humanity. For Pennies, it was a matter of minutes. I'm not sure what's happening, but one thing is certain. I'm not the same person who walked in here.

-22-

By the time we reach the next escalator, I can already hear them coming. The others aren't the least bit bothered, and I wonder if I'm the only one who can hear them this far off. They're above us, that much I can tell. Exact numbers are sketchy, but when have they shown up with anything less than a small army?

I warn the others, and we race down the escalator two steps at a time. It's littered with bones; most look like they've been gnawed on. We reach the bottom and the others catch the low, rumbling sound of what might be a few hundred Zees coming our way. The hissing is growing louder. At the foot of the escalator is a thirty-yard clearing which leads to a set of eight metal doors with push bars running across them. Above them is a sign.

"The train station is just beyond these doors," Oleg says, pointing, his voice trembling something awful.

We frantically try each one. They're all locked. We're boxed in with nowhere to go. If only we had another minute, Jinx would be able to blow a hole in that door and we'd have a chance.

"Check your ammo!" I shout, and toss Pennies' old pistol to Oleg. I'm breaking my own rules about guns in inexperienced hands, but at this point we don't have the luxury for rules.

My best guess is that they're working their way down the first escalator. Sneak grabs my arm. She's signing frantically and I'm shaking my head. Her fingers become more insistent. She has a plan, but it's too risky, and I shake my head at her. The others are watching, but don't have a clue as to what Sneak and I are talking about. That's when Sneak takes off up the escalator.

65

"Sneeeaaak!" I scream, but I know it isn't any use.

She's halfway up when the first glowing-eyed Zee comes charging down. I swing my repeater around. His arms are outstretched, but Sneak doesn't slow down; she means to go through with this. I squeeze off a short burst, hitting the Zee in the chest and knocking him down. Sneak runs past him and he tries to grab hold of her. I've missed his head, and he's back on his feet, giving chase. Another Zee reaches the top of the escalator, and I put one right between his eyes. Sneak disappears, but I can hear her trying to make noise as she goes. She's leading them away, but I'm terrified they're going to catch her somewhere in the darkness, and she'll die all alone, unable to cry for help.

It's hard to estimate how many Zees peel off to chase Sneak through the complex. The thought of racing after her almost hits critical mass, and another group comes pouring over the edge of the escalator. There's so damned many, and by the time the first one reaches the clearing, all I can see is a river of Zees stretching into the darkness.

Jinx is lobbing grenades from his launcher. He's timed the fuse to detonate right above their heads, cutting gaping holes in their ranks. The rest of us are waiting until they get closer. Reminds me of those pictures of how men fought hundreds of years ago, rows of them lined up with muskets.

"Wait for it!" I shout.

Twenty yards.

Glave's got his pistol pointed right at them, his hand bucking with nerves.

Ten yards.

I can see the details of their glowing eyes and leathery skin now. One female Zee has a formal gown on. She's got a net covering her matted hair, and it looks like she might've been wearing a wig at one time. They're all wearing gold watches and expensive jewelry, and I can't help but think of Pennies. And as much as I try, I can't tune their horrible hissing out of my head. I stick the repeater's butt right under my chin.

"Not yet!" I shout.

Ret looks over at me and gasps. "Azina...Your eyes...They're glowing."

-23-

Five yards.

Bron starts to turn my way when I give the order to fire. Suddenly, our little dead-end erupts with violent flashes of light and deafening gunfire. Zees disintegrate before us like snowflakes hitting wet ground.

Bron unleashes his 20mms, and the floor beneath us trembles from the concussion. The sound of pure destruction, rhythmic and exhilarating. Each round cuts through a dozen Zees. Heads torn clean off, bodies chopped in half.

But some other part of me feels a pinprick of pain as each Zee drops, as though someone were driving searing needles into my flesh. With each dying Zee, a flickering light has been extinguished and I'm distinctly aware of each one.

Bron sweeps back and forth, and it's a miracle that anything can live through such an awesome hail of fire. His 20mms choke up. Bron's arms are glowing red. He's overheated. Two spring-loaded blades eject from his palms and he wades into the remaining Zees, arms swinging, and in the dim light all I see are two sunsets arcing through the air.

My repeater clicks empty. There's no time to pop in another clip. Out comes the Katana. There's a Zee going for Ret, and I bring the blade straight down on the top of the thing's head. Its legs buckle, and it drops. Those pinpricks of pain are still there, and all I can do is ignore them, or we're all dead. I move into the group and hack another dozen, and I realize they're ignoring me completely. The patch of rough skin growing up my side has spread, and I'm aware that it's made its way up to my neck.

Ret's busy unleashing hell with his automatic shotgun. I can't help but notice him swivel to watch me every few seconds, and I'm sure it's my glowing eyes he's looking at.

I glance back to see a Zee in a cook's uniform heading for Oleg. The old man is pulling the trigger on his pistol and nothing's happening. I yank the knife from my boot and fling it through the air. The edge sinks into the puffy part of the cook's hat, and the Zee's dead before it hits the ground.

It takes us a few more minutes, and the last of them are no longer a threat. A number of Zees are little more than torsos, and Bron happily makes his way through the growing pile, finishing them off with the blade on his arm.

I hear another group approaching, and it sounds like this one's even bigger than the last. We're lucky that no one's been hurt or killed, and I'm sure that luck won't last another onslaught. "Jinx!" I shout. "We need to get through these doors."

He slides his pack off and reaches in. "I have just the thing." He smiles at me. It's a charge of C4. Old world ordnance, but it gives a nice kick and should do the job just fine.

I scan the darkness above. Still no sign of Sneak.

Ret touches my arm. His glare is intense and questioning, but my eyes are back to normal, I can feel it. Either way, he knows, and you don't need the brains of a Keeper to realize he's not sure what to do about it. I run this crew, but if I become a danger, Ret's my second and he won't have much choice but to take me down.

-24-

Jinx pulls the trigger on his detonator and one of the doors blows off its hinges. The Zees are at the top of the escalator now and we hurry through the opening. When we're all through, I realize the problem. Jinx's heavy hand has taken the door clean off. Now we have nothing to keep the Zees out. Bron snatches the mangled door off the ground and sets it back in place, but it's so bent out of shape it barely fits. Behind us is a counter, which Bron rips from the floor and jams against the opening to keep the door in place.

I should feel better seeing the barricade go up, but instead I have this sinking feeling, like we're never gonna see Sneak again. Part of me wants to go out there and fight through the Zees to find her. The other part of me knows full well that would be suicide.

That's when I notice Glave's hand is covered in blood. He's pulled it away from his tunic where there's a deep red stain on the shoulder. Oleg takes a step backward.

"Check that wound, Ret," I say. Personally, I'm not convinced it's a bite. Glave could just as well have shot himself during the battle or been hit by a piece of shrapnel when the door blew.

Ret peels back Glave's tunic, and the expression on his face leaves no doubt. Judging by the proximity to his head, he doesn't have more than a few minutes before he begins to turn.

Outside, the first Zees have made it to the barricade. This time, it won't be like it was in the movie theater. With the sheer weight of their bodies pushing against our makeshift door, it's just a question of time before it'll give way.

I see a glint off of Bron's blade. He's about to put an end to Glave.

"Wait a minute!" I shout. "Glave doesn't have any symptoms yet."

"Maybe not," Bron says, "but you saw the others, Azina. It's only a matter of time."

Glave seems to agree with Bron. "I don't want to turn into one of those things," he says.

"You won't," I assure him. Glave may have less than ten minutes. It's one thing to hack into a Zee like he's nothing more than a bag of meat, and it's something else entirely to kill a man in cold blood.

"I say we wait." I look over. It's Ret, and he throws a look that tells me I better know what I'm doing.

I don't, but I'll be the first to pull the trigger if I see the slightest sign that Glave's about to turn.

We shift our attention to this new area we're in and my breath catches in my throat. It looks like the pictures of old train stations I've seen in Sotercity. Two sets of tracks are laid out in even parallel lines. I shift my light and see that the tracks stop before a steel vault on my right that must be a hundred feet high. Even from here we can see the massive vault door is open. We head that way. A single, sleek-looking train sits on the farthest set of tracks. As we get closer, I see that things are strewn about haphazardly. Wooden crates have been toppled over, their contents covering the ground. The cargo is all the same – clear cases housing small, shiny discs.

We're looking at a scene that must have played out over two hundred years ago, and the sight of it is eerie and disquieting. The toppled crates paint an unsettling picture of how the complex's main lifeline became the very thing that killed it. And all it probably took were a few dozen Zees breaching this train tunnel. The way things seem to have been dropped, it was something the complex designers hadn't anticipated. Either way, at some

71

point, all hell had broken loose.

I motion to Ret and Bron. "I need you both to inspect that tunnel and make sure it's not blocked or crawling with Zees."

The two of them turn to head off, and suddenly the right side of my body feels like it's on fire. I stagger and sink to one knee, and Jinx grabs my elbow.

"Azina, this has gone too far. You need help."

He's probably right, but that voice in my ear is clearer now. The muffled quality from before is gone, and for the first time I can make out parts of what it's saying.

It sounds like gibberish. "BACK DASH FORWARD DOT DOT LINE HORIZONTAL LINE UP LEFT."

It's some kind of code, and the logical side of my brain doesn't equate it to a damn thing, but on some prehistoric, subterranean level, I know exactly what it means. What sounds like gibberish is a set of instructions broadcast to all Zees within range. It has something to do with us. Whatever's sending that signal doesn't want us to leave.

-25-

Oleg is anxious to make it into the library. I rise to my feet and pull him close to me. "I've been thinking about your Hive comment from before. Do you really think they could be communicating with one another on some mental wavelength we're unaware of?"

Oleg seems annoyed by my question. I'm sure all he wants is to head into the library. I squeeze his arm to let him know this is important.

He sighs. "Ants give off a chemical signal called pheromones that identify them to their group. But that's not to say instructions are sent via telepathy, per se. Even flocks of birds and schools of fish use a process called emergent behavior, where subtle movements made by individuals are picked up."

I feel that hand on my shoulder again, nudging me forward. When I turn around, Jinx has his head turned to our makeshift barricade, watching it buckle. Beside him is Glave, and his face is bone white. I notice one of his eyes twitching, and for a moment I wonder if he can also hear the instructions broadcast over the Zee airwaves.

"Let's make this fast." I say, and we head inside.

We find row after row of shelves. Each one lined with hundreds, maybe thousands, of discs. There are words on each shelf from top to bottom, all in the old tongue, and I can't make sense of it. Oleg, on the other hand, looks like a kid at Christmas. He's already got a stack of discs in his arms, all the way up to his chin. I just hope he has some machine capable of reading these things.

"What are they?" I ask.

"Digital Video Disks. They were used to store vast amounts of information."

"Like a book?"

"Yes, except each one of these can hold thousands of books."

I shake my head. "They sure don't look like much."

From behind me comes a thudding noise, like a sack full of beef being dropped on the ground. I turn. Glave has collapsed to the floor. He isn't shaking yet, not the way Pennies had, but it's becoming harder to cling to the dim hope that he'll pull through.

Glave looks up at me and whispers. "He's outside with the others…"

"Glave's losing his mind," Jinx says. "Azina, we don't have a choice anymore. We gotta waste him."

"Not yet."

Oleg's standing there, his mouth hanging open, probably expecting Glave's eyes to start glowing.

"Oleg." I snap my fingers. "Take what you can carry 'cause we're leaving."

I'm dragging Glave by the arm, and I see Bron waving at me from the mouth of the tunnel. Judging by the big, goofy smile on his face I'm guessing he and Ret have found something useful.

I hear a terrifying sound and the timing couldn't be worse – the clang of the metal door being flung onto the ground. Our barricade has just given way. Ahead of us is the train tunnel and home. On our left is the parked train, and just over that, the now shattered barricade. We begin to run and I can just make out Zees pouring into the station. My first thought is that they look like ants, but maybe that's because of what Oleg just said about emergent-whatever. They can't come directly at us, since the train is in the way, but solve that problem by simply going around. Half of them stream off toward the vault and around the front of the train, and the others toward the tunnel itself.

Jinx lobs a few grenades to stall them. Fat chance,

although it's worth a shot. Up ahead, blinding flashes erupt from Bron's heavy guns. Unlike before, he's being careful, trying to conserve his ammo. For a second, I allow my mind to consider the trouble we'll be in if his guns fall silent for good, and the thought terrifies me.

Then I see something emerge through the doorway. The Hive leader. I know it's him because his skin is blood red and he's a full foot taller than the others. The right side of my body feels like it's going to burn through my clothing. That hand that had been nudging me forward all this time is now pushing me backwards. He wants me to stay and I feel like I'm fighting through violent gale force winds. I look down and see Glave. His free arm is swinging wildly, trying to snag Oleg's cloak. The skin on his face is brown and wrinkled. He's turned. No doubt about it and I know there's no use avoiding what needs to be done any longer. I put him to rest by sending the tip of the Katana through his skull and into the concrete floor. Nice and fast. He deserves nothing less.

Jinx and Oleg are ahead of me. A sea of mangled Zees lies before Bron and Ret. Some of them aren't quite dead. The torso of a man in a business suit pulls itself toward them. It's nearly a foot from Ret when he notices it and turns the man's head inside out with the shotgun.

Oleg and Jinx reach the edge of the track and jump. Oleg lands awkwardly on his ankle and half the discs in his arms spill to the ground. He stops to gather them back up. Jinx grabs him by the collar and pulls him along.

I haven't even made it to the edge yet. I feel like I'm running in slow motion and for a moment I'm sure this is a nightmare and I'll wake up any second.

Ret and Bron retreat into the tunnel. They climb onto some contraption I've never seen before. A kind of device on wheels, with a teeter-totter. Looks like something people use to get water out of the ground. Except here, pumping the lever makes the wheels turn.

It's taking time to build up momentum; Jinx, Oleg and I will have to jump on while it's moving.

I finally reach the tracks and jump down. My feet hit the gravel running. Then, I realize Jinx isn't going to make it. There's a Zee right on his heels. I swing my repeater around, pop in a fresh magazine and squeeze the trigger. Oleg's a few feet away and so I've got to aim carefully. One round hits the Zee's chest and the rest ricochet off the walls. My next burst is lower, and it chews up his legs. He tumbles to the ground, but that's good enough for now. Oleg makes it to the cart and slides onboard with his few remaining discs.

Jinx is tired and slowing down, the pack of Zees are closing the distance. I pull out the Katana and swing left, hoping to cut them off. I can see Ret ahead, pumping that lever furiously, screaming at me to run. His face is filled with frustration. He doesn't understand why I'm so slow. "Run, Azina!" I'm almost certain he's about to jump down and help me, but he can't stop working that lever or he'll risk everyone's life. The pain in his eyes is heartbreaking.

I don't need to look behind me to know the Hive leader is doing his best to get inside my head. There are two of me now. Azina the Merc, running for her life and racing to stop these bastards from cutting down her friends, and Azina the Zee, eager to be a good drone and do whatever Papa Zee says.

Three of them grab hold of Jinx and I don't think I can get there fast enough. Jinx curses and flings his grenade launcher to the ground and tries to shake them off. I swing at the Zee closest to me and watch the blade cut an almost invisible line through the back of his skull. It's a killing blow. I know it even before his legs give out and he collapses. Then I realize it's already too late; the Zee on Jinx's right has its teeth buried in his forearm. Jinx shrieks and falls.

The others look on in horror, unable to do a damn thing but build up enough speed to get out of here.

I get to Jinx a second later. I know he won't make it, not with the horde so close behind us. There's only one thing to do. I swing down and then up again, killing both Zees. Even for me, the movements are seamless and beautiful. I don't have the heart to hear them tearing Jinx apart, and I save the final blow for him. When I turn, I can see Ret and the others shouting, but their voices sound muffled and distant. It's the other voice I hear now, the new voice, but my legs are still running.

Seven Zees.

That's how many it takes before I crash headfirst into a patch of gravel. They aren't biting me. Just holding me in place. My face hurts like a bitch and my vision's a blurry mess, but it's enough for me to make out hundreds of them leaping over us as they give chase to a small group of men on a strange cart. I watch as they become smaller and smaller before disappearing.

I can feel that red bastard coming up the tunnel, and I have no idea what he's about to do, but somehow, that has me less worried than the thought of what a swarm of hungry Zees will do to a world whose wounds haven't completely healed.

-26-

I awaken in a dank chamber. The smell of mold and rotting flesh is overwhelming. No way of knowing how long I've been unconscious. An ugly red face is staring down at me from out of the gloom and all at once I'm certain I've died and been sent to the underworld those superstitious Keepers are always blabbing on about. But I can feel my tongue sticking to the roof of my mouth and with it comes the dreadful realization that I'm not dead at all. No, it's far worse. I've finally gone and turned into a mindless Zee. But the mere act of thinking says otherwise, doesn't it? I think, therefore I am not a Zee. A Keeper is supposed to have coined that one. Probably the only one of that bunch with a decent head on his shoulders.

That face inches toward me and suddenly I know exactly where I am and who it belongs to. The Hive leader touches the patch of brown skin on the side of my face and I move at once to slap his grimy Zee hand away and all I hear is a clank. He's got me chained to some kind of old dentist's chair and so I do what any normal girl would under the circumstances. I swing my foot up between his legs. I can't wait to see those bulging red eyes of his start watering, but all I hear is another clank.

Leg restraints. Great!

The Hive leader smiles and I'm starting to think he isn't nearly as dumb as he looks. A series of thoughts trickle into my head, more of that coded gibberish and a second later the words bloom before my eyes.

"Save your energy, Azina. You belong to me now."

Easy for him to say, but all I can think about is escaping. I scan the shadows and see a few scattered Zees standing in the dim light. No way to know how far down

I am. More calming commands form inside my head. He's reading my thoughts, knows I'm itching to get out of here and leave him in a heap of red goo. But along with the code is another strand of information, one I'm sure he isn't even aware of. An image of that red bastard in real life, before he turned, before the world went to shit. He's dressed in a pair of blue overalls, mopping the floor in a gymnasium, just like the one in this very complex. In fact, the very same one. And in this image, a woman in a tight pink outfit traipses over his clean floor and suddenly his vision blurs with rage. He wants to strangle this woman. Wants to pull her into the closet where he keeps all his brooms and cleaning detergents and make her pay for what she's done.

There was something special about his – what did Oleg call them again? – his genetics. That's why he didn't become a drone like the others.

The Hive leader is over by a table with his back to me and I can see in the shredded rags he's wearing the vague outline of what was once his cleaning uniform. I haven't a clue what they used to call Grinders before the fall, but the end of the world has certainly been kind to him.

I see something that sends icy fingers dancing up my spine. That red prick's cutting open his own arm and wringing the blood into some kind of bowl. No, not a bowl, it's a drinking cup and something tells me it isn't for him. He's laughing now; the room's as quiet as a tomb, but he's in my head, laughing and telling me to be calm, that it'll all be over soon.

-27-

I know what's about to happen. He's going to make me drink the blood he's wringing out of his arm and then who knows what the hell will happen. If there are worse things than becoming a Zee, I'm about to find out.

I can't help thinking of that lady in pink, the one he wanted to dominate. My eyes scan through the darkness and I see that my things have been kicked into a corner; my pack, repeater, and most important of all, my Katana. Why didn't he leave them? Maybe because that sick fuck is collecting trophies.

I try to wrench my wrists free from the metal cuffs. The noise is kicking up a racket, but at this stage I don't really care. That cup is nearly full and I'm not in the mood to find out what will happen when it is.

Movement from the corner of my eye. A shape in the darkness, slight and hunched over and the movement strikes me as odd. Zees don't hunch.

The Hive leader's turning around now, but I'm not looking at him anymore. My eyes are locked on that shape. It's moving to the corner of the room, the one where my things are stashed, and a split second later it disappears. When I look back I see that the red bastard's heading my way, cup in hand, blood sloshing over the sides. Behind him I see a flash of steel and hear a thump as a Zee's head rolls off its body, then a second and a third.

The Hive leader turns around. The bodies of three headless Zees lay on the ground, their jaws gnashing at empty air.

"Sneak, watch out!" I scream.

I can feel the Hive leader trying to keep me pinned to the chair. He's calling for help, but all the Zees in the room are dead and it'll take time for his reinforcements to arrive. A blade cuts through the darkness. The Hive leader spins around, holding his belly. Sneak's opened his stomach like a can of worms and now his guts are spilling out onto the floor. More slashes and a deep line appears across his throat, releasing a waterfall of blood. Then another slash and off comes the hand with the cup. It falls to the ground, painting the floor red.

"Finish him," I shout.

Another blur of movement, but this time he's ready for her. She's in the top arc of her swing when he catches her by the throat. Sneak's legs are three feet off the ground, kicking at dead air. She's trying to swing at him, but he's shaking her like a ragdoll. The sword drops from her hand, clanking onto the floor. Even in the dim light I can see her eyes starting to roll up in their sockets. A sick gurgling sound is coming from her throat. In a few seconds she'll be dead.

-28-

Blood oozes from my wrists where the restraints are cutting into my skin. All I wanna do is pry his fingers off her throat. Tears well up in my eyes. I want it more than I've ever wanted anything in my whole life.

Then comes a snapping sound. The Hive leader's fingers are bending back on themselves at queer angles. And suddenly the room is lit up brighter than the full moon festival and I know right away what's doing it. My eyes are glowing.

Sneak falls to the ground, clutching her neck. The Hive leader turns to me, his guts dangling about him like a butcher's apron, his fingers bent back at odd angles. Blood streams from his throat and his severed hand, but it's his eyes that I see. They're wide and disbelieving. A flash of steel from behind and the Hive leader's eyes go wide. The first of his frantic thought waves hit me just as his head rolls off his shoulders and hits the floor with a wet slapping sound. I wanna hug Sneak so bad, but there isn't any time. I can already feel a group of those things nearby and suddenly my body feels so weak, I'm not sure I'll be able to stand up.

Sneak uses a key from the table to undo the restraints and I immediately fall to the floor. She's over me now, her face caked in blood and dirt, but I'm just happy she's alive though I'm still not entirely sure how she has survived. She grabs my pack and repeater and helps me to my feet. I feel her eyes linger over the patch of rough brown skin on the side of my face. The light from my eyes is gone, and already I can feel my strength returning. We're at the door, about to leave, when I feel that red bastard still trying to mess around inside my head. That's all he is now, just a head and I'm tempted to walk over and stomp his brains out, but there isn't time. The Zees are almost here.

-29-

We come out into a concrete structure. Low ceiling, filled with abandoned vehicles. The smell of oil and old rubber is strong. They used to call them cars, I know that much, but right now they look more like dust-covered coffins to me. Sneak's got her arm around me and I'm thankful, 'cause I know I won't make it five feet without her. Strings of Zee code are buzzing around inside my head, telling me to stay, ordering me still, but I'm muscling on. He isn't as strong as he was before Sneak sent my Katana slashing through his neck.

Up ahead is a red metal door with a small busted out window. Behind us comes the hissing. Sneak's face is a mask of calmness and it gives me strength. She managed to evade a horde of them all on her own. Only difference was, at the time, she didn't have any dead weight to carry. I glance back and my heart freezes in my chest. Lesson number one, I remind myself. When a pack of killing machines is nipping at your heels, never look back.

There must be well over a hundred of them, lumbering between the hulks of rotting cars, some scrambling over obstacles, all the while their eyes locked on the two of us with eerie determination. They're less than ten yards away when we reach the door and my only hope is that it isn't locked. Locked means we're dead, or worse. For a split second, as my hand reaches for the handle and my thumb pushes the lever, I'm furious that Sneak came back for me. Furious, because she had a chance to escape and now her life is in the hands of a rusted antique door.

I feel the lever begin to give and then jam. Sneak looks up at me like she knows this is it but at least she tried. They're less than ten feet away now and the smell they give off suddenly makes the homeless of Sotercity seem like the perfumed upper classes.

I give a final push and the sound of grinding metal gives way to a click and I swing the door open and shove Sneak in first. I'm right behind her, pulling the door closed when it stops short. One of the Zee's has his arm wedged inside and now the bloody thing won't shut. Another Zee's hissing at me through the broken window. His breath makes my eyes water. Sneak takes the Katana and lops off the arm in the door. There's a squishing sound as I pull it shut. I snatch the blade from her and give the one in the window a quick lobotomy. I feel that pin prick again and a pang of momentary guilt, like I'm killing my own kind, but I know they'd just as soon tear us both apart as look at us.

-30-

Stairs. Lots of stairs and I'm clinging to the railing like some kind of makeshift crutch. Each flight gets easier and easier and I'm suddenly aware of a pain at the back of my skull. My fingers dance around until they find a wet knot of flesh. Must have been when the Hive leader knocked me out in the tunnel. I can't help thinking about that blood he wanted to pour down my throat. It's obvious he isn't just another mindless drone. On some level he can still think, so what the hell is he after? I glance over at Sneak. Her hair is slicked back with some kind of motor oil and her clothes are torn in places. Then I see her neck, it's swollen where that headless sonofabitch was squeezing the life out of her. He didn't break the skin. I can see that even from here. Then I catch sight of the bandage on her right arm. Must have missed that in all the commotion.

"You're hurt," I say.

"I'm fine," she signs back.

I stop her and try to examine the wound but she shrugs me off. She's angry, I can see it in her face and by the way she's signing so fast her fingers are practically tripping over one another. She found an elevator shaft and cut her arm climbing into the car. Says the Zees kept chasing her and dozens must have stepped off into midair, only to splatter their brains below.

I'm still chuckling at the thought when we reach the top level and step out into what looks like the living quarters, except I don't recognize any of skeletons strewn about. I reach down and pluck a diamond necklace off one of the corpses. Sneak does the same. The instinctual part of me is saying forget the loot and focus on finding a way out of this deathtrap, but another part of me is

86

saying you never know when you're going to need a little cash.

It isn't long before I get my bearings. Soon we come to Glave's wife, still lying where Ret filled her head with buckshot. We pass through the theater and then the gymnasium.

We exit the gym and head down the escalators. There might be another way out of here. Hell, I'm sure we only scratched the surface of this complex, but right now I'm not interested in exploring.

It isn't long before we reach a mountain of dead Zees. Hundreds of them, maybe more. Their bodies clog the final escalator before the train station entrance and we don't have a choice but to climb over them.

I realize quickly this isn't as easy as it looks. Even a severed head still has the power to bite and turn you, but more important than that, if one of them sees us, all of them see us. Sneak and I hunker down and weigh our options. As we sign back and forth I spot the pile moving in places. More bodies lie at the foot of the stairs, but beyond that is the doorway to the train yard and the tunnel to freedom.

Sneak signs her opinion. She thinks we should just make a break for it. The look in her eyes tells me she just wants to get the hell out of here. So do I.

On my count we spring up and clamber over the bodies clogging the escalator. I step on a darkened Zee face in the tangle of arms and legs and see its jaw clamp down around the toe of my boot. Thing's trying to bite through, but his teeth can't penetrate the thick leather. Either way, they've seen us and the damage is already done. I send the tip of my Katana into his forehead and his lights go out for good, but not before I catch the mental warning he sends to all his Zee buddies. Almost in unison, the pile begins to ripple with movement.

"Run!" I scream to Sneak. The pile's become a mountain of clawed hands. We get to the bottom in a series of giant steps, trying our best to avoid getting snagged. A writhing mass of butchered Zees is the last place you want to have a fall.

The landing is littered with body parts too, but most of these ones are long gone, thanks to Bron and his 20mm guns.

Only seconds later and we're through the shattered barricade and into the station. The train is still there, its nose pointing at the vault door. To my left is a trail of dead Zees leading up to where Bron and Ret held them back before making off in that rail car contraption. Beyond that I see Jinx, or at least what's left of him, face down and looking like a rag doll. That's when I get another blast from Zee central. They're not far behind us and I'm about to tell Sneak that home is through that tunnel when I hear the voice.

-31-

"Halt!"

I spin around to find a Warden near the front of the train, his rifle drawn and pointing right at me. What the hell is he doing here? He's still a good hundred yards away, but for a trained marksman that's close enough. I raise my hands, as does Sneak. She's looking up at me now and in a calm whisper I tell her to stay cool. Another Warden appears by the first, with an armful of discs. They've come to clean the place out. That means Oleg, Ret and Bron must have made it home. I'm overcome with joy, until a shot sails over my head and into the concrete wall behind us.

"Hey, are you crazy!" I yell.

More shots, these ones even closer. Sneak and I hop off the platform and make a dash for the tunnel. The Wardens decide to give chase, but no sooner do they pull even with the complex entrance than a swarm of Zees bursts through. I turn only long enough to see the two Wardens disappear in a sea of dark flesh. More voices call out from the vault. Must be another group of Skuld's men and now the Zees begin charging in that direction. We're deep in the tunnel when the screams finally die away.

I'm still not sure why those Wardens were shooting at us. Zee's don't stop and put their hands up. Did they think we were scavengers from Sotercity? I pull to a stop and take a deep breath and listen. I don't have a sense that the Zees behind us are giving chase. My guess would be they're filling their bellies with Warden meat. Still, it's no reason to hang around.

Sneak and I reach the opening and when that first blast of sunlight hits my face, I'm blinded with pain. Feels like hot pokers are stabbing my eyes. Even Sneak's covering her face. We've been underground too long. Slowly, the pain subsides and I look around. I can just make out the edges of Sotercity in the distance. After that army of Zees got free, I was half expecting to find a pillar of black smoke rising up from the city. And the mental image reminds me of that story The Keepers used to tell about the old God and how he once destroyed a place called Gomorrah. Of course, I'm relieved it hasn't been touched. But if not toward Sotercity, where did the Zees go?

Part II

-32-

Hours after we escape the shopping complex, Sneak and I finally approach Sotercity, and right away I can see something isn't quite right. The bodies of four women swing from nooses, strung up over the eastern gate. They're too well dressed to be petty thieves or hardened criminals. Below them, in a long, ragged line are hundreds of people all waiting to enter Sotercity.

These aren't Grinders though, they're farmers from villages scattered throughout No Man's Land. Men and women who've struggled for years to eke out a living from barren soil. The Keepers say the land has been drying up slowly over the last fifty years and I can't imagine what it's like, waiting for seeds to grow in hardened clay. I also can't imagine living outside Sotercity's impressive walls: great slabs of steel that rise nearly a hundred feet into the air. The hulls from giant cargo ships that used to plow enormous lakes in the north. Some of that water's still there, but it's been a while since any ship was able to reach us. Even from outside I can hear the bustle inside the walls. As long as the overland trade routes stay open, anything you want can be had, for the right price.

A farmer in front of me's been bitching about the lineup since we arrived. He turns to commiserate and stops cold when his eyes light upon my face. Sneak digs her elbow into my side and starts signing. She keeps saying face, face and it takes me a minute to figure out what she's getting at. When it finally sinks in I yank my tunic up as far as it'll go, but even then a patch of rough darkened flesh remains visible. There's something else strange about these farmers. If they're coming to market, where's their produce? Hell, most of them are carrying trunks filled with clothes and strange bits of furniture. But the truth is they don't look like farmers at all. They look like refugees.

-33-

A voice behind me says, "You shouldn't be here."

My mind starts to race. I hope to hell he isn't talking to me. Maybe they've seen my face, think I'm a monster. The line shuffles ahead. The city guards are checking everyone over before letting them inside. I'm not sure what they're looking for, but I'm starting to wonder what they'll make of me.

"This line isn't safe for you," the voice says again.

I turn around. The man looking back at me is gruff and powerful. Shaved head. Square jaw, wild, bulging eyes. He looks like he's got a temper and the strength to back it up. This is no farmer.

"Do I know you?"

He smiles and two dimples form on his cheeks. "Your friend Oleg sent me." His voice is gravely and rough with a slight twang I can't place. A chunk from one of his ears is missing. If I didn't know any better, I'd say he was an outlaw.

"Oleg? Where is he?"

"We can't talk here. The city guards are looking for you."

The line moves ahead. The guards search through a cart filled with bundles of cloth, poking it with sharpened spikes.

"How do I know I can trust you?"

His blue eyes are shining like brilliant jewels and I can't tell if he's fearless or crazy.

"You don't, but I'm sure, by now, you know you can't trust them," he says, pointing at the guards.

We peel away and follow the city wall. The path leads down toward the dried lakebed. As we descend, the smell of raw sewage hits me like a shot to the gut. A second later, the source of the odor becomes clear. This is where the city's sewage system lets out. A steady stream of water pours from the tunnel. It's large enough to walk through upright and I can see the metal grate covering the entrance has been wrenched back.

I grit my teeth at the stench. It brings back memories, none of them good.

"I swore to myself I'd never walk through piss and shit ever again," I say.

"Get used to it," the man says. He's about to climb inside when Sneak and I stop dead.

"We've come this far, but we aren't gonna take another step until you answer some questions."

Impatience flashes across his face. "There isn't time."

"Unless you wanna make this sewer your tomb," I say, spitting on the ground for emphasis, "then I suggest you make time."

He stops. "What do you wanna know?" His arms cross over his chest and I notice the gloves he's wearing. They look like steel gauntlets, with spikes at the knuckles. Similar spikes line his boots, tied in place with thick leather straps.

"Never seen a Merc who didn't use a gun," I say.

"Let's just say I like to keep it out of sight."

"Who are you?"

"Krantz," he says coolly. His foot keeps tapping the gravel beneath his feet, the blades at the toe of his boot chiming softly.

"Where are my friends?"

"The Keepers have Oleg, Ret and Bron in the Citadel. They're scheduled to be executed tomorrow morning, unless we can do something about that."

My heart sinks. The same look of despair is mirrored on Sneak's grease-stained face. Then Skuld's haggard features loom before me and my fear quickly turns to anger. After killing that fifth Prospector, the only one to

95

escape the Hive, The Keepers more than proved themselves untrustworthy. It was the discs they were after. Those were our tickets to freedom, and knowing Oleg, he probably handed them all over to Skuld the minute they arrived back in Sotercity. No one from my crew would make such a rookie mistake. First rule of negotiation, never hand over the only bargaining chip you have. For all his book smarts, sometimes Oleg can be a damned idiot.

"So let me get this straight," I say. "We're going to breaking into a Keeper stronghold so we can free my friends?"

He nods. "And the best part? We're not going to kill anyone doing it."

I laugh. "Where's the fun in that? I'm assuming you have a plan?"

A slow grin forms on Krantz' face and I can see a light shining behind his eyes; now I know he's crazy.

-34-

We slosh through a stream of putrid waste. A hundred yards in and the smell isn't getting any better. The walls are low and cramped. Krantz is nearly a full head shorter than me and seems perfectly at home. I, on the other hand, need to stoop and the pain in my back and legs feels like burning wax is being poured over my flesh. Krantz tells us we aren't far now, but all I see is more sewer. I'm starting to wonder if this guy knows where he's going or if he's completely off his gourd. Maybe getting nabbed by The Keepers would have been a better option.

Krantz stops before what I assume is a door to an access tunnel. Three turns of a wheel and we're inside, but this is no access tunnel. This is a room, dry and not nearly as rank as the tunnels we've just come from. Krantz lights a lamp and our surroundings come to life. Bunk beds, dozens of them, as far as the eye can see.

Sneak begins signing. "What is this place?"

I ask Krantz.

"This is where Keepers come, when they've had enough of the corruption and the lies."

"Ex-Keepers," I correct.

"Not all, but most. Although once a Keeper, always a Keeper."

Sounds like drivel to me. "You're rebels," I say, with a hint of surprise. "I'd always thought The Keepers were one big happy family, but then aren't all families messed up, one way or another?"

"We stand for truth, learning, growth. Those are the true Keeper ways. Slowly, the brotherhood has fallen out of sync with those principles and has replaced them with deception, power and greed."

"Absolute power corrupts absolutely," I say and Krantz nods in agreement. His eyes are glistening.

"One day we will take back The Order and return it to its rightful heritage, but don't be fooled. I am more than prepared for a time when we too must be reminded. As you said, absolute power has a way of making us forget what we fought for in the first place."

Sneak stalks along the rows of empty beds. She's scouting, looking for a back door. A lesson hammered home in the Cartier shop and countless times before. Don't ever let your enemy box you in.

"So why us? What are you getting out of it?"

Krantz' eyes become cold and glassy. "Only one thing: Prior Skuld."

"Are you insane?" I cry. "You can't just execute a Prior. You'll have every Keeper within a thousand miles after you."

"He's a poison that has eaten away at the order since he first took office."

"Sounds like a suicide mission, to me. You're soft in the head, you know that?"

Krantz laughs. "When the people discover the extent of his evil, they'll rise up against him."

"And what does that have to do with me and my crew?"

"Everything. Once I help you free your men, you will help me to kill Skuld."

"Yeah, that sounds fair," I say, not trying to hide the sarcasm in my voice. "And when The Keepers come looking for us, where will we hide? In the sewers of Sotercity?"

"You won't need to hide. When Skuld falls and the list of his crimes is revealed, you'll be a hero."

There's something he isn't telling me and I can feel it, the same way I feel when those mindless Zees are close.

Krantz catches the skepticism on my face and looks away.

"You got a real hard-on for Skuld, don't you? What's say we cut the ideological bullshit you've been spewing and you tell me the truth."

A flash of anger crosses Krantz' face and, for second, I wonder if he's gonna come at me. His gaze falls to his hands and suddenly he looks like he's a million miles away. "I was only a boy when the Patriarch appointed my father, Julius, as Prior of Sotercity." As the words tumble out of his mouth, I notice the muscles in his forearms bunch into knots. "Skuld was his brother, my uncle, runner up for the position. They had been at each other's throats since childhood and this final blow had only served to fuel Skuld's already festering resentment. Perhaps hoping to ease his older brother's jealousy, my father allowed Skuld to act as sub-prior. which placed him at the head of security for all of Sotercity and her outlying regions. But my father misjudged Skuld's hunger for power and less than a week later, my mother and father went missing. Rather than allow this territory to fall into chaos, the Patriarch made Skuld prior and he's been ruling with an iron fist ever since. But I'm not the only one with demons," Krantz says. He's studying the patch of rough skin on my face and I'm suddenly not crazy about where he's going with this.

"I learned a long time ago, real trust comes from bearing one's soul. You've seen mine…"

I show you mine and you show me yours. Yeah, I played that game as a child and it always ended with someone getting hurt.

Krantz stands there waiting patiently.

My heart is hammering in my chest. He wants to know about my face and what happened. I tell him, but I can see he isn't sure what to make of it.

"You haven't turned."

"Not yet."

"Something inside you is slowing the change?"

I think of Pennies, Glave and Jinx and feel a sudden chill run up my spine. "That's the way it looks. But apart from this," I say, waving my hand in front of my face, "we're not so different, you and I. We were both orphans. Except my parents were Grinders, who worked in waste management. Every night they came home smelling like two sacks filled with shit. Guess now you know why I'm not a big fan of this subterranean paradise of yours. One day, there was an accident in the tunnel they were working in. Someone pulled a lever they shouldn't have and drowned a dozen workers, my parents included. After that, I was sent to The Keeper academy, to be raised as one of their own. There they tried to teach me the old tongue and how to behave and dress like a proper lady, but all that ended when I saw a group of Wardens training in the academy courtyard. I knew then what I was meant to do."

"You became a Warden?"

I laugh. "Never, but I signed up. Girls shouldn't waste time fighting. That's what most people here think. To you, we're nothing more than walking baby factories."

Krantz holds up his hands, palms out.

I take a deep breath. "One night, after basic, I was cleaning up when my commanding officer decided I'd make a better concubine than a Warden. Didn't matter that I told him to stop. You see, no one tells men not to rape, they tell woman not to get raped. Big difference."

Krantz' eyes dip and when they find me again, I can see he isn't like the others. "Tell me who did this to you."

"It was a long time ag–"

"Tell me."

"I could, but it won't do you much good."

Krantz looks puzzled.

100

"It won't help you because they found the sonafabitch the next morning wearing his balls for earrings. I learned then that men who underestimate women do so just once. It was soon after that I left the Wardens and joined a group of Mercs."

Krantz is nodding with approval. "Then I have something to show you I think you're going to like."

A tapestry with a strange symbol hangs on the wall behind him. Krantz yanks on the edge of it and the curtain disappears into a hollow cavity in the ceiling. Beneath it, the wall is jammed with weapons, enough hardware to outfit a small army.

"Take your pick," he says. "Just remember, speed and agility over firepower. The trick will be to get in and get out without anyone knowing, or getting hurt. Remember, there's only one man we want dead."

"Fat chance," I say. "There's an old saying I learned as a child. Better to have and not need than to need and not have."

Krantz' laughter echoes throughout the room, his entire body gyrating and I can't help but join him.

"Azina, I'm starting to like you."

Krantz opens a nearby trunk and comes back with a black and red Warden's cloak. He wraps it around me and smiles.

"What's this?" I ask.

"Our ticket into the citadel."

-35-

The sewers beneath Sotercity spread out like a spider's web, connecting every major building. Krantz keeps our Warden cloaks in a bag, nestled amongst cloves and pine needles, so we don't pop out smelling like a bunch of Grinders. I couldn't help but snicker watching him cut more than a foot of cloth from the robe Sneak was wearing. She looks like the world's smallest Warden.

It isn't long before we come to a ladder that leads to a grate. We creep up and find ourselves in an indoor pig farm and the sewers smell like a bouquet of roses by comparison. Sneak is last up and lowers the grate while trying not to breathe. A pig, nearly the size of a man, scurries away grunting madly. Krantz tells us we're inside the pens. This is the bottommost level of Sotercity, where a group of specialized Grinders maintain food and livestock for The Keepers. Faint light trickles in from an adjacent room, but otherwise this place feels like we've entered a dark patch of hell. Ahead of us, an old Grinder in rags is hosing out a pig stall. He sees us approach and salutes. Krantz returns the gesture and tells him to carry on. For a minute I watch the Grinder's eyes as they study the dark patch of skin on my face. Then out of nowhere I feel long fingers skitter up my back. There's no one there. The feeling's gentle. Almost like a hand that's just come up short and I hope to hell it doesn't mean what I think it means. That Grinder's looking at me real weird now and I'm sure I'm gonna need to feed him to the pigs, but he doesn't say a word and I let him live.

In the levels above us is a barracks, housing hundreds of guards and Keepers we're desperately trying to avoid. We follow a set of stairs that lead up two levels and into a narrow and dimly lit corridor. The sound of a siren cuts the ominous silence. Low at first and building to an incredible whine, like one of those antique air raid jobs. A door up ahead swings open and my body tenses. Four Wardens come rushing out, straight at us. Krantz is just ahead and I've agreed to follow his lead, but I won't be taken down without a fight, that's for damn sure. They're getting closer now and I can hear them shouting. Sneak looks back and I'm sure she sees the steely look in my eyes and turns around at once. They're only a few feet away, but I can already tell they're focused beyond us. They rush past, the one in front still barking commands to the others moving with him. Something's going on outside and, judging by the anxious looks on the men we just passed, it isn't good.

-36-

That siren is still squalling when we make it through the first bulkhead. The room on the other side is stacked to the walls with computing machines.

Two men in long black cloaks are poring over reams of paper. A third crosses the room with a clipboard in his hands and a look of acute annoyance on his face. On his cloak are two red initials.

S.I.

Sotercity Intelligence. Shadowy types who get a kick out of poking around in people's trash and looking for 'threats against the public good,' whatever that means.

He points up with the edge of his clipboard at some invisible point above us. "You should be at your stations, are you all deaf or just stupid?" Of course he's referring to the sirens that are giving me one hell of a headache, but all I wanna do is shove that clipboard down his throat.

Krantz speaks up. "We're on our way to the holding cells to retrieve prisoners for Prior Skuld."

The man's hair is slicked back and he's sporting a matching mustache that looks just as greasy. He's looking at my face now and his mouth tweaks into a sour expression.

"What happened to you?"

"Flamethrower accident," I say without missing a beat.

The weasely man shakes his head. "Fine, fine, just don't touch any of the equipment on your way through."

Krantz nods and we weave past tables covered with maps and booklets marked 'top secret.' On our left is an open door. I glance inside and gasp. They've got a Zee, jammed inside a glass tube with a tight metal bowl around his head. Wires dangle from the cap to a machine beside him. It's spitting out trails of ticker tape, like those old pictures you see of dusters checking stock market prices. Even from here I can see words printed on that length of paper. They're listening in on the Zee signal.

I can't believe my eyes. Oleg said The Keepers knew nothing about the Zees still being around. So then how long has this one been here? Could they have built a machine like this in the short time since Oleg's been back? A layer of dust covers the top of the glass dome and I realize that this has been here a while. But how can that be? Just then the Zee's eyes see me and its mouth starts moving a mile a minute, spitting out that ticker tape like ribbon candy. I wasn't expecting any of this and now the Zees know where I am and it's only a matter a time before they come and find me.

-37-

The room falls away and Krantz tells us the holding cells aren't far off. I stop and tell him what I saw, what it means.

"Now do you believe what I told you about Skuld?" he asks.

I nod, but inside I'm still reeling; I mean, I knew Skuld was no good. Even a child could sense the guy's rotten inside.

"But how did they nab a Zee and bring him back here without anyone knowing about it?"

Krantz has a look on his face, like he doesn't want to say. "They didn't bring him here. They made him."

My jaw falls open.

"They've got needles of the stuff, Azina. One little prick is all it takes."

Even Sneak's eyes are wide and disbelieving.

"They're doing worse than that," Krantz says, "far worse, and I can't fight off the inclination to go back and kill everyone in that listening post, the Zee included."

Skuld's men, grabbing innocent people off the streets and turning them into Zees before they know what's hit them. I've spent a lifetime trying to stay hard and uncaring and now I'm turning into a mushy suck. That's what I try and tell myself, but through the thick haze of anger I don't even realize I've turned and started heading back. Back to kill them all.

Krantz' fingers close around my arm. I break free with ease, which surprises even me, considering Krantz is certainly no pushover. He grabs me again.

"Azina. What's more important, killing a bunch of Keeper spooks or freeing your friends? There'll be time later to make things right, I promise you."

106

I take a deep breath and feel my blood pressure begin to stabilize. He's right, of course and for a moment I'm just thankful my eyes didn't start glowing.

-38-

Up ahead is another bulkhead with the letters BRIG stenciled in bold red letters. A single Keeper stands guard outside. But this isn't a Warden, not that it will matter much in the end. Krantz approaches him. The guard's on edge. The alarm's got them all on edge.

"We're here to escort prisoners Oleg, Ret and Bron to see Prior Skuld."

The guard spins the door wheel and swings it open. The place smells of sweat and piss. Rooms are on either side of us and in the distance are a series of jail cells. I can hear a man screaming and I hope – for their sake – it isn't one of ours. We reach the cell block and find another guard, seated at a desk to our right. This one's nose is all bandaged up and bent outa shape, like someone took a metal pipe to his face.

Krantz gives him the same spiel he gave the guard at the door, but it doesn't look like he's buying it and suddenly I'm calculating how quickly I can grab the Katana stuffed under my robe and bring it down on this drone's head. Out of the corner of my eye I see a cell with the bars all bent out of shape. It's dark in there, but there's a large figure inside and I'm sure it's Bron. Next door, a face peers through the bars. It's Ret. His face is bruised, and filled with defiance.

More echoing screams and this time I know now it isn't coming from Bron or Ret.

The guard rises.

"You lot stay here while I run this past the supervisor. He's in with the old man now, or what's left of him."

And suddenly I've had enough of this charade. The guard turns and I reach for my blade. He hears me coming up behind him, and as he turns to tell me to wait at the desk the edge of my sword splits the top of his skull and doesn't stop until it hits his jawbone. He blinks once and then withers like a dead leaf.

The one who let us in is walking back to his post at the brig entrance. I fling my six inch blade and catch him just above the neck.

I can hear Krantz behind me, telling me this isn't the way, but I won't sit back and play games while my friends are being killed. The screaming's coming from a room two doors down. The metal booms as I bang against the door with my fist. A second later the screaming stops and a bored looking man in overalls opens up. He gets it right in the throat. I pull out and he falls, gurgling. The supervisor rises, hands up, palms out. I can see it all over his ugly face. He wants to say, "Who are you and what is the meaning of this?" I know the type, but he doesn't. Beside him, Oleg's strapped to the wall with thick chains. His robe's been torn open and wires trail from his nipples and the lobes of his ears to a battery on a nearby table.

"Fast or slow?" I ask the supervisor. My voice is calm and it's taking everything I've got to keep it steady. The man's name is embroidered on the breast of his uniform. Hankel. Just a regular jailhouse drone with a sadistic side.

"I was following orders."

"I'm sure you were. Now I'm gonna ask you one more..."

"Fast," he says before I can finish. I swing the Katana in a wide, sweeping angle from right to left. Instinctively, he raises his hand to block the move and I watch as his fingers fall away, one by one, a split second before I see the thin red line stretching across his forehead. He's stares at me, mouth flapping open like a giant fish, for the length of time it takes to bring the sword back to my side. But staring or not, I know he's already dead.

There's a strange cracking sound as the back of his head hits the wall on his way down. He's damn lucky we're in a hurry.

Sneak pulls the wires off Oleg's ears and chest. The skin there is charred and, for a moment, I regret giving Hankel the easy way out. Krantz grabs the keys from the supervisor's corpse and heads off to free Bron and Ret.

Krantz is pissed. "I told you I didn't want any unnecessary bloodshed."

"Trust me," I say. "That was necessary." But I can already feel the guilt settling in. I mean, killing Zees is one thing, but nothing ever really prepares you for that septic feeling you get after turning a man's head into a salad bowl.

The supervisor has the keys to Oleg's shackles and we free him and sit the old guy down. He doesn't look good.

"Oleg," I say.

His eyes are glassy. His face is a canvas of sweat and streaks of dried blood.

Bron and Ret enter the room, followed by Sneak. I grab Ret and squeeze him tight.

"I thought you were dead," he says. He holds me at arm's length and tries to wink, but his eye is too swollen. Seeing him up close now, I realize what truly made me snap.

"Thought you were dead too," I say.

Bron's looking at me funny and you don't need to be the sharpest blade to figure out he sees my face and isn't quite sure what to make of it. The change had already started in the complex, but who has time to notice the little things when you're being hunted by an army of Zees?

I reach out to him, but his arms remain lifeless at his sides.

"Bron, don't be like this," I say, unable to stop the feeling growing inside: that I've become some kind of monster.

Ret lifts one of Bron's arms and lets it fall. "It isn't you, Azina. Those assholes switched them off when Bron tried to redecorate the bars of his cell."

"But I'll bet they didn't count on me using my head." There's a patch of dried blood on his forehead where he must have broken that guard's nose. Bron is smiling and I can see one of his brown teeth is missing. Oh boy, coming here didn't do much to improve anyone's good looks.

There's a low humming noise and Bron's fingers begin to twitch. Sneak's behind him, closing the access panel between his shoulder blades. He lifts one of his gleaming arms and balls his fingers into a tight fist. The fist opens and he holds it out to me. I slide my hand into his and feel a chill run through my body from the cold steel.

"Thank you," he says.

I blink stupidly for a second. I've never heard Bron thank anyone for anything. He never even felt indebted to his mother for giving birth to him, even though squeezing out an eighteen pound baby Bron nearly killed her.

-40-

"If we're done with all the hugging and kissing," Krantz snaps, "we need to get a move on."

He's right and it isn't just the wail from that siren shrieking overhead that brings his point home. We've got to get these guys back to safety.

Bron bends down and scoops Oleg into his arms. The old guy's head flops back and forth and I'm certain he won't last much longer.

We stash the bodies in the makeshift torture chamber and head out.

Two levels down and we're just about to reach the S.I. listening post when I feel my body being thrust forward and I know right away it's got nothing to do with anyone behind me.

I turn to Ret and the dim pool of light makes his battered face look like some kind of creature's.

"We've got a problem," I say.

Ret stares back with a puzzled look, but there's no time to explain how I know when Zees are close. I pull open the door and I'm assaulted at once by the smell of blood. It's been sprayed all over the walls as if someone nicked a jugular and spun in circles like one of those old fashioned sprinkler systems Dusters were so fond of. Then I see what's caused it. One of the technicians is behind a metal table. All I can see are his legs and they're twitching madly. We swing around and the sight startles me. There's a Zee trying to bite through his skull. The man's throat's been torn clean out. Right beside the body is a blood-soaked clipboard. The Zee glares up from his kill and I see past the dark leathery skin covering his face and recognize the same testy little man who approached us as we entered the listening post. He hisses through a

113

mouthful of blood and blackened teeth. He's about to spring. The muscles in his body tense and then release. He's halfway through the air when Bron's hand arcs down, shattering his skull and sending his mangled Zee body crashing to the ground. Bron doesn't have a stitch of ammo on him, but it's just as well. The last thing we need are those big guns of his drawing any more attention. But something else is growing more certain within me. That Zee seemed to be coming directly for me. Back in the complex, as the chemical began creeping up my leg, they had largely ignored me. Things seem different now. Then the truth settles over me like a suffocating gas. The Hive leader is in the city and he's come to get me back.

-41-

Two other bodies litter the ground, but that Zee is still in his glass tube so it couldn't have been him that started this massacre. Bron sees the Zee attached to the metal cap and ticker tape machine for the first time and laughs. "What's he supposed to be doing? Getting a perm?" He shatters the glass and crushes the Zee's head.

"I guess we know now why that siren's blaring," Ret says.

"I tried to warn them," says Bron from the other room as he wipes his hands on a lab coat. "Tried to tell them something big was on its way, but they wouldn't listen."

"They didn't need to listen," Krantz says, "because they already knew." I remember the refugees lined up before the eastern gate and how on edge the guards were. Krantz may be right, but I'm still not sure what it all means.

Back through the stench of the pig farm and into the sewers. We make it to Krantz' hideout without seeing another soul, Zee or otherwise, but I only really feel safe once the door is locked tightly behind us.

Bron lays Oleg on one of the bunks and I quickly see that we're not alone. Two men in red robes sit at a nearby table, looking listless and shell shocked. The larger of the two is thick and muscular and has a long scar running down his face. It's an old wound, the skin around it puffy and cauterized. His face is smeared with blood and I'm sure none of it is his. The one beside him looks far more frail with a head of hair so blonde it's almost white. He has soft, rounded features – a child's face – and he's mumbling to himself, the way new recruits often do after their first kill. Krantz points to the one with the scar.

"This is Gunnar. The one beside him with the snow-colored hair is Vasser. Where are the others?" Krantz asks them, and the concern in his voice is obvious. Gunnar looks up from the drink in his trembling hands, his eyes taking their time to focus. "If they're not here, then they're probably dead." Gunnar's eyes find my face and he springs to his feet. "You let one of them in," he screams and raises his rifle like he means to put a few dozen rounds between my eyes. His barrel's nearly on target when Bron grabs the end and turns it into a pretzel.

"Stand down," Krantz shouts to Gunnar.

I wave my hand to tell him that no harm is done. I'm more worried Bron's going to put the man's head in a vise and it's quickly becoming clear we're going to need everyone we can get.

"Don't hold it against him," I tell Krantz. "A few days ago I would have done the same."

"If you're not a Zee, then what are you?" Gunnar asks. His voice is cold.

"I'm not sure," I say.

He goes to take a sip of his drink and stops. "Well, your friends are outside the city walls. Thousands of them. I'd say no more than a handful managed to get in and look at the chaos they managed to cause. I'm not even sure how they got in. Refugees have been streaming into the city all day with wild stories of monsters coming down from Mount Kepler. And most of The Keepers have been running around trying to pretend like everything was business as usual, even the few of us embedded in the ranks, but anyone with a brain could tell something was very wrong. Wasn't long after that we saw a dust cloud appear on the horizon, maybe ten clicks out. Something big headed this way. Turned out to be those things. Thousands of them."

The more I hear, the more the pieces start falling into place. All those Zees that had chased Bron, Oleg and Ret

116

from the complex must have veered off once they were free. No Man's Land is a rough and unforgiving landscape, but even so, thousands have fled an overcrowded Sotercity to strike out on their own. Small communities struggling to stay alive in the harshest conditions. And how many of them are now Zees, clawing at those same city walls they so desperately wanted to leave?

Gunnar swallows hard. "They closed the gate on women and children. I lost count how many. Right before those things arrived in force." He paused and buried his face in his hands. "I'll never forget those screams."

-42-

I hear Oleg begin to stir behind me. Ret's by his side.

I kneel beside them. "Will he be okay?"

"He'll live," Ret says. "He's just dehydrated and in plenty of pain."

Oleg opens his eyes and I can see Ret's right about the pain.

"We've given you something that should take the edge off," Ret offers.

Oleg tries to wave us away. "I need that edge," he growls. "Need a clear head. If it's not already too late."

"We know," I say and fill him in on the Zees ravaging the countryside and their numbers swelling. "We don't think more than a handful got into the city. So far, the walls are holding."

"I'm not talking about that," Oleg spits through a shudder of pain. "The discs we retrieved. I couldn't see the full extent of it at the time, what Skuld was up to."

Now Bron, Ret and Krantz are standing over the old man. The other two hold their distance, still not sure about me.

"What was on those discs?" I ask.

"Blueprints."

"What do you mean?"

"The design schematics to a machine. A powerful piece of old world technology. I remembered what you said in the complex about using the discs as bargaining chips. I knew it was our only hope and I hid them away without ever realizing that I should have just destroyed them when I had the chance. Within hours of entering Sotercity, I was picked up by a group of city guards and dumped into a cell next to Bron and Ret."

"Those discs," I say. "What was on them?"

118

"A genetic accelerator."

More of Oleg's techno babble. "Great, but what does it do?"

"Exactly what it says. It accelerates genetic mutations by hundreds and thousands of generations. In minutes it can accomplish what it took mother nature millions of years to do."

All our faces are masks of confusion and Oleg sits bolt upright. He's pissed that we're not getting it, looking at us like we're a bunch of buffoons; a part of me is glad to see he's inching back to his old, crotchety self.

"Don't you get it? The chemical that made the Zees in the first place caused a severe genetic mutation. If Skuld builds that machine, he intends to use it on himself."

"To do what?" Bron asks. "Grow himself a bigger pair of balls?"

"I wish you were right. No, Skuld is going to inject himself with the Zee chemical and use the machine to become a God. After that, he'll awaken every hive within a thousand miles.

"But what on Earth for? Ret asks. "Is he mad?"

Oleg sneers. "You don't need me to tell you that Sotercity's a political backwater. Any Prior with dreams of advancement wouldn't be caught dead here. Unless, that is, they'd fallen out of favor with the Patriarch."

Bron's shaking his head. "So you're telling us, we don't just live in a dump, we also happen to be the scum of the known world."

"Skuld hopes to use the Zees to remove the Patriarch from power and have himself crowned Emperor of The Ten Territories."

The Ten Territories. Shorthand for what remains of the civilized world. They were formed after the fall, each with varying amounts of wealth and power. And at the head of it all is the Patriarch, who runs the show from behind the walls of Attica, a former prison turned palace and capital city. How fitting.

On the far edge of that mess is Sotercity, the capital of the tenth territory. Officially called Noma Landis, but popularly known as No Man's Land.

Krantz' whole body seems to be sagging. I can only imagine the way Skuld's plan must be eating him up inside. First the man murders his family, now he wants to kill everyone else too.

Beside him, Ret is shaking his head. "And how is it you know all of this? You lied to us before, about the true purpose of our mission. How do we know you're telling the truth now?"

"I was instructed to locate and remove specific discs, but I wasn't told what they were for. Surely now that you see Skuld's plan, you can understand that all of us are expendable."

I try not to sound like an interrogator, for fear that Oleg will clam up. "You still haven't told us how it is you discovered Skuld's intentions."

"How about from the man's own lips? When I refused to speak, he came down to question me himself. You'd be amazed what people will tell you when they don't expect you to be around much longer."

I can still see that smug look on Skuld's face when he hired us. "I knew The Keepers were a bunch of crooked–"

"No, Azina, not all Keepers, just Skuld and his inner circle."

Bron snatches the pewter mug out of Gunnar's hand and squashes it. "And I'm sure he's promised them a piece of this new Zee-infested kingdom he intends to build. I'd sooner die."

Gunnar stands and Krantz puts a hand on his shoulder to ease him down.

There's a grave look on Oleg's face. "You may get your wish, Bron. We estimate there may well be over a hundred thousand hives, spread throughout the ten territories and beyond. If Skuld manages to wake and bind even a fraction of them to his will..." Oleg's voice trails off, but we get the point, loud and clear.

Sneak's fingers start to dance in midair. She's asking a question. I translate.

"Why are they sleeping in the first place?"

Oleg leans back on his elbows. "I wasn't lying when I told you that long ago The Keepers fought and defeated the Zees. I never said we exterminated every last one of them. Frankly, I wonder if that's even possible; but our ancestors did what they thought was the next best thing. They lured the Queen out into the open and killed her. Destroy the brain and you stop the Zee. After her death, the hordes retreated back into their hives and became dormant."

121

Oleg looks right at me. "Azina, have you not wondered why you haven't succumbed entirely to the chemical?"

His eyes are scanning up and down the rough patch of skin on my face and now everyone's looking and I can't help feeling somehow shameful. "I have, but what can it be, besides dumb luck?"

"Her body is fighting it," Ret says. "Like an infection."

A bolt of inspiration smacks me square in the face. "Oleg, this machine you describe, the accelerator. If we made the right kinds of changes, do you think it could be used to reverse my... the condition?"

He falls silent and I feel a knot of anxiety growing in the pit of my belly.

"It might," he replies cautiously, "but you'd need to find an engineer with an unbelievable level of expertise."

Bron lifts one of his shiny arms high into the air. "I know just the person."

-44-

Of course, Bron is talking about the genius who made his arms, but I also know he hasn't seen him in years. But if this works, it may be the key to ending the Zee menace for good, as long as we stop Skuld in time.

At Krantz' feet is a wooden chest with the word 'requisitioned' stenciled across the top in big bold letters. He pops the lid, reaches inside and tosses Ret his automatic shotgun. Ret catches it and cradles the gun in his arms.

"Oh baby, I thought I'd never see you again." He showers it with kisses and I almost scream. Hell, even I didn't get a greeting like that and just as suddenly I wanna slap myself across the face for feeling jealous of a shotgun.

"Got anything in there for me?" Bron asks.

Krantz picks up a 20mm five inch shell and drops it back inside the chest. He reaches into an ammo case at his feet and produces a red-tipped 20mm round. "What do you give a person who has everything?"

Bron's face lights up like a child during Winter Solstice.

"These are next generation explosive rounds," Krantz says. "If you ever wanted to know what a Zee looks like in a million pieces, this'll tell you."

Bron's discolored and newly gap-toothed smile stretches clear across his face.

Then Krantz hands me my repeater. "Not the best weapon around, but it's gotten me out of more than one jam in my life."

No sooner do I grab the stalk than a string of Zee code fills my head. It quickly forms into an image. Thousands of figures staggering through a dark tunnel.

123

"They've found a way inside the city," I cry.

Krantz isn't sure what to make of my comment, but the others know by now not to waste time with silly questions.

"Grab what you can," I say. I try my best to sound calm, but on the inside, a million different scenarios are racing through my head.

Krantz unlocks and pulls open the thick metal door. Even from back here I can see them, clogging the sewers, a literal wave of darkened flesh. Gunnar and Vasser are by Krantz' side and together they try to slam the door shut before any can get inside, but the Zees are too fast. It's almost like they were waiting there, waiting for that door to open so they could get inside. Another painful jolt and now I know that somehow the Hive leader is in the tunnel with them. He's come for me and has brought every Zee he could muster with him.

-45-

Leathery Zee hands snatch at Krantz' Keeper robe. Sneak and Ret rush forward to help slam that door shut, but already I know there isn't any hope. There are too many of them and in a few seconds they'll be inside and all over us.

"Get down," Bron shouts, as Oleg scrambles to his feet and out of the way. The door swings open and Bron opens up with a deafening hail of shells. I watch in slow motion as the concussive force pulls back on his arms after every shot. The first shell enters a Zee's open, hissing mouth and detonates, sending blackened gore and splinters of lethal bone into the faces of the others around him. Shattered torsos fall to the floor in heaps of quivering flesh. The Zees in the sewer behind them get a taste and I can feel tiny pricks of pain as Bron's exploding shells tear them to pieces. The carnage is unbelievable. With so many corpses clogging the open doorway, there's absolutely no chance of closing it now. Krantz, Sneak and Ret crawl back toward us as tracers from Bron's heavy guns cut through the air mere feet above their heads. The Zees are still rushing forward, scrambling over the wall of death. Then Bron's guns jam. He scrambles to my side, working each bolt, trying to free the jammed shells, but I know it isn't any use. He's got them overheated.

I swing my repeater around. Half a dozen Zees are clawing over the pile and I hold down the trigger, sweeping from left to right, riddling their skulls with holes that ooze a dark, foul-smelling liquid.

The entire room erupts with gunfire. "We can't stay here," I shout over the roar.

Oleg's got that terrified look in his eyes again, probably wishing old Skuldy had let him die when he had the chance.

Krantz is right there beside me, eyes wild and glaring, blazing away with twin .50 caliber pistols. He's wearing a maniacal grin, as though he hasn't felt the blood pump through his veins for a very long time.

Behind the growing mound, we can hear the Zees pulling at the bodies, trying to clear the doorway. That isn't the act of mindless drones, and right on cue the Hive leader's back in my head. He must be right outside. I can feel him tinkering around inside my brain. I saw his head roll off his body so I'm not sure how this is even possible. He's knows we're trying to escape, wants to find out where we're going. I try to block him out, try to keep him from seeing our plan, but there's so much going on.

"Follow me," Krantz hollers.

We storm down the rows of bunks. Bron's at the back, toppling beds, trying to put some obstacles between us and the shambling horde. To buy us time.

This part of the room is bathed in darkness. I see the others groping with their hands, but while they are blind, I can see a ladder up ahead, leading to a manhole. Then the Zees burst through the door behind us.

Bron turns. "We're gonna be dead in another minute unless you find a way outa here."

I scramble up the ladder and pop the manhole out with surprising ease. A thick shaft of light bleeds down from above. I slide back down to help the others up.

Sneak, then Oleg and Ret.

The Zees reach the barricade of beds and Bron's running backward. Beside him are Gunnar and Vasser.

"Krantz, you're next," I say and up he goes.

It doesn't take the Zees long to scale the barricade. Then, in the distance, I see the Hive leader enter the room. Even from here it's obvious his head isn't on the

126

floor where Sneak left it. He's stuck it back on and the bloody thing's healed in place. He's even managed to stuff his entrails back into the hole in his belly. I can't help but curse, knowing I should have stomped his brains into mush when I had the chance. I scale the ladder into bright sunlight, Bron and then Gunnar right behind me. Once at the top, I reach down and take Vasser's hand, but no sooner do I feel his fingers then he's wrenched violently from my grasp and is dragged into a sea of shrieking Zees. When I try to dive in after him, Bron's hand closes around my belt and jerks me out. Vasser is still screaming when Bron slams the manhole back in place. There's a scolding look on his face and he's right, I should have known better. The minute those Zees yanked him off that ladder he was a dead man.

Bron drags a heavy trash container over the manhole cover to keep them from crawling up after us. We move away quickly and I can feel the Hive leader trying to pull me down. He would pull me through the slab of concrete that separates us, if he could. With force of will I return my focus to the alley and the intersecting street up ahead, where people are running and screaming. Close behind them are a group of Zees in dresses and bow ties, some in tunics and rough woolen pants. The streets of Sotercity have always bustled with life, but now they've become a slaughterhouse.

"Where's this engineer of yours?" I ask Bron.

"He's in the industrial sector."

"That's two sector's over," I say in disbelief. Sotercity's made up of four sectors. Commercial, entertainment, and industrial are packed in neat blobs in the center. Surrounding them is the residential sector, where most of the Grinders and small business owners live. The entertainment sector's a different beast altogether and this kind of fun's got nothing to do with Oleg's movie theaters and work-out rooms. No, entertainment in Sotercity means gambling, alcohol, bare-knuckle fights and ladies of the night, or as Bron likes to call them, 'horizontal refreshments'.

"All right," I say. "We need to move low and fast." I look at Ret. "We're not here to save every poor sap we come across, not when Skuld's making ready to finish off the rest of us."

We duck into the shadows as another group of Zees shamble past the alleyway's entrance.

"Blades only," I say and pull out my Katana. "Last thing we need is to draw any more of these things."

I'm the first one out. Behind me are Ret, Krantz, and Sneak, who's helping Oleg along. Pulling up the rear are Gunnar and Bron. They're comparing battle wounds, trying to find out who's tougher. Gunnar's drawing an index finger along the scar on his face, probably making up some wild story even though I'm sure he got it falling down in a bout of drunkenness. It didn't take long working with muscle bound Mercs to discover that they aren't men, but little boys trapped in men's bodies.

We're in the commercial district and the street is brimming with little stalls selling everyday items. From noodles to tunics, from religious statuettes of Newton and Copernicus to pewter mugs of warm beer. Except nearly every single one of them are closed and shuttered and most of these poor saps haven't a clue that in a few hours, all their earthly possessions won't be worth a damn.

We come to one shop that isn't closed up and I see a bunch of Zees inside, bent over, tearing at something or someone. No matter where you go there's always one stubborn asshole who refuses to run when things turn to shit. Those are the damn fools who either die crying for help, or get labeled heroes for dying valiantly. Hell, I'd rather be alive and smart than dumb and dead.

A second later we run head first into a frightened crowd of women and children.

They must think we're Keepers who can lead them to safety, 'cause right away they start to follow us. I catch sight of Gunnar, Krantz and Oleg, all in their Keeper robes, and wish I hadn't been right. I turn and shout. "You people better find some place safe. You don't wanna follow us, not where we're going."

An older woman with pale skin and a pair of fine silk coveralls looks like she's about to lose it. "Where can we go? We just came from the keep and it's been overrun by those things."

She looks like she used to be rich enough to afford servants, but no amount of money in the world can protect you when a pack of Zees are running through the streets.

I signal to Bron and he rips open the metal shutter to a grocer's shop.

"Hide in here," Bron says, ushering them inside. "There's enough food and water for all of you. And when you've cleaned the place out, leave a big fat I.O.U. in the money box." He erupts in a bout of thunderous laughter and I wanna smack him.

Gradually, the stalls give way to a row of brothels. Rising above the rickety sheet metal roofs I see the top of the keep and trails of thick black smoke pouring from the upper levels.

We haven't seen a single Zee since we hit the streets and I'm starting to wonder if that's where they've gathered. Then a terrible thought occurs to me. Maybe the Hive leader knows we'll be heading there as soon as we get our hands on this engineer. I only hope he'll be able to make Skuld's machine reverse my condition and whatever Skuld manages to do to himself.

I spot ladies in skimpy clothing. They've climbed up onto the brothel's rooftop and are waving for help, but there's nothing we can do. Above them is a billboard with a picture of Prior Skuld and a cheesy caption underneath. Join The Keepers and make your world a better place.

Now I wanna kill Skuld more than ever.

Streets whiz by. I grab hold of Oleg and help him along. All around us, bodies are stacked like cord wood. Some of them moving, twitching, others, newly turned and feeding on the human flesh beside them. I wait until I can tell for sure before using the Katana to cleave their heads in two. It's a horrible business, but the number one rule of watching your back is making sure nothing can sneak up behind you. It isn't long before we reach the industrial sector and spot our first smoke stack. It's still belching out the same dark clouds that have slowly turned Sotercity into a smog-filled cesspool. I also know those furnaces are running on their own and the feeling is an eerie one. Soon the fires will peter out and grow cold. The city's becoming a tomb before our eyes, and it reminds me of the cavernous underground complex we so narrowly escaped.

-47-

The workshop has a sign with a wrench and a bolt on it. I normally make it a point to stay as far away from the polluted industrial sector as I can, so all this is new to me. Two solid oak doors with engravings and metal studs. Bron pounds his fist against a carved picture of a master and apprentice hard at work, pummeling the image out of existence.

No answer.

Oleg starts to squirm and I decide to knock this time, using the butt of my repeater. I hear bare feet shuffling through the street and realize the time for manners is long gone. I look at Bron.

"Do it!"

He grabs each of the handles and pushes with so much force his face turns a deep purple.

Those footsteps are getting closer.

From behind us comes Gunnar. "Move aside," he bellows, "and let the real men have a go."

Bron releases, shaking out his metal fingers. "Be my guest."

Gunnar grasps the door handles, makes like he's about to push and then casually pulls them open. Ret doubles over in laughter.

Gunnar has a gleeful look on his face. "Next time, try pulling first, big man."

Bron isn't a fan of being made to look silly and I can see he wants to put Gunnar's head through the wall.

We close the big oak doors quickly behind us. There's a thick chain on a nearby workbench and Ret and Sneak busy themselves with weaving it through the handles so whatever's shambling down that street won't be able to come in after us.

I glance around the gloom, weak shafts of light spilling in from a set of high windows. All types of gizmos and contraptions litter the workbenches and hang on hooks suspended from the ceiling. Oleg points to a weird looking machine with two wheels and an ugly chunk of metal stuck between them. "By Newton, I haven't seen one of these in years," the old man says. He looks around at us and then shakes his head in disgust at our ignorance. "It's a motorcycle." Sneak's face squishes up. "You know, small combustion engine."

"Yes, I've heard of them," I say. "And I also know they're illegal."

"Oh phooey," Oleg spits. "The Patriarch has done everything in his power to stop information travelling faster than he can control it, including outlawing these wonderful machines. Just imagine the potential. You could barrel across the twelve districts in hours instead of weeks."

A sudden noise above us. Our eyes trace up to a second story loft and find a figure crouched there, glaring down at us. He's holding some kind of weapon and I reach for my repeater, but by the time I swing it around I'm already too late. A concussive noise rings out as he fires. It's some sort of net gun and it's aimed at Gunnar, who raises his arms to fend it off. A split second later, the weighted ends twirl around, entangling him. Gunnar tries to take a step and falls to the ground, twisting and pulling and generally making his predicament far worse.

I don't tolerate being shot at, no matter what the weapon is, and when the shooter disappears, my first instinct is to find and throttle him; but if this is our engineer, we might not have that luxury. And besides, I remind myself, technically speaking, we're the ones who are trespassing.

The shooter sails down a short flight of stairs and it looks like he's heading for a back exit. We swing around the corner, breathless – Gunnar still on the floor behind us, cursing at his predicament – only to find Sneak sitting on the squirming body of a young boy who doesn't look a day over fourteen.

"Well done," I say. "But who the hell is he?"

Sneak shrugs and signs back indignantly, "How the hell should I know?"

Ret and Krantz lead the boy back to the room with the benches and gizmos.

Bron's poking at Gunnar who's throwing all kinds of obscenities his way.

"Cut him loose," I say.

Bron starts whining. "Do I have to?"

I toss him the 'do what I say' look, mostly out of respect for Krantz. Gunnar is one of his men, after all. Bron's now pouting like a child who's been told he can't play outside anymore. A blade slides out from the palm of his hand and he frees a thoroughly disgruntled Gunnar.

The boy's wearing a ratty, grease stained tunic and a floppy hat; from here he doesn't look like much more than a teenage Grinder. His fingers are trembling, but I notice they're strong for someone his age. He's more than just a stowaway.

"What do they call you?" I ask.

"Dhal," the boy replies. His features are sharp and symmetrical. He'll be handsome when he grows up. If he grows up. Gunnar's got a grim expression on his face that tells me he's hoping for option number two.

"We're looking for the engineer who owns this shop," I say.

"Master Lund? You're too late." His tone is filled with false bravado.

"What do you mean too late?" This time Bron speaks and he can't manage to hide the worry in his voice.

"Keepers came by and grabbed him, bout the same time all hell broke loose outside. Those things are eating people, in case you haven't noticed." He looks at Oleg, maybe because he looks old and wise or maybe it's because of the Keeper robes he's wearing. "Is this the end of the world? Sorta like the big bang those Keeper priests are always talking about, only in reverse?"

Oleg shakes his head quickly, but it would take a blind man to miss the fact that the boy's got the old man thinking.

"Enough of this," Gunnar barks. "Where did they take him?"

The boy recoils. "To the Keep. Least, that's what they told him. But how do I know, maybe they were lying."

Sharp as a steel blade, this one. I sit down beside him, my repeater slung back over my shoulder and I can see him looking at my face, wondering the way Gunnar did, whether I am one of them; wondering whether I'm human.

"Is Lund your father?"

Dhal spits out laughter. "That crotchety old nog? Hell no, I'm his apprentice. Mother and Father work for Sotercity. I got a knack for mechanical stuff which is how I ended up here, I guess."

I turn to Ret. "Should we take him with us?"

Ret studies the boy, who watches us from his seat at the table, trying to make out what we're saying.

"You really think this kid'll be capable of making the changes to Skuld's machine? Besides, we don't even know what state it'll be in by the time we reach them. He could be a lot of dead weight."

"If you reach him," Dhal whispers under his breath. Kid's smirking now and none of us are liking it one little bit.

"Something funny, little boy?" Gunnar asks.

135

"No. It's just that if Skuld's bunker underneath the Keep is where they've taken Master Lund, then unless you're all on some kind of suicide mission, there isn't a chance in hell you're gonna get anywhere close."

I look over at Oleg who nods. "The child is right."

"I'm not a child," he whines, but all eyes are glued on Oleg.

"There are rumors the Keep's underground sanctuary has recently been greatly bolstered. Skuld may be very well protected indeed, although in what ways no one really knows."

Ret crosses his arms. "This has 'bad idea' written all over it."

Sneak's in total agreement and her fingers are doing a mad jig through the air to drive the point home.

I'm not happy either. "Why are we only hearing about these defenses now?"

Oleg's face begins to flush and for a moment I can't tell if it's anger or embarrassment. "Because I haven't seen them. Rumors, that's all they are, and I certainly wasn't going to alarm you with make believe tales of encrypted passageways and machines capable of ripping a man in half."

Dhal raises his arm like a schoolboy.

"What is it?" I say, not even trying to hide my exasperation.

"What the old guy just said. Those aren't rumors."

"And how would you know, young man?" Oleg replies, sounding snippy and I'm not sure if it's the 'old man' comment he doesn't like, or being shown up by a kid.

"Master Lund was the one who designed the place for Prior Skuld and who the hell do you think helped him?"

-48-

We aren't two minutes from the workshop, Dhal struggling under the weight of a backpack loaded with who knows what, when I feel a tingling in my gut. We head down a narrow street, a gauntlet of small factory-type structures and shacks, even a billboard or two showcasing Skuld's ugly face. Ahead and to the left is the Keep and somewhere inside is Skuld. I'm the first to turn the corner and the first to come skidding to a stop.

Zees. A sea of them, stretching out in a line that leads all the way to the Keep. They must have cleared the upper levels looking for us and now they're moving on to other places. Dhal's eyes grow wide in amazement and fear.

"We need to find another way in," I shout as we turn and run back the way we came. Krantz is in front now, maybe twenty yards ahead. He must know this area better than any of us. He turns a corner and then reappears a second later.

"It's a trap," he screams. Behind him is another swarm. A queer mixture of Zees from the complex, dressed up all nice and pretty in antique clothing, and alongside them the recently turned from Sotercity, a veritable snapshot from all walks of life: bakers, shop owners, Keepers and rich merchants. Men, women and especially children. An angry mob of dark leathery skin and bared teeth, with one thing on their insect-like minds: feeding.

We're completely surrounded. I hear the first bunch scrambling up the other street and it won't be long before the two groups merge, with us sandwiched in the middle. Sneak points upward and my jaw drops. Zees on the rooftops are poised to leap down on top of us, but they don't. They're waiting. But for what? Orders? Then I see in the distance, toward the rear of the second mob, is the Hive leader. That big red melon of a head is on his shoulders like he never lost it in the first place.

Both groups are now within visual range. The walls of the buildings are too high to scale and we're in a spot void of doorways to duck into.

"Stand back," Bron says and levels his guns, but he's not aiming at the oncoming Zees. Even he must know there are too many of them to fight. The barrels of his guns are pointing at a brick wall on our left.

"Buy me some time," he hollers and opens up, showering brick and mortar down on us as his explosive shells tear away at the masonry.

One chunk hits me in the head and for a moment I'm seeing stars. Ret, Krantz and Oleg fire into one crowd of Zees. Me, Sneak and Gunnar fire on the other. Dhal huddles at our feet, his hands clamped over his ears. I can already see a breach in the wall and I'm sure in another second we'll be able to squeeze through.

Then I hear the command, Zee gibberish flickering before my eyes. The Hive leader has given the signal to his drones on the roof to leap down on us. If they manage to break up our firing lines we won't stand a chance. Then I remember what happened back in the complex, when that red SOB had Sneak by the throat. Through sheer force of will I'd managed to send my own rogue Zee command to wrench his fingers from around her neck.

I try to do the same thing now, but it isn't easy in the chaos of battle, with hordes of mindless drones bearing down on us. I do my best to slow my breathing and allow a picture to form in my head. I imagine the Zees diving down, but head first and I send the signal out in a process that feels as normal as sending a signal to my legs to take a step. The Zees approaching from either side are nearly

138

on top of us, but right now I'm not paying any attention to them. I squeeze my eyes shut in concentration and when they open again, I catch Dhal and Gunnar watching me with the kind of terrified expression on their faces that tells me one thing. My eyes must be lit up like one of Skuld's billboards.

I raise my arms and then jerk them down violently. The Zees jump, and for a moment I'm not sure if I've managed to do anything more than waste time with my finger off the trigger.

Then more than half of them dive head first, their skulls hitting the ground and exploding in a spray of black goo. My legs begin to give out and Sneak grabs me before I can fall. I'm trying my best to stay up, but I can see plain as day the other half of the Zees from the roof have landed on their feet. Now we're surrounded. Sneak puts me down and pulls out two eight inch daggers. Her movements are so graceful she looks like she could be dancing. She spins and lunges out faster than the eye can see. Three Zees around her drop to the floor. Even Krantz has a few tricks up his tunic. He's doing his own dance, albeit not nearly as fast or elegant, but nonetheless making good use of those blades on his boots and the others bound to his knuckles. Now Bron pulls his attention off blasting the wall and unleashes holy hell. It's the perfect killing zone. He's got each arm pointed in opposite directions. Zees barely ten yards out on either side are torn in half, but on they come.

"It's now or never," Bron growls just as a Zee appears before him, his arms stretched to either side. I'm worried he won't be able to maneuver in time. I reach for the knife in my boot, but I already know I'm too slow, too tired.

Bron begin to shift his fire and, even from here, I can tell he isn't going to make it.

Ret notices Bron's situation and slides feet first between the big man's legs and opens fire. The blast from his automatic shotgun knocks the Zee backward. A final shot to the head and it stops moving.

Bron helps Ret up off the ground and then cups his balls protectively. Robotic arms are one thing, but some bits can't be replaced. We hear the piercing scream. I turn to find a Zee latched onto the side of Gunnar's neck. Another sinks his teeth into the soft flesh of his forearm and Gunnar's face is a mask of panic as he tries in vain to shake them off. Krantz sends the blood-soaked blades on his knuckles into their brains, killing them both. I can't help seeing Jinx flash before my eyes. He had that same look on his face when they got him.

Gunnar stumbles and then drops to one knee. Blood from his neck is spurting between his closed fingers. Already his skin looks pale and deathly. He's not going to make it and judging by the height of that wound, he's got only seconds before he joins Zee central.

Krantz crouches to tend to him, but Sneak pushes him aside and buries one of her daggers in Gunnar's forehead. His eyes roll up to whites and it's all over. Painless.

The rage in Krantz' eyes looks like it can melt steel. But Sneak did the right thing. I just hope that if we manage to make it out of this, Krantz will see it that way too.

We evade the grasping hands of approaching Zees and rush through the hole Bron had cut in the brick wall. Sneak and Ret help me along and I can only hope that no else has been bitten. A few quick shots from Bron's 20mms and part of the ceiling crashes down behind us. That should hold them off for a few precious moments.

-49-

We're inside a dimly lit factory. Stacks of sheet metal and pressed wood lie in piles around us. The basic household building blocks for most of the Grinders living in the outer ring. It's cool and dusty in here and I want to rest so badly, but we can't, at least not until we reach the Keep. That's what I'm repeating to myself over and over. And by the looks of things, our only hope is to make a run for it while those Zees are busy forcing their way through the debris behind us.

Ahead is a shaft of light from outside.

"This way!" Bron says pointing.

He bursts through before I can tell him to be cautious. Only a few Zees are milling about. They won't be hard to get through, but he still doesn't understand, that letting them see us is like ringing a giant dinner bell.

Out we charge. Above us are the Keep's imposing battlements and stretching higher still are swirling plumes of black smoke spilling out of her many upper windows. The main gate hasn't been closed in many generations and I can't help but wonder what it must have been like for the Keepers manning the gatehouse to see a horde of Zees rushing toward them with no way to shut them out.

Krantz is still shaken from Gunnar's death and no doubt still upset with Sneak for speeding it along. He's not the only one reeling, though. The full impact of forcing those Zees off the roofs and onto their fat heads hasn't completely sunk in yet. I struggle on with Sneak's help, becoming more and more frightened with the implication of it all. Every time I merge with the signal and make them obey, do I take a step closer to becoming one of them?

The open ground is easy to cross. It's one of the few bits of an otherwise cramped and dilapidated city where you don't feel hemmed in. Krantz is out front, relieving some of his aggression on the scattered groups of Zees that come our way. My legs are still a bit weak and rubbery and I can only hope that they hold out until we get ourselves somewhere safe. But even I know I'm fooling myself. In a world like this there's no such thing as safe, and I'm starting to wonder if I might be a bigger part of the problem than I care to admit.

Almost on cue, Krantz' slicing and dicing triggers a flood of signals.

UP, DOWN. MOVE, MOVE, FORWARD, DASH, SEVEN.

And I don't even need to hear it to know that it's about us. About me. The horde knows exactly where we are, and unless I've been able to block them out sufficiently, they also know where we're headed.

-50-

We hit the Keep's main entrance not a moment too soon. Surging behind us is a mass of darkened flesh, ebbing and flowing like a flock of birds, thousands of them, eyes glowing, mouths gnashing at empty air in anticipation of the time when those teeth will close around our throats. I feel a chill run through my body as Ret struggles to close the reinforced door behind us. It may hold them off for a time, but it can't be the only way in here.

Dhal's chest heaves and his face looks ashen and deathly. The only color comes from the streaks of Zee blood smeared across his forehead. Sneak lowers me into a chair. Oleg sits across from me and I can see him sucking in wind and favoring his side. We're in a kind of waiting room, but this place isn't like Attica, the Patriarch's walled palace. The Keep is purely utilitarian, an army barracks on steroids. Except I wonder where the guards are? Almost in response, I catch sight of a severed leg poking out from an adjacent room, a shaft of white bone glinting off shafts of light. Yes, the lights are still on. Not much of a silver lining, but I'll take it.

Outside the Zees are piling up against the entrance, doing their best to follow us inside. Even with inches of stone and wood between us, I still can't help hearing the horrible noise they make. Sounds like a sickly cat being strangled.

Bron is checking us over for bites and none too gently I might add. He sees the bandage on Sneak's arm and I catch the change in his expression at once.

"She's fine," I say, already feeling the strength coming back into my body. "It isn't a bite." Ret's standing over me. He's got that same look on his face he had years ago, on the Holson job. A wealthy Trader had hired us to rescue his eldest son from a band of kidnappers. We found the kid all right, except he was stuffed into a chest, his legs folded in at odd angles. A note on his body said: "This is what happens when you don't listen."

Ret had been the one to deliver the bad news and that somber look he's wearing now is nearly identical. Like somebody died.

I look him square in the eye. "Something tells me that concern on your face doesn't have anything to do with losing Gunnar."

"I don't like losing anyone," he says. "Especially not to those... things. Not that way."

"Sneak did what she could."

"I'm not worried about Sneak. You've trained her well."

I catch his fingers fiddling with the loose straps on his ammo vest.

"You wanna know what's happening to me, that it?"

He nods.

"And if I tell you I don't know?"

His voice is quiet now, just below the racket coming from outside.

"I'll find it hard to believe. You don't think I saw those Zees break their heads open? Maybe you take me for an idiot. Bet you probably didn't have a clue that your hands were in the air before you yanked them down like a troupe of marionettes."

My hands slide up to the curve of my hips, a defensive posture I'm barely aware of. "They communicate with one another, the Zees," I say. "If Oleg wasn't trying to catch his breath, I'd pull him over and have him explain it to you. They're all connected to one another." I point to my face. "And now so am I."

"Like that Zee we found in the laboratory?"

"Yes, plugged into the signal. I see that signal too, but I don't need a salad bowl on my head to tell you what it's saying."

"And what is it saying?"

"Let's just say they think of me as the one that got away."

Ret's eyes drop. "That Zee in the listening post. He could only send and receive signals. He wasn't able to…intervene."

"That's right, once the ones that turn completely become passive receivers and transmitters."

"But Azina, I saw you control them. Make them bash their own brains into the gravel."

"And it nearly killed me."

"Maybe, but let's cut the bullshit. You know as well as I do what this means."

I catch the glare in his eyes and I'm sure the others can hear us just as well. My hands rise, the urge to plug my fingers in my ears and block out what he's about to say is strong, but I've got to face it, face what I've become.

That grieving look settles over Ret's face again as he says it.

"You're becoming a Hive leader."

-51-

We gather our things and head through the room with the severed leg. Bodies are piled everywhere. Most of them Zees or Keepers, killed in the process of turning. Oleg keeps mumbling about Skuld's doomsday machine, that we need to stop him and I'm worried the old guy's gonna give himself a heart attack. I'm feeling more and more myself with every step. Threads of my conversation with Ret are still buzzing around in my head. That's when something occurs to me. That very first time I'd tapped into hive central and used it to pry that red scumbag's fingers from around Sneak's throat, I'd recovered in a matter of minutes. This time took so much longer, and for a while my thoughts had been cloudy and almost muffled. Shouldn't I be building up a tolerance to it, the way people build a tolerance to alcohol? Whatever the full scale of this ability is, with every use, I seem to be losing more and more of myself.

I'm up at the front of the group. Dhal's beside me, looking over some kind of diagram he's pulled from the sagging cloth backpack strapped to his shoulders.

"I thought you knew this place inside out?"

"So did I."

I reach over and flip the map around. "For starters you've got it upside down."

"I knew that," he chirps back and I'm wondering whether it was a mistake to drag this kid along in the first place.

"You will be able to reverse the effects of this thing Skuld's building, right?"

Dhal smacks the bottom of his backpack with his free hand and all I hear is the metallic clang from a bunch of tools banging together. "Hardware's in the bag and I'm the best coder I know."

He isn't even that short, but he's talking directly to my breasts. I've never met an adolescent boy who wasn't boastful or oversexed. According to them, they're the best at everything they do and think they're going to live forever. Reminds me of a younger Bron.

"Here," he shouts and draws to a stop. At our feet are more bodies, these ones Wardens. One of them is rough-skinned and stirring, ever so slightly, and I use the six inch blade in my boot to make it stop.

From the rear, Bron pipes up. "Why are we stopping? There isn't anything here but a few dead shitsacks."

The boy's gliding his hand along one of the smooth white walls. I'm starting to think he's lost his mind when Oleg steps up and explains. "He's looking for a seam. Apparently there are secret entrances to the lower levels all around here."

A distant booming noise makes us all freeze. Sounds like it's coming from behind us.

Sneak's already backtracking down the hall, head tilted slightly. A second later she signs back. "They're inside."

And I don't need to ask who she means by 'they'. I turn to Dhal. "I really hope you know what you're doing, 'cause sometime in the next two minutes, things are gonna get real crowded around here."

He nods, removes that floppy hat of his, and uses it to wipe away the layer of sweat that's beading his forehead. "I know it's around here somewhere."

I send Ret in the other direction to keep watch. We're like sitting ducks in this hallway. Ret clicks the safety off his shotgun and looks at me with those piercing eyes of his and I feel the sudden impulse to pull his head back and kiss him right on the spot. And just as quickly I'm struck with a horrible epiphany. The Zee chemical isn't

147

only surging through my veins, it's also in every ounce of my saliva. A kiss from me is a kiss from death itself. As a child I remember The Keepers reading us a story they said was thousands of years old. About a king named Midas whose touch turned everything to gold. Seemed like a blessing, at first, until he touched his daughter and she was turned into a golden statue. Even the food that touched his lips turned to gold. Devastated, the king prayed to an ancient god named Dionysus for help. Dionysus told Midas to bathe in the river Pactolus and when he did, it washed the curse away. If this kid's as good as he thinks he is, I'm hoping Skuld's little apocalypse machine can become a kind of Pactolus River for all of the infected.

The racket in the distance is growing louder and tiny bits of Zee code are zipping through my mind. They're honing in on me like a beacon. I should leave the group, but I know Ret, Sneak and Bron will have none of it. Dhal's fingers tremble as he sweeps them across the wall, back and forth, muttering to himself like an old drunk, swaying from too much hooch.

Then hissing from down the hall. They're close and I watch the blood drain from Dhal's face. Out of nowhere he shouts in triumph. "Here it is! I found it!"

Ret and Sneak are on their way back, Sneak at a brisk pace and I know the Zees only seconds away. Dhal reaches into his knapsack and pulls out an eight inch prybar. Bron snatches it from his hands and digs the tip into the thin groove. Bits of plaster fall away as he works it in as far as it'll go. Ret and Krantz take up defensive positions.

"Any time you're ready, Bron," Ret snaps.

"If you think you can do this any faster, medicine man, give it your best shot."

There is a sound of metal under stress, but this noise isn't coming from Bron's arms. It's coming from the prybar, which snaps in two.

Bron curses. "I should have known better than to play with a child's toys," he says and punches a ten inch hole in the wall. His eyes grow wide.

He must have found a clump of metal rods in the reinforced concrete wall and he uses them as leverage to wrench the door open.

"It's moving," Dhal says. He's ecstatic, and only I can see that the legs of his trousers are stained with piss.

"Course it's moving," Bron snaps. "But no thanks to you."

I hear the breath hitch in Oleg's throat. Zees turn the corner and Ret and Krantz open fire. The hallway is narrow and the first few Zees are torn to shreds. Dark blood fans out behind them, painting the walls with a horrible image of death. But the stream doesn't end. With Zees it never ends, and it won't until every single last one of them lies on the ground with their brains pouring from their ears.

They're less than twenty feet away when Bron jars the cellar door wide enough for us to slip inside. He's the last one in and lays down a volley of punishing fire to buy us some time. The rest of us are descending into darkness when I feel those flashes of pain stop stinging me. Above us, the door slams shut and it takes the others a few minutes for their eyes to adjust to the ambient light. All but me. The darkness is where I see best now. Details jump out at me. The low, recessed ceiling. The precision of the stonework. Our feet whisper down the cool steps as we make our way into blackness.

-52-

Up ahead a glimmer of light. We're inching through the darkness, single file, with me in the lead. Oleg is right behind me. Someone at the rear, maybe Ret, trips on something and curses. Bron bellows laughter. The big guy lives for others falling flat on their faces. Slapstick, they used to call it, although I don't see how the two words relate to the kind of joy Bron experiences seeing someone stumble.

I tilt my head back to Oleg and whisper. "You've been quiet since we freed you from Skuld's men. We usually can't shut you up."

Oleg's hand tightens its grip on my shoulder and his body begins to spasm.

Uh oh.

"It's your family, isn't it?"

His voice is heavy with emotion. "Yes."

"You don't just want to stop Skuld from waking the Hives, do you? You want revenge."

"He tortured them and then hung their bodies outside the city gates. Wouldn't you want revenge?"

I remember seeing them strung up like a pack of thieves, although at the time I hadn't a clue who they were. "Want it worse than you know. It's because of Skuld that Glave and Pennies and Jinx are dead. Because of him that I've become…" My voice trails off.

"Then you see."

"Oh, I see. But you and I are gonna have to get in line. Krantz wants a piece of Skuld too and no doubt Bron is anxious to blow him into tiny bits, even if it's just on principle. Ret may be the only one who's let it go."

"Yes," Oleg whispers. "He'd make a fine Buddhist."

The light's getting closer, we're almost there.

150

"Buddhist?"

Oleg laughs, more to himself. "Oh, nothing. One of the old religions. They believed in pacifism and were one of the first to go when the human race began to devour itself. Some were said to have sat in blissful meditation as they were eaten alive."

I grimace and ask what is probably a silly question. "What's the opposite of a Buddhist?"

Oleg doesn't miss a beat. "The man we're trying to kill."

The light in the room is dim, two emergency fixtures on either wall. Inside everything is white, or at least used to be, making it appear brighter than it really is. There's a heavy gray film coating the walls, desks and chairs. Dhal's checking his map again, a confused look on his face; he doesn't have a clue where the hell we are.

I look at Oleg and Krantz.

"The Keeper museum has a display room that looks an awful lot like this," Oleg says.

I run my finger along a table, stacked with shriveled pieces of what was once paper. My finger comes away dark and then I feel stupid. The skin on that side of my entire body is dark and shriveled, just like the stuff in this room.

"What do you make of it, Oleg? You're the expert on that dead world."

He's already busying himself opening squeaky drawers and shuffling through bundles of rotting paper. "It looks like an old office. Special rooms within tall buildings, where Dusters used to busy themselves moving papers around."

"Sounds thrilling," Ret says.

Dhal clears some room on one of the desks, spreads out the map, and traces his finger along the path we've already taken.

151

"So I take it you've managed to get us lost already?" I offer encouragingly.

"There's more than one way to the underground bunker," he replies. "Weird thing is, this room isn't showing up on any of the schematics."

I peer down. He's right, but I can see that each entrance leads to a central room.

"What's this?" I ask, tapping my finger on that point.

"That's the main access elevator."

"How deep down are we going?"

"All the way."

Behind us, Krantz emerges from behind a desk, waving something in the air.

Oleg rushes over and the others follow suit.

I'm the last to arrive. "This isn't the time for a museum field trip," I say, but no one's listening. Oleg and Krantz are blabbing to each other like a couple of old ladies.

"What have you found?" I ask.

"This was an administrative office for a company called Kempers Inc."

Bron's eyes light up. "Did they sell chicken?"

"No," Oleg replies curtly. "They were a bio-chem firm."

I can practically see that one sailing over my head.

"Bio-chem?" Ret asks.

"Biological and chemical."

"And look at the company logo," Oleg says. "In the old world it was called the atomic symbol. A powerful, and luckily for us, a lost technology."

I study it and realize I've seen that symbol somewhere before.

Oleg notices and asks: "What does that look like to you?"

I'm drawing a blank and frankly, not in the mood for games. "Just spit it out old man."

Oleg lowers the paper until the company logo falls in line with The Keeper symbol on the breast of his robe. They're close enough that I can't believe I missed it. Three overlapping elliptical rings and eleven empty spaces within. One for each of the territories radiating from a central core. The Patriarch.

Krantz calls out from the other side of the room. He's elbow deep in the bowels of a filing cabinet. "You're not going to believe this."

-53-

He lugs over a number of heavy manila folders and plunks them down on the table. Dust motes swirl around us.

I'm not sure what point they're trying to make, and right now all I can think about is getting to Skuld before he manages to finish off the human race for good. And if that weren't enough, somewhere above us is an army of Zees, led by something that will sooner or later figure out how to open that trap door and catch us here with our pants down, holding reams of crumbling paper.

Krantz is flipping through page after page, handing them to Oleg one at a time.

I peek over his shoulder and see that dead language arranged in neat columns from top to bottom, enough to give me a headache.

"What does it say already?" I ask.

Krantz scratches his forehead. "An initiative called Adam 930. Looks like the people who worked for Kemper Inc. were really pushing the boundaries."

Oleg's face suddenly looks ten years older. "One of the old world's creation myths spoke of a man called Adam, who was created in the perfect image of their god. A man who lived to the ripe old age of 930. That was what they wanted, for men to become gods, to never grow old or get sick and die. They wanted to play almighty Newton and instead, their arrogance destroyed the world."

"Kemper Inc. poisoned the water supply to help kick start their version of Heaven on Earth?" Ret asks.

I shake my head. "I thought you said the Duster governments were responsible?"

Oleg glances up at me, looking dazed and shell-shocked. "That's what we were taught."

"Yes, and when things went horribly wrong," Krantz says, disgusted. "My forefathers were there to pick up the pieces, weren't they?"

"We need to burn this," Oleg says.

Bron stiffens. "Are you crazy, old man? Do you know what you're holding in your hands? Proof that The Keepers killed billions of Dusters and then hung around to scoop up what was left."

"Yes, but you can't convict a group of people for something their ancestors did two hundred years ago. You start down that slippery slope and you can make a case for every one of us to hang. Besides, who are you going to show this to? The Patriarch? Ha! You're better off digging a grave now for yourself and everyone you've ever known."

Ret glances at the folders on the desk and then looks away. "Judging from what's going on upstairs, I'd say that right about now everyone I've ever known is either dead or a shitsack. No offence, Azina."

"Oh, none taken," I say without meaning it. "Believe it or not, I tend to agree with Oleg on this one. Right now, our real enemy is Skuld and the few misguided saps who were foolish enough to follow him."

"But what could he have promised them in exchange for turning the world into his own personal Hive?" Ret wonders.

Now it's my turn to laugh. "You'd be surprised what men will do for nothing more than a fistful of empty promises."

"And all the Zee concubines a man could ever want," Bron says, laughing uncontrollably at his own joke.

"Skuld's gotta go," Krantz says, "no question about it. But Oleg might be right. These documents don't indicate Kemper Inc. was trying to lay waste to the world.

They were trying to create a sort of utopia and on some level, I admire what they were trying to accomplish. A world free of sickness, starvation and death." Krantz flips through a half dozen sheets, then runs his finger down one of them until he finds what he's looking for. "And by the looks of things. they didn't pump barrels of the stuff into the water supply as we thought. Hell, it didn't take more than a single jug of the stuff to start a chain reaction they were powerless to stop. Sounds more like a Keeper Science Academy project gone wrong than a group of evil geniuses."

I gather up the folders and put them in Dhal's pack. "Look, if we don't stop Skuld, then it won't matter one damn bit who started this mess. Ret and I will take lead. Bron, you and Krantz watch our backs."

-54-

It isn't long before we come to the intersection of four separate hallways with an odd looking platform in the center of it. We approach and Oleg shouts out from behind. "It's a freight elevator. A box attached to cables that transports people and goods between the floors of a building." He doesn't even wait for us to ask anymore.

"But there aren't any doors."

"No, but it looks like there's a grated roof, so we'll need to hang on tight."

Heights are not good in my book and I can already feel my teeth begin to grind with anxiety.

We're less than twenty feet away when I feel an electrified tingle jolt through my body. Then comes a signal. The Hive leader's pushing them on, as if he can already feel me within his grasp. They're close, no doubt about that, but I haven't the foggiest idea how they could have broken through that doorway so quickly.

Then movement up ahead. Past the elevator and through the hallway on the other side. It's dim, but even from here I can make out figures scrambling through the shadows.

"Zees straight ahead," I bark. "We can't let them cut us off from the elevator."

And almost on cue their eyes fill the hallway with beams of dancing light. Their hissing is growing louder and I know it's going to be close.

Dhal's running directly behind me and I shout at him. "For everyone's sake, I hope you know how to work that thing."

I glance back for no longer than a second and catch the panic on his face.

We reach the elevator first and I swing my repeater off my shoulder and into my hands. I'm about to fire when I realize that our situation is so much worse than I originally thought. Dhal's hunkered down over the control panel, trying to make head or tail of the buttons, while Oleg hovers over his shoulder, pointing and shouting. Before them is a number pad and below that more buttons, presumably one for each floor.

The Zees are less than fifty feet out and closing fast, but not from only one direction. Each of the four corridors is jammed with masses of darkened flesh and electrified eyes. They're coming from everywhere and for a second I'm not sure where to fire. The elevator platform is huge, more than big enough to hold our entire party, but all of us are bunched together.

Thirty feet away now. Dhal and Oleg are yelling at each other. Oleg's trying to press buttons and the kid's knocking his hands away. "You plug in the wrong password and the system will lock us out."

Bron springs to his feet with a savage grin on his face. "Ladies and gentlemen, please keep your heads and arms in at all times," he barely gets the words out before he howls with laughter. His own arms are pointing in opposite directions when he opens fire. The concussion nearly knocks me over. Zees in two hallways are torn clean in two. Shells that miss their mark detonate overhead and decimate groups of them with loads of deadly shrapnel. I'm doing what I can with my repeater, but even on full auto the lack of firepower is humbling. Bron switches corridors and resumes firing, but already his barrels are starting to glow and I know he can't sustain this for more than another few seconds. The Zees are less than fifteen feet away and I draw my Katana. I nod to Sneak and Krantz. Once those things reach the elevator, close quarters is all we'll have left. Bron's guns choke up and he ejects the blades from the palms of his hands.

A Zee dressed in a Sotercity guard's uniform is about to make it onto the platform when it starts to descend. Cries of triumph rise up from Dhal and Oleg and they're hugging each other as though they just landed a man on the moon. Then the platform jerks violently, sending us all on our asses. Now there's a gap between the corridor level and the platform and that uniformed Zee flings himself on top of me. He grabs my ankles and starts dragging me to the edge. The Hive leader's probably told them to take me and kill the rest, but this drone's too stupid to realize we're going down. I swing the Katana and sever his arms at the elbows then stick the point up through his nasal cavity. My foot digs into his gut for leverage and I push him off the blade. The gap between the top of the elevator grate and the floor above is quickly diminishing, but that doesn't stop the Zees. Nearly a dozen of them are on their bellies, trying to crawl in after us. But none of them manage to get farther than their chests before the elevator roof descends on them. The platform buckles as their bodies are torn in half. Soon it's raining Zee heads and mangled torsos. One, severed right below the rib cage, grabs Dhal's pack and starts clawing up his body, entrails tumbling out of it like lengths of loose rope, its jaws snapping and oozing thick black liquid.

Dhal starts spinning in circles. "Get it off me, get it off me!"

Bron stomps out the brains of a Zee at his feet and points to Dhal, bellowing laughter.

"Please someone grab that thing before I piss myself."

Krantz does a spinning kick to kill it, but instead sends it flying toward me. The Zees jaws lock onto my forearm and I howl with pain. A second later, the knife

159

from my boot opens a window into his skull. The light in his eyes begins to fade and I wedge the blade into its mouth to pry the dead Zee's jaws apart. Blood gushes from the wound and now Bron isn't laughing anymore. Ret's by my side in a flash, bandaging my arm. I flex my fingers, thankful it didn't sever a tendon. Suddenly, from out of the silence, comes a crashing sound that violently rocks the platform. One of those stupid ass Zees just stepped off the edge after us and landed on the caged ceiling, splattering his brains all over us. A second later there's another crash and then another. We're all thrown to the ground and with every jolt I become more certain that thin cable holding us up is about to snap and send us freefalling to our deaths.

-55-

Peering through the grated floor of the platform I can see we're almost there, but every meter we put between us and the Zees above us only magnifies the impact of their bodies landing on the elevator roof. The ceiling of the metal cage we're in is beginning to buckle. Bron jumps to his feet, trying to brace the supports and I warn him to avoid the Zee blood oozing down from above.

Another jarring impact, but thankfully this one is us reaching the ground floor. We collectively sigh with relief and no one needs to be told to rush from the platform.

We're in a darkened hallway with low lighting. Ahead is a blast door and beside that, another keypad. We find that this one doesn't have any numbers at all, just a bunch of squiggly lines.

Oleg leans in for a closer look. "Letters A through I in the old tongue. It's an alphabetic cipher."

I glance over at Dhal who fidgets through his packsack and comes out with a small black notebook. That smug look is plastered all over his sweaty face. "Master Lund had me write down the important door codes and it's a good thing, 'cause this door is booby trapped."

"What do you mean, booby trapped?"

"I mean we have three shots to key in the proper code, or else." Dhal drags his thumb across his neck.

"That really doesn't help us," Ret says. "Can you be a little more specific other than..." He mimics the gesture.

"No, because I haven't the foggiest idea what will happen."

Bron looks just as pissed as I feel. "I thought you said you built this place?"

161

"I never said I built it, I said I helped to design it. Master Lund and I recommended cyanide gas and Prior Skuld vetoed it. Not enough suffering, he said."

"But you already know the password, so we're fine then, right?"

His lips twitch. "Should be."

"I hate the word 'should,'" Bron says, "especially coming from a bratty little puke like you."

The sound of metal squeaking and grinding interrupts us.

"What just happened?" Oleg asks, examining the lock combination.

Sneak races to the other end of the hall and quickly signs back.

"The elevator just lifted off."

"Is that bad?" Krantz asks. "I mean, these things don't have brains; no offense, Azina."

Ret can see the annoyance on my face and smiles.

Oleg looks squarely at Krantz. "Our research shows the Hive leader has the mental faculties of a five or six year old. Some basic reasoning, although even he runs mostly on instinct."

"Then we're okay," Krantz concludes.

I rest a hand on Krantz' shoulder and catch a flash of jealousy from Ret. "No, it means we gotta get this door open cause this hallway's about to become a highway."

56

"H-E-F-F-A," Dhal says as he inputs the letters. He's reading off the grease stained pages of his notebook. He's about to hit the enter button below the keypad when Oleg stops his hand.

"Are you sure this is correct?"

"Heffa is Skuld's wife. I'm sure it hasn't changed since we installed it."

His finger mashes the enter button and three quick beeps ring back which doesn't sound good. Dhal grabs at the door anyway, jars it violently, but the handle won't budge.

"I don't believe this!" he says, exasperated.

Ret's shaking his head. "I do."

"What other passwords you got?" I ask him.

"That's it."

Bron wiggles his index finger at Dhal. "Little boy, I love a good laugh as much as the next man, but please tell me you're kidding us."

Beads of sweat form on Dhal's forehead and it's about all the proof I need. From down the hall comes the faint sound of the distorted elevator grinding to a stop far above.

"I'll have to use the decoder," Dhal says, his voice cracking.

I help him get the pack off. "Yes, do that."

"Only problem is it may take several minutes."

"Then stop blabbing and start getting it done," I say.

Dhal pulls out a strange looking device with a suction cup and attaches it to the metal next to the keypad. Then he uses a screwdriver to undo a bolt at the bottom and attaches a set of red and blue wires to a circuit board of some kind. The device has tiny windows for each possible letter. Suddenly the machine comes alive with letters whizzing by at lightning speed. I hear the elevator begin its lumbering descent as the first letter appears.

"It's an A," Dhal says gleefully.

Oleg lets out a long breath. "All right, it seems to be working."

I can still hear the elevator rumbling at a decent clip when another letter appears: I.

"A. I.," Dhal says as though he expects one of us to guess the rest of it.

Bron leans over and shows me the ammo gage on his arms. He's almost empty. Blasting through that wall must have done it.

Ret catches on to what we're talking about and all the color goes out of his cheeks. "What are we supposed to do, fight them back with sharp blades and curse words?"

"How many you think are on that platform?" I ask them.

Dhal erupts into cheers. "Another I. A.I.I. No clue what it means. I hope this thing is working properly."

Ret loads more shells into the barrel of his shotgun. "Not sure, knowing those Zees it could be as many as a hundred if he packed them in like sardines."

The rattling sound from the elevator shaft is getting louder and so is another sound, one that was barely audible before. Hissing. Lots of it.

"D. We got a D."

"Gotta make every shot count."

Bron flicks his head in Dhal's direction. "Kid thinks he's running a bloody game show in the entertainment district."

"They'll trade flesh for distance," I say ignoring the comment. "That's why we gotta hit em hard the minute they touch down."

"E," Dhal shouts and inputs the code. "Anybody know what an AIIDE is?"

164

Even Oleg ignores the boy. He's spinning the barrel of his revolver, no doubt wondering whether one of those six shots has his name on it. Beside him, Krantz racks the bolt on his assault rifle.

"I want clean lines of fire. We can't afford to waste a single shot."

Dhal starts shouting that he's got another A when the elevator touches down and it's packed with Zees with glowing eyes and suddenly all of them turn in our direction at once – they're less than a split second away from breaking into a run.

Bron raises his arms and opens up right over us. Boom, boom, boom, boom. Four shells go flying over our heads. The few hairs clinging to Oleg's scalp go whipping back and forth. A dozen Zees out front and funneled through the narrow darkened hallway have their insides splattered against the walls. Arms and legs and bits of skull are all that's left and then, just as fast, comes the ominous sound of Bron's guns growing quiet. He only has a few shots left, and he's probably reserving those for when things get really bad. Now it's our turn and we rise to our feet and fire. Krantz, me and even Oleg with his pistol. Only Ret and his shotgun hold back for when they get in too close for comfort.

Some of Krantz' shots are missing their mark, hitting Zees in the body and a few below the waist. "Aim for the head, damnit," I shout.

I'm doing the best I can with my repeater, but the truth is we just don't have enough firepower. Stopping a horde of charging Zees is about as easy as trying to shoot water up a hill.

57

They're close enough now that I can see their blackened mouths hissing back at me and nearly all of them are new Zees, turned in Sotercity or the outlying regions, dressed in roughhewn tunics and bits of shredded fabric. Only a few are wealthy looking Duster types from the complex.

I hear Dhal hollering behind us.

"D. Final letter's a d. AIIDEAD. AII DEAD. All dead." His voice trails off.

He inputs the final letter and a long single beep follows, but most of this is drowned out in the chaos of battle. The door opens a moment later and that part we hear just fine. Krantz and I are still firing. We're trying to stagger it properly so both of us aren't reloading at the same time. The Zees continue to stumble forward, the walls around them oozing with gore and there's more of it at their feet but they trample over it without even noticing. We're trying to pull back and doing our damndest not to trip over each other. Tripping would be bad but this is not an easy maneuver, especially when you can't see what's behind you...

Oleg, who must have run out of bullets long ago, rushes for the open door, as do Dhal and Sneak. But Sneak isn't running from battle. She's scouting up ahead, making sure the way is safe for the rest of us to follow. In the distance, the elevator lifts off for another load of Zees.

Krantz and I stop firing long enough to slide behind Ret. Together we snag Ret by the belt and start pulling him toward the exit as he fires into the crowd, his feet sliding along the dusty floor as though hovering on a cushion of air. Buckshot works best against large numbers of Zees packed tightly together and from over his shoulder, I have a ringside view of packs of them, only feet away, being turned to pulp.

We scoot inside and Bron slams the door shut, except instead of the sound of a lock clicking into place, all we hear is a sick crunch. I look back and gasp. Dozens of Zee arms bristle in the opening. Bron pushes harder and I see the veins in his neck beginning to bulge. We all pile on, pushing with everything we've got and even still the door is inching further and further ajar. The sheer weight of them is what's causing the problem and if we can't get this door closed, we're finished. I slide out the Katana and start hacking at any leathery arms and legs poking through. Soon only a handful of bloodied, squirting stumps remain, but still we can't get it shut.

I take a step back and now the others turn to me, probably wondering if I've given up, ready to accept whatever that red bastard has in store for me. Really though, I'm trying to quiet the frantic thoughts swirling around in my head, trying to quiet my pounding heart. My mouth feels like it's filled with a bucket of sand and my chest is heaving wildly, but I try and put all of that to the back of my mind so I can pluck out the thread of Zee chatter, buzzing in the air all around me. The door's inching open and I know full well the consequences of what I'm about to do, that it's slowly changing me into something more Zee and so much less human.

I close my eyes nevertheless and imagine the horde outside backing away. Can see their feet in my mind, retreating, one behind the other along the cold hard floor until the entire mass outside begins to look like a horrible dream being played in reverse; all the while I feel that patch of dry, leathery skin, inching further up my face and toward my brain like a dark, evil hand.

There's a loud boom as the door slams shut and Ret and the others stare at me in mute horror. My eyes are

167

glowing, that much I know, but when I look down I see the reason for their horrified expressions. I'm hovering nearly a foot off the ground.

-58-

I hit the ground hard and it feels like every ounce of energy's been sucked right out of me. The Zees are banging on the door something fierce. Sounds like wet rags slapping against metal and it takes me a second before I realize it's the sound of bloody stumps knocking out a dreadful beat. I also know the Hive leader's probably heading down on the next elevator and I'll bet 50 to 1 Dhal didn't wipe that code before we all ran through. Made it real simple for him. All that red prick'll need to do is turn the handle and push. I glance over and find Dhal crouched down beside me. His pants reek of piss and I know better than to even bother asking him.

Krantz is eyeing me like I'm some kind of alien. "What is she?" he asks Oleg. He's not even trying to be discreet. I feel like a patient, laid out before a group of young Keeper med students.

"She was bitten," Oleg replies. "Days ago, but didn't turn; not fully, at least."

"Not only once," Ret adds undoing the bandages on my arm. "But twice." The bandages fall away and he shakes his head. "Just as I thought."

I glance down at my brown, almost mummified arm. It's ugly as hell but, more importantly, it doesn't have a single scratch.

"We need to keep moving," I croak.

Ret helps me to my feet. I'm little more than a newborn baby on a pair of rubbery legs, learning to walk anew.

Now Oleg's talking to me directly. "You don't only hear them do you, Azina? You can communicate, make them obey you."

169

The fear on Bron's face is hard to miss. "I saw you floating in the air, defying almighty Newton himself. Please tell me you won't snap and attack us when we're not looking?"

"Course I won't," I spit in mock anger at the suggestion, "don't be silly." But the truth is I have no idea what I'm capable of, especially if Skuld's machine manages to turn him into some kind of Hive emperor. If that should happen, I hope they kill me quickly before anyone gets hurt.

We gather our things and head out. Sneak in the lead, maybe ten yards up. The rest of us follow behind. With every step, the act of planting one foot in front of the other becomes easier and easier.

Tiny rooms are on either side of us. We've entered some kind of research area. Large windows, set twenty feet apart, reveal operating theatres and tables filled with strange glass containers. There's no sign of life, even though the faint echoes of recent human habitation are all around us. Up ahead, Sneak comes to a T intersection, stops and peeks in both directions. Her hand stabs the air behind her and she begins to signal frantically.

I translate what she's seeing. "Left clear. Right, twenty yards. Three Wardens in full battle gear."

We move up behind her, just as she walks into view of the soldiers. I reach out to yank her back, but my arm's too sluggish to respond in time. Besides, any second now, that door to the elevator room at our backs is going to burst open and spew out hundreds of Zees. If these wardens raise the alarm, then everything we've done will be for nothing.

Around the corner I hear Sneak crying and whimpering and it's the first time I've ever heard her make a noise.

Rifles snap to attention.

"Halt! How did you get down here?"

She doesn't answer.

A new voice. "Easy boys, she's just a little girl."

Then a third. "I coulda swore we swept the science sector clean as a whistle. I don't see how we could have missed–"

The first voice again, trying to whisper. "She must be a Grinder. How did you get down here, sweety?"

Pause. Sneak is sniffling.

They repeat the question, but still no response.

"Maybe she's deaf."

Laughter, then three sets of heavy boots approach her and stop.

"What's wrong little girl, cat got your ton–"

Scuffling and blades, two of them, slicing through flesh. Gurgling and garbled speech. The sound of something heavy hitting the ground, then another. We rush around the corner and find Sneak standing over three dead Wardens.

Her fingers zip through the air. "They called me deaf!" She looks more hurt than angry.

I'm about to ask her which one said it when I see she's sliced the ears off the fat one.

Dhal tries to wipe the awe off his face, but he isn't quite fast enough. "I coulda done that you know," he says.

"Really?" Bron replies and taps one of his metal fingers on the top of Dhal's head.

"Ouch," he squeals, clutching the top of his skull.

Bron's heavy frame gyrates with laughter. "You'll be better off sticking to your gadgets and your toys, pipsqueak. And if the shit hits the fan, then get behind lil Sneak over there, she'll protect you."

Dhal gives Sneak a crooked smile. She smiles back and wipes a smear of blood off her cheek.

-59-

After passing through a set of double doors, we come to a cavernous chamber. It's circular with a high arched ceiling and even Oleg looks impressed. "Do you realize these marble floors predate the fall?"

Maybe so, but frankly none of us are in the mood for one of Oleg's history lessons. Built into the walls of the room are stone pillars that reach up to the domed roof. They're purely decorative, and not load bearing, even I can see that, but what does catch my eye is the source of light wedged between two of these pillars at the opposite end of the room. It appears to be a large window, with figures moving about on the other side. Ret and Bron see it too.

We approach and my heart begins to race, but that's good, because it means I'm almost back to normal. That cloudy feeling in my head is almost cleared away and my muscles are becoming tight and responsive once again.

I'm finally able to see what's going on behind that glass wall and the sight of it nearly freezes the blood in my veins. It's Skuld, dressed in his Keeper's best; robes of deep violet, trimmed with snow leopard fur and some sort of tall white ceremonial headdress.

The word 'pharaoh' comes spilling out of Oleg's mouth, but I haven't the faintest idea what he's talking about.

Men in white Keeper lab coats scurry all around him. Some are fiddling with buttons and knobs on the wall. Others seem to be making last minute adjustments to a machine in the center of the room. They begin to strap him into it. It's bulky at one end, filled with blinking lights and levers. On the other is a ring of thick metal, taller than a man and housing four restraints. It almost looks like a torture device.

The scientists are binding Skuld's ankles and wrists with leather straps when he sees us. The glare from his black, dead eyes is piercing and somehow humiliating, all at the same time. We must look like a bunch of poor Grinders with nothing to eat, gawking at him from outside. His lips move, but not a sound makes it through the thick observation glass that's protecting him. The room he's in must be sealed as tight as a drum. Two Keeper scientists look at him and then at us. The alarm in their faces is immediate and suddenly they're shouting to one another. A short pudgy man with a large nose and bad skin goes to mash a large red button on the wall and then stops. I follow the direction of his gaze and it leads me to Dhal. The boy's wearing the same expression of surprise and sadness mirrored. Suddenly it becomes clear. The short man with the big nose is Master Lund. Now Skuld's entire demeanor changes and he seems to be shouting at Lund, ordering him to push the button, but Lund isn't listening. One of Skuld's deputies raises a pistol and fires, dropping Lund to the floor. The deputy crosses the room in three great strides and hits the button. Dhal lets out a desperate cry just as the room we're in erupts with bursts of yellow light. Now a siren begins to wail and I can't tell if we're about to be incinerated or if he's just summoned a battalion of Wardens.

Beside the observation window is a stout metal door with a keypad lock and I tell Dhal to snap out of it and crack that code. He isn't listening and I grab him by the collar of his tunic and shake him vigorously. His eyes look dull with shock and I slap him twice across the face. Yellow light splashes across his narrow features. The siren is blaring in my ears. He finally comes around and I see his eyes are filled with terror.

173

"We've got to get out of here," he stammers, "right now."

"What are you talking about? Skuld's in there," I shout, pointing in the other direction.

"You don't understand. They hit the button. They activated the Goliath. We won't stand a chance."

Yellow emergency lights still pulse in my eyes. The siren echoes off the walls and assaults my eardrums. The feeling of acute nausea comes on fast and I suddenly feel the urge to retch all over the floor. Behind us, Skuld, still flanked by Keeper scientists, preps the machine that's about to end all life on Earth for good.

I hear the sound of a gate clanging shut. It's just come down over the entrance to this giant round death trap of a room and suddenly I know we're in serious trouble. Ret is fumbling shells into the barrel of his shotgun when I hear boots charging down the hallway outside. Then the voice of a commander barking orders.

Bron's smirking and I can't tell if he's nervous for the first time in his life or if he knows something I don't. "This is about to get interesting," he says.

Any second now I'm expecting to see red Warden cloaks through the bars that are blocking our exit. Then their assault rifles, poking through and firing indiscriminately. Rats caught in the granary. That's exactly how I feel right about now.

"Skuld's only minutes from activating the machine," Oleg shouts. "We need to get in there."

I glance over to find Dhal's already at the panel, working on the code.

Bron lifts his arms and prepares to fire at the glass.

"Don't bother," Dhal snaps. "Master Lund and I designed that glass to withstand a direct hit from an RPG."

From outside, just as I'm expecting those Wardens to start pokin' their guns through the bars I catch sight of something I never thought I'd be so happy to see.

Zees, hundreds, maybe thousands of them, tearing past, hissing, some snarling, one even crawling on its belly, probably split in two by one of Bron's shells. Over the sound of the blaring siren I make out screams of panicked men as the horde of Zees crashes into the Wardens. The sounds are horrifying, frantic gun fire, blood curdling cries for help.

Behind us, Dhal seems to be making headway on the lock, and for a moment I allow myself to feel a pinch of optimism, but then I see Skuld's expression. They're nearly done prepping him and he's got a smug smile plastered all over that pock-marked face of his. The scarring is the remnants of a disease that nearly killed him in childhood. Even natural order tried to kill him and failed.

I hear a slab off stone sliding away and see a hidden doorway opening up in the far wall. Then comes the sound of grinding gears, squeaking metal and thunderous footfalls. I swing my repeater around just in time to see it emerge from the opening. It's the color of polished brass and must be nearly ten feet tall. Almost looks like a man, too, except for the color and the plumes of thick black smoke chugging out from a pipe behind its neck. All of us watch in amazement. Three thoughts fire through my brain at nearly the same time. The first is that this metallic monster reminds me of old pictures I once saw of a train, black smoke and all. On the heels of that is the dim realization that we've just met Goliath. The third is that we're all about to die.

-61-

Goliath scans the room and its cold, metallic gaze settles on Dhal as he works frantically on the lock. It turns in his direction and Krantz levels his assault rifle and unloads an entire magazine. Sparks fly off of Goliath's metal belly and head. I see dents appear, parts where the brass finish is chipped off, but even from here I can tell that every shot ricocheted and didn't do anything more than make it angry. In four crushing strides it closes the distance between it and Krantz, a trail of black smoke belching out behind it. I send half a dozen shots squarely at its head, knowing they won't do a damn thing to stop it, but hoping somehow to draw its attention. Even Ret is firing, being careful not to catch any of us in the wide spray from his shotgun. Between Krantz and Goliath is Oleg and he falls to the ground; for a moment I'm sure it's about to squash the life out of him, but its focus stays on Krantz.

Inside the lab, Skuld has a gleeful look on his face, like he's got front row seats to a bare knuckle boxing match in the entertainment district. In a flash I remember the terrible things Skuld did to Krantz' parents and I'm scared he's about to finish what he started.

Goliath is faster than any of us could have imagined and as Krantz drops the empty magazine from his rifle, he turns to run, to give himself a chance to reload. But Goliath sweeps out and snatches the back of Krantz' cloak with one of its powerful hands. Without the slightest discernible effort it whips him off his feet and into the air, looking like a child twirling a sack of food from the market.

Bron grunts in anger and opens fire. Three shots ring out before his guns click empty. One grazes the back of

177

Goliath's head, cuts through the swirl of black smoke rising above him, and explodes against the far wall, creating a gaping hole. The other two hit Goliath in the side of the chest, just below the shoulder, and detonate – nearly knocking it over. Krantz is being spun through the air as though he were a human sling shot, shouting for help. There's nothing we can do and the feeling of powerlessness is devastating. I see a hole in the machine's side and thick, black oil trailing down its left leg. Goliath rocks back on its feet, staggers, but doesn't fall. Instead it swings the terrified Krantz higher into the air and then whips him down violently against the ground. I turn my head even though the sound of Krantz' skull being crushed by the impact is enough to tell me he's dead.

For a moment, the mechanical giant studies Krantz' shattered body, before turning toward Bron.

Bron balls his gleaming hands into fists and nods. "This will be a good death," he says and charges Goliath before I can try to stop him. For a moment, even the machine looks surprised before it too breaks into a charge.

Goliath raises its arms to crush Bron, but he sidesteps the blow as the machine's two giant arms strike the marble floor, kicking up clouds of powdery dust and bits of pulverized rock. Now Goliath is open and I see Bron eject a blade from the palm of his hand and drive it into the wound in the machine's side. Goliath brings its fists up from the ground in a sweeping arc toward Bron, who tries to block the blow. The clang of metal on metal is almost deafening as Bron is sent tumbling across the floor. His blade has snapped off and is lodged in Goliath's side. I see that trail of black smoke billowing out from the pipe behind its neck sputter, which gives me an idea.

Goliath is closing in on Bron when I signal Sneak. She's with Dhal, by the door, watching over him as he

178

works the lock. She nods when she gets the message and snatches the cap off Dhal's head and bolts in my direction. I look past them and gasp. One of the attendants is injecting something into Skuld's neck and he begins to writhe violently, struggling against his constraints, thick yellow foam frothing from his lips. They've injected him with the Zee chemical.

-62-

Bron staggers to his feet as Goliath barrels down on him. There's a metallic clang as Bron rocks back on his heels after blocking a sideways blow from the machine. Bron's already looking tired and I can see his arms are badly dented. Goliath's next shot sends him to the ground again. This time the machine steps on Bron's right arm and pins him in place. There's a sound like metal being flattened in a press. When Goliath's foot comes away, Bron's arm is a twisted mess. Goliath lifts him into the air. It's trying to tear him apart, rip his arms right off his body and I race toward them, just as Sneak tosses me the cap. Bron is screaming in pain now, something I've never heard in all the time I've known him. I run up from behind and jump on Goliath's back. It notices me at once and releases Bron, who tumbles to the floor.

It's reaching for me now, its dented metal hands cutting through the thick black smoke chugging out the top of it and I do all I can to stay on. Soon it's spinning in circles and I feel my feet in midair. Dhal's cap is in my free hand and I jam it down that exhaust pipe, as far as it'll go, trying to ignore the searing pain as the flesh on my arm begins to melt. Finally, I pull free and let go, hitting the floor hard. I skid into the wall with a painful thud and a cloud of starbursts blurs my vision. Goliath is still trying to reach behind it, as though a knife were stuck between its shoulder blades, but Dhal's hat is deep inside the exhaust pipe and I know he'll need to rip himself apart to get it out. A wheezing escapes Goliath, as if the machine is suffocating; it probably is, because the black smoke is now a mere thin thread, trailing from the wound in its side. Goliath lets out a deep, bellowing moan, and falls forward, its head cratering the marble floor.

The rest of us run to Bron's side and the lights begin to dim. They've turned on Skuld's genetic accelerator machine and the room behind the window swirls with bright blue light. I can see Skuld inside, chained to that contraption, his body whipping back and forth. His new dark and leathery Zee skin is changing again. It's slowly turning red, but something tells me it won't stop there. He even looks taller now, his headdress split open at the crown and protruding above the ring holding him in place. Slowly his skin goes from red to black and the blast from Zee central is like nothing I've ever felt before. I've heard The Keepers talk of how Dusters used to explode bombs capable of destroying entire cities and now I understand what they meant. My hands rise to my temples. Blood trickles from my ears and eyes. Feels like my brain is being scrambled. A million messages flooding in all at once. Can't block them out. Skuld's done it. Activated all the Hives. I crumple to my knees, bending to his will, the others watching me without a clue as to what's going on. Only Sneak knows. Knows exactly what's about to happen. Then, mercifully, Skuld's body goes limp, the lights in the chamber go out, and like a switch, that pain in my head – like my brain is about to implode – suddenly fades.

-63-

I come to as I'm being dragged along the marble floor, now pockmarked and torn up from the battle. The gate that was blocking the room is still down and more importantly, a veritable sea of Zees are behind it, arms pushed through, reaching for us. Some of them are dressed in heavy Warden gear, the product of the struggle that was raging between the Zees and Skuld's men right outside. The lucky ones, I realize, are already dead.

Dhal finally cracks the lock and the door swings open and he disappears into the blackness within.

"Stop," I shout, but Sneak and Ret think I'm speaking to them and they halt. I clamber to my feet, Sneak steadying me as I rise. Nearby is Krantz' mangled body and Bron, cradling his shattered arm and looking rather dazed.

"We can't let Dhal go in there alone," I say. Sneak nods and rushes off ahead and even the thought of keeping up with her right now is much more than a fantasy. Ret, Oleg and I finally make it into the lab and I've got my repeater drawn – Ret his shotgun – but it's quickly apparent that Skuld is gone, along with most of his scientist lackeys. One or two terrified men in white lab coats remain and Sneak is already herding the stragglers into a corner. Dhal is on the ground, hovering over Master Lund's body. The whole time he's been with us he spoke of the old man with an almost tangible contempt, but I should have known he was only putting on a brave face.

Bron enters, cradling what's left of Krantz under his good arm. He sets him in the corner and removes Krantz' Keeper robe, placing it over him like a shroud.

The air in here is still electric and it draws my attention to the machine. Oleg looks as hopeless as I've ever seen him.

"What do we do now?" I ask, not entirely sure I care to hear his answer.

His shoulders rise and then fall listlessly. "They turned him, didn't they?"

He's talking about Skuld and I nod.

"And do you think he had time to–"

"Awaken the Hives before he blacked out?" My eyes dart away quickly and Oleg's lips scrunch together.

The yellow flashing stops as does the siren. All welcome changes, until I realize the full significance.

It doesn't take more than a quick glance through the observation window to see we're back in a pot of boiling water. When the emergency sequence ended, so too did the need for the heavy gate that sealed off the chamber we were in. Now, thousands of hissing Zees are heading straight for us. In the lead is an old woman in a blood-smeared tunic with a dark, distorted face and she's coming fast.

"Bron, get the door, quick!"

He looks at me from a million miles away.

I curse and stagger off to do it myself.

They're more than half way across the chamber, flooding around where Goliath collapsed, when I see the Hive leader enter the chamber, doubling my resolve to stop them from getting in.

I get there and slam the door just as the haggard old Zee reaches out for me.

But even as it closes I don't feel the magnetic seal yank it shut. She's smearing her face up against the glass, her mouth opening and closing as she tries to bite me. The door kicks open an inch and I shout over to Dhal.

"How do I lock this thing?"

Panic in his eyes. "It should lock on its own."

Bron drags over an aluminum table filled with scientific instruments. I leap out of the way, right as he slams it in place with his one working arm and wedges the other end against a row of machines with blinking lights. But the door doesn't close all the way and it's only a matter of time before they smash their way in.

"Dhal, fire up the machine," I bark.

He looks at me like I'm crazy and maybe I am.

"You heard me, now do it."

Oleg is nearby, wringing his hands like a nervous grandmother. "Tweaking the machine to reverse your condition will take hours we don't have. In fact, it won't be more than a matter of minutes before those things break in here and then what?" He points to a greatly diminished Bron who's doing his best to keep the table in place. "Your own heavy weapons expert is wounded and completely out of ammunition. There must be an escape hatch hidden in these walls somewhere that Skuld and his men used."

Oleg stops pacing when he sees the look on my face.

-64-

"Oh no, Azina, you have no intention of trying to reverse anything, do you?"

"Once Skuld gathers his strength, there's no telling how many millions of these things he'll be able to summon. By that time there won't be a weapon on Earth that has a chance in hell of stopping him."

"Except you," Ret says, deep sadness descending over him like a cloud. He knows that for the second time in as many days, I'm about to die.

Ret hands his shotgun to Bron and begins to strap me in. With a knife in each hand, Sneak manages to persuade the two Keeper scientists huddled in the corner to be of some use. Even Dhal is flicking switches and bringing the machine back online.

Bron fires a few shots through the growing gap in the door. It's only a matter of minutes before they force their way inside. I see the Hive leader working his way through the mass of darkened flesh, his twisted red face looming like a shark's fin in shallow water. A moment later he's up against the glass, trying to get into my head, using every trick in the book. My hands and feet are struggling to break free but I'm tied in place, luckily. The others around me pause when they see his red body and twisted face. Dhal looks like he's about to shit his pants and I tell them all to get back to work.

That aluminum table's starting to crumple from the pressure of the Zees pushing against the door.

Every time one of them manages to squeeze their hissing face between the crack, Bron sticks the barrel of Ret's shotgun between their lips and pulls the trigger.

"Ten seconds," Oleg calls out.

Sneak is over on my left, signing to me.

"Don't worry," I tell her. "I'll be fine." It's a bold faced lie, but if I tell the truth they'll never let me do it.

A shattering boom fills the room as Bron kills another Zee and glances back with that goofy smile of his, one arm hanging limp by his side.

"Seven seconds."

"Are you sure about this?" Ret asks me. "It isn't too late to stop it."

I smile. "Positive." Another lie and part of me feels like I'm about to be executed. "If something goes wrong," I tell Ret, "I want you to be the one who pulls the trigger."

"Three...two..."

He nods, and for a second I swear I can see his eyes tearing up before the room is bathed in deep blue light. Then the shock hits me and I hear my own voice hollering at the top of my lungs. The skin on my hands starts to blister and turn red and then slowly black. There's a humming noise from the machines and my mind is suddenly ejected out of my body and for a moment I wonder if I'm dead. I'm looking back at myself, through a thousand sets of eyes, and this feeling is foreign and yet somehow perfectly familiar. I can see myself strapped to the machine, arms and legs splayed, my skin oil black, my body convulsing violently. Ret's waving his arms and shouting for them to stop as the others look on in amazement. Then in a flash I realize what's happening; I'm seeing through the eyes of every Zee around us. We're all connected in an indescribable web. They're a physical extension of me, a finger, a toe, an arm and a leg, and to them, I'm their mind.

A second later the machine cuts out, as do the lights. I'm back inside myself and my body falls limp, suspended by the leather straps holding me in place. We're in darkness, but I can see just as well as if the sun itself were in the room with us. It's the others around me and the way they're fumbling about which tells me it's dark. The table finally crumples from the weight of the Zees struggling to get inside and the force sends Bron tumbling onto his back, the shotgun sliding across the floor.

They're on him in a flash, the teeth in their blackened mouths bared and ready to tear him to shreds. One of them is less than an inch above Bron's face, a stream of dark drool trailing out of its mouth in a long filament, when they freeze. The lights snap back on and Ret dives for Bron's hand to pull him away. Oleg, Sneak and Dhal scramble to stem the flood of Zees but they've all stopped dead in their tracks. The picture is almost surreal. We're surrounded by more than a thousand Zees, a handful in the room hovering over Bron's prone form, and not a single one of them is moving an inch. Not even that Red bastard outside. Why? Because a single word is pulsating inside my head over and over.

STOP!

My eyes lift and so do the Zees over Bron. Bron grabs hold of Ret's hand and scrambles to his feet. My eyes trace back toward the door and now the Zees are backing up. The haggard old Zee I saw earlier is the last one out and she closes the door gently behind her. Now I turn my attention to that red sonafobitch. He's not smiling anymore. Looking inside his Zee brain isn't any harder than looking into my own, and I understand now why he wanted me so badly. He wanted a queen and he thought making me drink his blood would accomplish that. Well, in a manner of speaking, he got his wish, for that's exactly what I've become, although I'm not quite sure he's gonna like what comes next.

I give the command and the Zees outside descend on the Hive leader like a pack of wild dogs and they tear him to shreds, one chunk at a time. His beady little eyes widen with panic and disbelief. He opens his mouth to utter a guttural Zee scream, but the Zee hands are in his mouth too, ripping and tearing. It isn't more than a matter of moments before the red smear running down the observation window is the only sign he ever existed. No one says a word except for me. "That was for Gunnar and Vasser, but most of all, it was for Jinx and Glave and Pennies."

-65-

Ret and Sneak are the ones who untie me. Judging by the way the others are keeping their distance, I can tell they still aren't sure what exactly I've become. Hell, I'm not sure. But some things are clearer now than ever. The Azina who entered the complex only days before feels like a stranger to me now. There are three parts of me, all battling for supremacy. The Azina I've been all my life, Azina the emerging Hive leader I was slowly becoming, and now Azina the queen.

Without all the pressure, it doesn't take long for Dhal to find the false wall and we make our way out of here. Sneak reaches out to hold my hand and then recoils. I look down and see that the hairs along my body have become tiny spikes. If I wasn't a monster before, without a doubt I've become one now. As we make our way out, Dhal's discussing Bron's shattered arm and his ideas for improvements. Bron pretends not to care, but even from back here I can sense his excitement. He pats Dhal on the shoulder, but the worried look on Oleg's face brings me back to the task at hand. Skuld is still out there and so are millions of Zees, stirring awake from a slumber that's lasted nearly two centuries. Fighting fire with fire was the only choice we had. That's what I keep telling myself. I just hope to hell it'll be enough.

Part III

-66-

The dead lie scattered in the streets of Sotercity like pieces of discarded trash. It's the silence that gets to me most. I glance over at Oleg, Dhal, Ret, and even Sneak, and it's clear they feel the same way. Bron is the only one who's oblivious. I want to say the streets are still, but that isn't entirely true. There's movement in and amongst the corpses. Some of them aren't dead, only chewed up enough to be turned into Zees, and now many of them are pulling their brown leathery bodies along the ground. None of the ones we see are able to walk. One has both legs bent at odd angles. Another is just a torso. All of them, however, are clawing over the dead with a single-minded purpose: leave the city. As though they're being summoned.

Bron stomps one skull into mush and smiles, seemingly unaware of his battered arms, especially the right one which hangs limply by his side. "Squashing bugs never gets old, wouldn't you agree, Azina?"
The big man's eyes drop to my arms and the dark skin and spiky hairs bristling there like the flesh of a cat's tongue. I'm sure he's trying to goad me because, to a guy like Bron, anything that baffles or frightens is bad and needs to be destroyed. Not understood. That's why Ret's presence is so important. He tempers Bron's impulsiveness and closed-minded ignorance with reason and tolerance. I know how I look. This is what I chose. It's just too bad Bron can't see that deep down I'm still the same old Azina who started this group of ragtag Mercs.

If it were anyone else, I probably woulda clobbered them by now.

But, right now, we have bigger problems. Skuld is calling those Zees. I don't tell the group because I don't see the point in alarming anyone, but I can hear the signal as loud as that bell in the Sotercity clock tower. And when I glance down the deserted street behind me, I can almost see a faint mist, snaking off into the distance. It's part of Skuld's signal, that much is clear. The one all of these gimps are trying to follow out of Sotercity. Only the Zees trapped underground in the dome-shaped chamber remain and for a very good reason: they aren't smart enough to call the elevator to free themselves.

But seeing where Skuld is going, or where he's ordered these Zees to assemble, is another matter altogether. I'll need to follow it for myself and as soon as possible.

A legless Zee reaches out for me and I know right away he isn't trying to make me his breakfast. He senses a master is present and is eager to do my bidding. I try and tell him to just die, but the Zee only pauses. A direct command to commit suicide is something they don't seem to understand. A shame really, because it would avoid me having to do this. I draw the Katana from my back and run it through the thing's skull. It continues reaching for me for an instant, locked in a sort of religious ecstasy, before it slumps and the light in its eyes goes dark. But religion isn't an entirely misplaced idea.

To them, I'm something of the minor deity. But if I'm a deity, do they see Skuld as a full-fledged God?

Sweat pours down Ret's face. He's carrying Krantz' body, covered in a Keeper robe, and it's clear Bron's enjoying every second of his suffering. Especially since Bron is normally the one tasked with doing the heavy lifting. He would be too, if it weren't for those shattered arms of his. I love the big guy like a brother, but sometimes I wish he would quit being such a baby.

192

We arrive at a small patch of loose ground, just outside a temple to Newton, and begin hastily digging a grave. The earth is full of hard rocks and the others are having a rough time of it. Ret's trying to use the butt of his automatic shotgun and cursing with every flick of dirt. Oleg's muttering under his breath and it's hard to tell from here if he's bitching or saying a prayer. Soon enough we cut a deep enough hole and lay what's left of Krantz inside. He wasn't with us for long, but the sting of losing one of our own is real nonetheless.

"He had a good death," Bron says and I'm suddenly not so angry with him anymore. In five words, Bron manages to sum up what would've taken Oleg an hour. A good death is all any of us can really hope for.

67

We arrive at Dhal's workshop, weary and craving rest. I figure it belongs to Dahl now, since he was Master Lund's apprentice and the old guy's lying under the keep, stiff as a board. I can tell the kid wanted him carried out and buried, as we did for Krantz, and if we make it through this I promise to lug the old bastard out myself. But I'm not running a funeral home. Over the next few days the few survivors in Sotercity will have their hands full, preventing this place from becoming a rotting cesspool of disease. Corpses scattered in the streets have a funny way of doing that.

The group is barely inside long enough to sit down before Dhal begins tinkering with Bron's arms.

"Are they salvageable?" I ask the kid and immediately catch a look from Bron.

"Of course they are," Bron cuts in. "Right, little man?" There's an almost pleading quality to his voice that makes me feel suddenly sorry for him.

"Doesn't look good." The kid says, his tongue poking out the side of his mouth in concentration as he loosens a bolt and removes Bron's crushed right arm. It lands on the workshop table with a clang. Dhal moves to unscrew Bron's other arm and the stout Norseman jerks away.

"Don't worry, I'll give you something in the meantime," Dhal assures him. "Master and I were working on something special right before he…"

The kid doesn't say the words, but he doesn't need to for the pain in his eyes to shine through, making all of us pause for a moment. All of us except for Bron, of course, who's more worried about his new arms than silly things like feelings. Ret may look stoic, but I know him well enough to see he hasn't hardened completely.

194

Dhal disappears into the back room and returns with what looks like a pair of kitchen utensils. Ret's already snickering. Even Sneak is beside me, grinning widely. All of this has the effect of making Bron even more upset.

"What the hell are these?" He asks.

"Why, your replacement arms. That is until I can finish the others."

"But what can I do with these? They look like glorified spatulas."

The room bursts into spastic laughter. Sneak's slapping her leg, signing to me that she's about to bust a gut. The straight-as-a-board Oleg can't help but give in and this may be the first time I've ever seen him smile. But soon that smile fades and I know why. He's thinking about what Skuld's just done to the world, and more than that, what he's about to do. Oleg stands and it's clear enough that we're about to get a lecture for fooling around. Dhal begins attaching Bron's temporary arms while Oleg speaks.

"All of this laughing tells me none of you have grasped the severity of our present situation."

See, I knew it. I rise as well. "Oleg's right. Skuld is in the process of summoning every Zee he can get his grimy hands on…" I'm no more than a few words in when I feel a tingling sensation run up my left arm. One that begins to grow and, before I have a chance to stop it, my left hand jerks out and closes around Dhal's soft throat.

Right away, the kid's eyes go wide with shock and fear, his pupils dilating in terror. The others are stunned too. If I were trying to shut the kid up, that'd be one thing. He was only attaching those hideous arms to Bron's shoulders. But, the thing is, I'm not the one doing this. Somehow, Skuld's pushed his way into my mind and has taken hold of me. And this new me, I'm discovering, is infinitely stronger than the old Azina. Won't be more than another second before my grip closes, crushing Dhal's windpipe, sending him to join Master Lund.

68

Gurgling noises are all that's coming from Dhal's throat when Ret jumps in and grabs my hand with both of his. I join him and the scene almost looks surreal, the two of us trying to pry my left hand off Dhal's neck. It wrenches free a moment later and the kid gasps for air. Oleg's leaning against the workshop table like his heart's about to give out.

Already that tingling sensation is beginning to dissipate. I'm still wringing my hand when Sneak signs what everyone else in the room is probably thinking.

"That was Skuld, wasn't it?" She asks.

"I'm not sure," I reply, but that isn't too far from a boldfaced lie. Of course it was Skuld. Leading a group of Mercs without trust is like trying to wipe your ass with your feet. You might manage it, but you'll make one hell of a mess in the process.

Bron looks worried. "First the glowing eyes, then the levitating, and now this. Where's the old Azina?"

"She's still here," I try and reassure him. "Got this under control, trust me." Wrong choice of words, because I can see the doubt on their faces as clearly as I can see the pained expression still clinging to Dhal's. I put a hand on his shoulder and the group flinches.

"Sorry kid, won't happen again."

"An apology from Azina," Bron says. "Now we *know* something's wrong."

Weak smiles all round and it doesn't do a damn thing to cut the tension in the room. Slowly, still rubbing his neck, Dhal returns to attaching Bron's temporary arms and I tuck my hands into the pockets of my leather tunic and do my best to continue where I left off.

"Skuld is building an army," I say.

197

"Yes," Ret adds. "That part is clear enough, but for what?"

"Maybe to prove his pecker is longer than his pinky," Bron says, holding his new spatula arm in the air and then quickly retracting it in embarrassment.

Sneak is about to laugh again and I give her a nudge.

"If you're right," Ret says, "then there can only be one place he's heading."

"The capital." Oleg may be the one to say it, but the words are everyone's lips.

Bron spits. "That damn bastard wants to turn everyone in the ten territories into bloodsucking Zees."

I shake my head. "That may be, but I sense there's more to it than that."

"Course you sense it," Bron snaps back. "He's been whispering in your ear since he turned. For all we know, the two of you are in league with each other. But don't think I'm gonna sit by when you turn on us. You know the code, Azina. Kill or be killed."

"Enough!" Ret shouts, with uncharacteristic force. "Azina is one of us."

"For now," Bron mutters and walks over to a bench crammed with tools so he can sulk.

"I believe there's only one way to get to the bottom of what Skuld is after and what we might be up against," Oleg says.

I'm doing all I can to not slap the old man upside the head. "Stop the foreplay and get to the point, will you?"

Oleg grumbles for a moment, probably about what a bitch I've become, before he spits it out.

"We must head to the archive."

"Oh, great," Bron whines from the far end of the room. "We're going on a Keeper field trip."

"Oleg may have a point," I say, ignoring Bron's jab. "Skuld's just woken thousands of sleeping Zees, but who knows what's down there with them?"

"What can be worse than a Zee?" Sneak signs.

"I'm not sure," I say. "But I have a feeling we're about to find out."

-69-

The Keepers have a real hard-on for libraries and a bigger hard-on for books, which makes the cramped space of the archive so much more surprising. Oleg tells us it was once the basement of a bank, which he says was a place where Dusters stored their wealth. Frankly, I can't imagine allowing anyone to put their filthy hands on my hard-earned USCs. That said, it's difficult to imagine having too much to handle yourself.

Oil lamps on the wall cast disturbing shadows along the narrow corridors. Everyone's with us except Dhal, who stayed behind to finish Bron's new arms. As we left, the big oaf couldn't let Dhal tinker without offering the kid a final warning.

"When we get back I wanna see something great. And nothing girly. I don't need arms to end you."

"The documents are down one more level," Oleg says and descends into shadow. We catch up to find him standing before a Keeper guard.

"No one may enter without written permission," the prick says.

Ret's fists curl into fists. "You turd. Don't you know what's happened? Nearly the whole city's been wiped out by Zees."

The skeptical look on the guard's face makes it clear enough has no intention of being tricked. More than that, the word Zee doesn't seem to mean a thing to him. At this very moment, his entire family is probably either dead or shambling toward Skuld's rendezvous.

The guard's eyes light on my face and the muscles in his expression go slack. "What in Newton's name is she?"

"We don't have time for this idiot," Bron says and when he lifts his arms in a threatening gesture, all they

200

produce is a tiny squeak. The guard's face splits with a smile and Bron's face turns the color of a giant radish.

"Are those spatulas? Oh, I get it, you're some kind of cook."

"That's it," Bron growls and brings his forehead down on the guard's nose. There's a loud crunching sound before the man crumples into a heap.

"Did you have to do that?" I snap.

A thin drop of blood rolls down Bron's forehead. "He's not dead, least I don't think he is."

The guard is breathing, that part's clear enough, but the big guy's missing the point. In the coming days we're gonna need everyone we can get. Even idiots can pull a trigger.

Slowly, we make our way inside and find rows of tall shelving, stocked with boxes. Each is labeled with numbers. I spot a box marked 2158. Another reads 2057. "What kind of filing system is this?" I ask.

"It isn't," says Oleg. "Those numbers represent the year the document was created."

Oleg's gotta be wrong about this one, 'cause the current date is 223. There's an extra two in there.

He sees my confusion and sighs. "Not long after the fall, the Keepers reset the calendar. The death of the Zee Queen became year one. Before that, Dusters kept their own dates and they got up to somewhere in the early 2000s. But the reset date was only intended for the masses, so they wouldn't long for the decadence of the past. A fresh start, you might say."

"So Keepers have their own calendar, then," Ret says, wiping a coat of dust off one of the boxes. "That sure explains a lot."

Oleg waves at a cloud of motes floating before him. "Sometimes, knowledge of the past can be a dangerous thing."

"Dangerous for who?" I shoot back. "Only the monkeys in charge utter that kind of drivel."

Bron is making a mess of a box labeled 'Banned Female Attire,' when Ret calls out. We head over.

"I was searching through box 2025 when I found this.' He hands a document to Oleg, who begins reading, his brow furrowing as his eyes scan down the page.

"This is a battle report from a Duster general named Dempsey. It's about the final confrontation with the Queen."

Now Oleg is in that same box, digging around. He comes up with a paper and the longer he stares at it, the whiter his face becomes.

"Don't keep us in suspense, Oleg," I say hotly. "What is it you've found?"

Oleg swallows hard and his throat makes an audible clicking noise. "The Queen," he says. "She's isn't dead."

70

"How's that possible? I bark, starting to feel the blood flow into my face. "You said yourself, they lured her into the open two centuries ago and killed her."

The stern look on Oleg's face tells me he remembers exactly what he said and has no need of being reminded. "That was what we were told."

"It's what we were all told," Ret adds. "Leave it to the Keepers to weave a tale that never happened."

"Propaganda." That's what Sneak is signing and I can see her hands ball up into tight fists as soon as she's done.

"So those Duster pussies never finished her off after all?" Bron says. "Now I've lost all respect for them."

"Not killed, she was captured and imprisoned," but even as Oleg says the words, his head shakes in disbelief.

Ret laughs, but there isn't an ounce of humor in it. "They locked her away, like some Grinder caught stealing a loaf of bread."

"Not exactly," Oleg corrects him. "She was driven into deepest recesses of a Duster prison and there she was sealed, presumably forever. In order to ensure she would never be disturbed or reawakened, our ancestors chose that as the very site upon which to rebuild the human race."

Ret blinks his eyes hard. "You're saying she's locked somewhere beneath the capital?"

Oleg nods. "According to these documents, yes."

"Well isn't that just great," Bron snorts, looking like a man with two dinners before him. "So, who do we go after first? Skuld or the Queen?"

"I have a feeling we won't need to choose," I say and Oleg knows exactly what I mean.

Bron looks bewildered and ready to head butt someone else. Outside, I hear movement and realize it's the Keeper guard waking up. He's moaning, which means he's touching his nose and trying his best to remember how it got bent so far out of shape.

"Skuld's heading for the capital," I say. "We knew he would, sooner or later, but what we didn't know, until now, was why."

"Or that he'd have an army of Zees with him when he arrived."

I glance over at Oleg and spot the concern deeply etched on his face. I ask the question, although it's clear enough he's already wondering the same thing. "What will happen if Skuld manages to kill the Queen?"

The old guy reaches down and ruffles the edges of the papers he's holding. "Then there would be nothing left to stop him, Azina, not even you."

Oleg grabs a wad of papers in his arms and signals that he has everything he needs. One of those things is a map of the catacombs under Attica, and a tunnel that supposedly leads to the place where the Queen is being held. Which raises two disturbing questions. Rule number three of being a gun for hire is 'never rely on outdated maps when your life is on the line.' Those discolored papers, that Oleg's clutching like a newborn child, are probably two centuries old. The capital city has grown a lot since then. They've built structures and crude plumbing and who knows how many of those tunnels are still there. But that isn't my biggest concern. From the corner of my eye I catch Sneak watching me, and I know full well she sees the worry on my face. She knows me well enough to realize it doesn't have a thing to do with fretting about my own life. I would never have strapped myself to Skuld's little machine if that were the case. I glance down at my inky black arms, bristling with prickly hairs, almost as if to drive the point home. Already I've attacked one member of the team and I can't fight the terror, nagging inside of me, that the closer we get to Skuld and the Queen he's so desperate to kill, the more of a danger I become.

71

It's dusk by the time we start heading back to the workshop, and it isn't long before the full devastating effect of Skuld's plan, on the people of Sotercity, comes into clear focus. A woman in a shredded tunic, her face a mask of shock, wanders the streets, calling out the names of loved ones. She doesn't appear to have been bitten, but the chances are good whoever she's calling out to has, and whatever's left of them is surely heading toward Skuld's gathering point as we speak. Her eyes spot me as we approach and the sudden change in her expression is dramatic. She thinks I'm a Zee and shrieks, searching the ground for a weapon. Doesn't seem to matter one bit that I'm surrounded by a half-dozen others. Another survivor nearby picks up on the commotion and follows suit. They're heading our way, a handful of new stragglers swelling their ranks by the time Ret raises his shotgun. "Looks like things are about to get sloppy."

"Don't hurt them," I say. How can I possibly blame these people, after what they've gone through? If the tables were turned, I'd probably be leading the charge. I'm a monster. On the outside, at the very least, and perhaps shortly on the inside too. Sneak's tapping a finger on the hilt of one of her twin blades and I know for a fact if they get too close – even wielding makeshift weapons – she won't hesitate to kill them all. She would lay down her life trying to protect me. I spot an intersecting street and we turn down it. The detour will add a few minutes to the journey, but it isn't worth risking any more bloodshed.

The mob is far behind when we make it back to the workshop and the sound of hammering. "They should be burying the dead," Bron says. "Instead of making trouble for the rest of us, who risked our skins trying to stop Skuld."

Oleg's staring into his hands as though he were reading something terrible etched into the grooves of his flesh. "Sotercity's been reduced to a mob of lowly Grinders." The elitist old bastard looks positively beside himself. I'm the one that crowd would hang from the city walls, not them. Shouldn't I be the one in despair? If anyone ever needed more proof the world's a screwed up place, this is it.

The hammering stops and Dhal glances up from a pair of gleaming metal arms he's got laid out before him. The kid's face is a patchwork of grease stains and sweat. These new arms are bigger than Bron's broken ones, and a universe apart from the comical looking spatulas he's wearing now. Not surprisingly, the big guy looks positively elated.

He nods in their direction "For me?"

Oh boy, now he's a child opening gifts on the Winter Solstice.

"They were meant for the son of a high-ranking Keeper," Dhal says. "Only other pair in existence." The kid says, nodding to what remains of Bron's shattered arms beside him. "I salvaged as much as I could from the old units, but you have to understand, they were so badly damaged…" Bron's only half listening. Details like how and why roll off of him like water off a feathered back. "Get these things off me, would ya?" he snaps.

Dhal shrugs and begins loosening the bolts to remove the makeshift arms. The boy pauses and winks at me. "You know," he says pensively. "Maybe I shouldn't, I mean, I could get in a lot of trouble giving these away. That Keeper paid a lot of money for these arms."

"Never mind any of that," Bron barks. "That crusty old Keeper and his snot-nosed kid are either dead or new members of Skuld's new shitbag army. Get moving."

207

It takes Dhal nearly 30 minutes to make the final attachment of Bron's new and improved killing machines. The big guy stands and holds one in the air, rotating his wrist, flexing the fingers into a fist. He almost reminds me of a woman trying on the new pair of gloves.

"Whaddyathink?" he asks, knowing full well they're an impressive spectacle by any measure. He snatches a three inch metal bar off the workbench and bends it as easily as a child might bend a piece of tall grass.

"They're certainly shiny," I tell him.

Ret's shaking his head. "Zees'll see us coming from miles away now."

"So, you like them then?" Dhal asks and despite the boy's phenomenal expertise, his adolescent insecurities are hard to ignore.

"Like them?" Bron bellows, snatching those flimsy temporary arms and crumpling them into a mangled ball of steel. "I'd marry them, if I could."

Dhal smiles. "Wait till you see what else they can do. I know you recently lost your demolitions expert, Jinx, so I've added a 40mm grenade launcher to your left arm." Dhal holds up what looks like a child's marble. "Might not look impressive, but they pack as much power as a full-sized grenade. Tilt that arm into the air and you become a one-man mortar team."

Ret's got his head buried in his hands and I know just what he's thinking. If Bron's ego wasn't overinflated before, it sure as hell will be once the kid's done explaining these upgrades.

"What about my old firepower?"

"All there. And, like the grenades, I transitioned your arms to fire slightly smaller shells. Just as powerful but you can carry more ammo."

"Good, but will they be as loud? I mean, I'll be disappointed if everyone's ears aren't ringing after I lay down a barrage." Bron's famous brown-toothed smile is back in full force.

"Guaranteed to deafen within a dozen yards."

Bron thinks he's being funny, but those guns of his have already impacted my hearing by at least 30%.

Dhal taps a compartment at the base of Bron's right palm. "Right below your blade ejection port I added something special. Go on, give it a try."

Oleg and the others hurry out of the way just in time. Bron aims his palm at a thick wood beam and fires a spear point across the room. It thuds into the solid oak, trailing a thin cord behind it.

"The cable has a tensile strength greater than steel. Oh yeah, there's one last thing that I added and I think you're really gonna to love this one."

"A built-in toilet roll dispenser that wipes his backside for him?" Ret asks. Bron flicks him a look that says 'why you trying to ruin my birthday party?'

Dhal flips a switch on Bron's left arm, revealing a nozzle.

"I hope that's not for moonshine," I say, only half joking. "Bron after a few drinks isn't pretty."

Ret concurs. "Once, after six shots of something called Grinder's Delight, Bron ripped out the entire bar and sent it through the window."

Dhal suddenly looks like he isn't so sure arming Bron to the teeth was a good idea.

Bron taps the nozzle. "Never mind them, what does it do?"

Dhal swallows hard. "It's a flamethrower that fires something Dusters used to call napalm. A combustible gel that burns at over 2000 degrees Fahrenheit. Doesn't matter if they're human or Zee, whatever you point this at stops living. There ain't much in there, so use it sparingly."

Tears form at the corners of Bron's eyes. The thought of that much death and destruction always makes him emotional.

Oleg's been patiently listening to all this and now stands to speak. "As impressive as this is, let me remind you even the mighty Bron is no match for the sheer number of Zees Skuld is drawing to him. An army is forming and we don't have anything powerful enough to throw at them."

"What about Azina?" Ret says. "You saw how she made those Zees tear the Hive leader to pieces."

"I did," Oleg concedes. "What remains to be seen is how she will fare when she enters Skuld's effective zone of control. Who are the Zees likely to follow?"

"That's a question none of us can answer," I say. "Not until we're there."

Oleg's brow ruffles like one of those cranky Keeper professors. "Is that the kind of plan in which the future of the human race will depend on Azina? Let's wait-and-see?"

As always, I'd love to crack Oleg in the head, but I can't deny the sour old bastard does have a point. We're gonna need more than wishful thinking if we want any chance of stopping Skuld from enslaving humanity or worse, driving them to extinction. Dhal's got his hand propped in the air again like a schoolboy.

"What is it?" I ask, hoping to hell it isn't another fun fact about Bron's arms.

"I know what we can do," he says.

72

"We need to go to White Rock," Dhal says and pauses, as though any of us have a clue what he's talking about.

Ret's still nodding, waiting for the rest to spill out, when Oleg pipes up. "The testing ground, you've been there?"

"Of course," Dhal replies.

Now I'm really starting to get pissed. "You wanna fill the rest of us in on this private conversation you two are having?"

Oleg clears his throat. "Any new tech recovered by the Prospectors is first sent to White Rock for secret testing and implementation."

"Goliath," Ret blurts out as the pieces of the puzzle begin fitting together.

"But I destroyed that worthless hunk of metal," Bron offers proudly.

Ret tsks. "You *hurt* Goliath. Technically, it was Azina who killed it by shoving Dhal's hat down its exhaust pipe."

Almost on cue, Dhal's hand pats the top of his head. "I miss that hat."

"It's still there, if you want it," Bron offers, a mouthful of rotting teeth winking back at the boy. "Might be a touch dirty, but anything is better than looking at that mop you call hair."

I cut through the chatter and address Dhal directly. "What's at White Rock?"

"The Titans," Dhal says. "Goliath's prototypes." And that's when it begins to make sense. Even a genius like Master Lund didn't get it right the first time.

Ret doesn't seem convinced. "So we're gonna risk our lives over two heaps of scrap metal?"

Dhal shakes impatiently. "Goliath's predecessors aren't scrap. With each generation we made improvements, until we arrived at exactly what Skuld was after: The ultimate killing machine."

Sneak starts signing and she raises a good point. I translate for the others. "But can you get the Titans working?"

"Probably, but that isn't our biggest problem," Dhal says, wiping a smear of grease from his hand. "White Rock is heavily defended."

Oleg straightens his robes. "One thing you must remember, White Rock is the storehouse for the very technology Skuld has sought to keep from the general population. You won't find Wardens there. The men who guard White Rock aren't conscripted, they're born in White Rock and that's where they die."

"An elite force, cut off from the outside world, that shoots first and doesn't bother asking any questions," I say. "This keeps getting better by the second." And even as the words come rolling off my tongue, I feel that strange sensation wash over me again. A tingling that courses through my body. I glance down and see those sharpened hairs on my arms standing on end, as though an electric current is running through every fiber of my being. That's when the deep timbre of a man's voice calls out to me. It's Skuld, I'm sure of it and he's trying to get inside my head and make me do things. From a great distance, I hear Oleg say, "cut off and likely unaware the Zees are about to destroy what's left of the human race."

Then Ret speaks and it sounds like he's talking through an old tin can: "All the more reason we'll need to convince them."

Oleg's about to say something else, when that pulse firing through my body becomes too strong to resist.

Sneak is the first to realize there's a problem, followed by Ret; but, by then, it's already too late.

It doesn't matter that my hands are clasped together as tightly as I can squeeze them. My right whips out and hits Oleg square on the chest, knocking him across the room like a child's doll. My own strength, after the transformation, is unbelievable and I'm doing everything I can to regain control, but already I know deep down it isn't going to be enough. The tingling is surging even stronger and there isn't any doubt: unless I can stop it, whatever's inside me doing this is about to kill everyone around me.

-73-

Ret doesn't get a single step closer before I snatch him by his ammo vest, raise him two feet off the ground, his legs kicking wildly in mid-air, and fling him over the workshop repair table. The sound of clanking tools fills the room as he rolls over bits of pipe and copper shavings before hitting the ground. Dhal might be next, but the kid's already gone, probably learned his lesson after I tried to crush his throat.

To my left, Bron raises one of his arms, intent on frying me to a crisp, when Sneak snap-kicks his wrist. An orange gout of flame spews from the nozzle and douses the workshop ceiling. Sneak only meant to stop him from killing me but, with no way to tell him that, it's clear Bron thinks Sneak and I are the enemy. The big guy's about a second away from opening up with both his 20mm guns and tearing this place and everyone in it to shreds. Already I can feel Skuld's grip weakening, but the damage is done. My choices are clear and each one is worse than the last. Either plead with Bron and risk being blasted into mush, or stand and fight. I've never been one to beg and, with that, I lunge across the room, reaching him in a single powerful leap, grabbing hold of his thick metal wrists as he opens fire. My hands vibrate wildly as shells tear past my head. He's so incredibly strong I won't be able to hold him for long. Both blades eject from his palms and now I know I'm in trouble. Sneak's trying to get between us, desperate to stop this before one of us is hurt or killed, and her concern might just have something to do with the fact that the roof's on fire. Before Sneak can do much, Bron sends the heel of his boot into my stomach, knocking me backward. I reach for my Katana, just as I spot one of his blades slicing toward my head.

The Katana gets there just in time and the force of it nearly knocks the sword from my hand. I realize then that I'll never have enough time to recover before the next strike and, as I see it coming, all I can do is hope the end is quick.

The loud clang beside my head makes my ears ring. I open my eyes to find that Sneak's blade deflected Bron's killing blow. Both of us take a half step back and I know right away she's in trouble. Bron goes at her, swinging madly, and with unmatched grace she dodges his vicious attacks as he first chops the workbench in half and then cleaves a solid Oak chair in two. Wrenches and screwdrivers scatter. The bloodlust in his eyes tells me he won't stop till we're dead. I move behind Bron and swing the tip of my boot up between his legs. My foot connects and almost at once Bron doubles over in pain, moaning. I use the narrow window of time to gather my things and burst out of the front door, running as fast as I can down the street.

Smoke is billowing out of the workshop's upper windows, but even as I leave I can see Oleg and Ret getting to their feet. I would sooner let Bron kill me than watch them burn. In a strange way, it is comforting knowing that Sneak will get them to safety. Although I can't deny the very thought of what has just happened is tearing me apart. How could I have stopped it? The force rumbling within me, right before I lost control, felt about as uncontrollable as an approaching tsunami. Maybe if I'd run away before it seized me completely… But, as the Dusters used to say, 'hindsight is 20/20,' although I haven't a clue what 20/20 means. Just one of the many enigmatic expressions we cling to from a bygone era.

Making my way through the ghostly streets of Sotercity, the residue from Skuld stomping around inside my mind is still there. A tingling vibration, along the edges of my fingers, and something that feels like his hot,

215

stinky breath warming the back of my neck. And the thought makes me wanna wretch. Not just from the sensation, but from what I almost did. Skuld has tried to destroy us before we could move to stop him and I'm suddenly sure he may have just succeeded.

-74-

Skuld's stink is still all over me when a sound reaches my ears. Angry voices and they aren't far off, around the next corner at the end of the street, but the noise is bouncing off the walls, making pinpointing the origin next to impossible. And you don't need to have studied under the Keepers to know that it's the same mob that chased us earlier. Now that the real threat has left, they're anxious to relieve their frustrations on the first intact Zee they can find. Which means they'd love to get their grimy little Grinder hands on me. But I haven't made it this far by being taken down by a group of people who can't even spell their own names.

I'm assaulted a moment later by a series of pin pricks. I've been feeling them since we made it back to the workshop; I assumed it had something to do with Skuld's mind games. Except it's starting to become clear. Those Zees, crawling through the streets on shattered limbs, are having the life stomped out of them by the mob. It shouldn't anger me, since I did the same myself and, more importantly, since it's the only real way to stop the Zees from spreading their chemical mutation, but somehow it does.

I reach the intersection of a major boulevard and practically bump into a pocket of men and women, stomping a Zee body into mush. One of the bastards spots me, before I can disappear around the corner, and I take off at a run, feeling more and more certain that this is likely how the rest of my life will play out. Chased from one gutter to the next by people more interested in knocking the brain from my skull than listening to my attempts to explain the fact that I'm not a Zee.

217

As I backtrack, it's apparent some of them are moving around to cut me off. A moment later my fears are realized when I see a clump of them tear around a corner, hatred flashing in their sunken eyes. They're threatening to cut me off and force me into a corner, where I might need to fight back. Many of them will die, but they'll get me eventually, especially now that Ret, Bron, Sneak and the others aren't here to back me up.

The breath is wheezing in and out of me, my heart charging along at a frantic pace. A memory of seeing the Hive leader being torn apart by Zees flashes before my eyes and I vow to not suffer a similar fate.

An alley looms up ahead and I duck into it, frantically praying to one of Oleg's imaginary gods that I haven't been seen. I get no more than a dozen steps before I see I've made a terrible mistake.

A Keeper pulls back the bolt on his rifle with a threatening click.

"Don't move a muscle, bitch, or I'll spray your brains all over the walls."

Behind him are three other Keepers. They look like guards, not Wardens, but in tight quarters like these, one hardly needs to be a marksman to land lead on target.

I remain still, as instructed, ruminating about how much I hate being called a bitch, when I recognize the guard tucked behind the cocky bastard with the gun. He's got a broken nose and a trail of blood crusting his upper lip. Dark hair, mid-twenties and now I know where I've seen him before. He's the Keeper from the archive. The one Bron head butted into a groggy sleep.

"She's some sort of monster." the cocky one says, nestling the rifle butt into his shoulder and taking aim.

"How's your head?" I ask, distinctly aware of the angry crowd drawing ever closer.

One of them, with dark skin, turns to the prick with the rifle in my face. "I thought you said these things didn't talk?"

"I'm not sure what she is," says the fresh faced Keeper with the broken nose. "But she isn't one of those things, I know that much."

Those footsteps are getting louder and the Keepers can hear them too. From a low hanging rooftop I spot a glint of metal and a wisp of movement. A smile grows on my lips and suddenly I don't feel so alone. But the Keeper guard with the gun is arguing with his friends about what to do with me and the grin on my face isn't making him happy.

"You find something funny, bitch?" he asks

There's that word again. "Only that you're too stupid to realize we might just be on the same side."

"I'm stupid, am I?" His finger squeezes the trigger peppering me with automatic gunfire and I twist out of the way; but no matter how fast I am, I'll never be able to dodge a bullet. The first shot slices through my wrist and slams into my chest. Another breaks my collarbone and exits the other side. The last two riddle my abdomen and it feels a lot like the time Bron thought it would be funny to sucker punch me in the gut. I fall to the ground, fully aware that I'm dying. That glint from the roof drops down among them and I see Sneak, perhaps for the last time, and the rage on her face is like nothing I've seen before. The first one to die is the Keeper who shot me. Sharpened steel plunges through the back of his neck and into his brain, finishing him faster than he deserves. The dark skinned Keeper moves to raise his rifle and in the process accidentally discharges it, shooting the man beside him. A blade to the spine paralyses him and now there's only the one with the broken nose left. The only one who stood up for me. I try and tell Sneak to stop,

219

that this one should live, but death closes in before I can tell if she heard me.

-75-

Prior Skuld

Councillor Plak fumbles over a mouthful of words like a child caught telling a fib. "I've come before you, Prior Skuld, on behalf of the other council members. These creatures…"

"Make you nervous," I say, motioning to the senior member of Sotercity's General Council.

"Is that what you're trying to say, Plak? That you don't feel safe? That you're having second thoughts?"

Plak swallows hard. "These creatures," he continues, "want nothing more than to tear the flesh from our bones…"

I snicker, still surprised at how deep my voice has become. The two of us are standing in the ruins of a village that just happened to lie between Sotercity and the capital. Smoke rises from the buildings around us, engulfed in flames. And yet the most dazzling sight is the ocean of dark skinned Zees, standing shoulder to shoulder, as far as the eye can see.

"Let me ask you something. Have any of the council members been harmed by a Zee in any way, shape or form?" The words come out as a question, but it's clear by the look on Plak's face, he knows perfectly well I mean it as a statement of fact.

Plak shakes his head, his eyes lowering with what I can only assume is the same spineless streak that made him betray his fellow Keepers in the first place.

"We would march straight on the capital, depose the Patriarch and you would do away with all of these monstrosities at once, that's what you said, Prior Skuld. All we're asking is for some assurances that you can…"

221

Ever the politician, Plak pauses, searching for the least offensive words.

"Control them," I say, putting him out of his misery. "You want me to guarantee you and your colleagues won't be eaten by Zees. That's really what you're asking, isn't it? You've seen how they watch you and it's made you nervous. Well, it should. Our fates, I suppose, are tightly bound, Councillor Plak. Because if something unfortunate should happen to me, there won't be a thing holding those Zees back from devouring you and your fellow councillors. And believe me when I tell you, the Zees are so very hungry."

The sight of the blood draining from Plak's face is absolutely titillating.

I dismiss him and his petty concerns with a wave of my hand. Watching his crimson robe brush the ground as he leaves, I can't help marvelling at his rather pathetic obsession with mortality. Over the years I learned to tolerate the Council's incessant whining and petty squabbles, for one simple reason. I needed their support to maintain my grip on Sotercity. Once the Patriarch is deposed and each of the ten territories falls under my control, I'll need someone to take care of the day to day affairs. It's just too bad those small minded Council members could never grasp the bigger picture.

The Zees are the best disciplined army the world has ever known and, unlike the Council, they will obey my every command without ever asking why. I would never have subjected myself to Master Lund's horrendous contraption if another option had been available. The transformation into Zeedom was more shockingly painful than even I was prepared for. Every cell in my body was ripped apart and fused back together, into something that's barely human. Any doubt of that requires only the smallest glimpse in a mirror to be believed. I'm not

222

human anymore but, then again, in many ways, I never was.

In this new and exalted state, with powers beyond my comprehension, the pettiness of men like Plak and the old world are all far behind me.

Zees don't cry or conspire when they're passed over for promotion. A nearly imperceptible order no sooner forms in my mind than some measure of it is being eagerly carried out. That's when Azina comes to mind. For a while, after the transformation, I'd been distinctly aware of her and the unique threat she posed, which was why I'd reached my hand across the gulfs of space, in that special way only Zees can, and plucked at her stings like a master puppeteer. So, when all sense of her suddenly vanished, there could only be a single explanation. She was dead.

Not that the thought bothers me. The key to taking control of the ten territories begins with the Queen, locked beneath the capital, not with a lowly mercenary.

Krall, my nearly eight foot tall Zee general, approaches from out of the gloom, lowering himself onto one knee. The truth is, Krall's little more than a Hive leader, with a particularly strong signal. He doesn't speak, but he doesn't need to. Speech between Zees isn't burdened by anything as crass and barbaric as words. At once, bundles of Zee code begin unravelling before my mind's eye. Krall's asking about the humans we're holding and what we're going to do with them. I know exactly what he's getting at. He's talking about the brave men and women who were trying to defend this sorry excuse for a village from the hordes. But there comes a time when an army has grown large enough. "Feed the villagers to the Zees," I say. "We won't need them. Not where we're going."

76

Azina

My eyes peel open and it takes a minute to drink in my surroundings. Above me is a wall of earth-toned threads, arranged in neat rows. It's a mechanism of some sort and it takes another second before I realize its purpose. I'm in a textile factory, where they make tunics – not that there are any customers left to buy them. Slowly, Sneak comes into focus. She's bent over me, like an old mother hen, and I try and shoo her away, but she won't have any of it. My clothes are folded in a neat pile on a chair next to me. Sneak has made a bed out of tunics. I glance down at my naked body and shudder. I'm still tightly muscled, except the skin around those muscles is dark and as coarse as tree bark. White bandages cover my abdomen, wrist and collarbone, where that Keeper prick riddled me with bullets. No sooner does the thought register than I spot the guard with the broken nose. Sneak must have heard me call out for mercy as she turned his comrades into mounds of useless flesh.

He had tried to save a stranger, even after Bron bent his nose at an odd angle. Not a common quality, for sure.

Sneak's signing slowly, like I was shot in the head and turned into some kinda halfwit.

"I'm fine," I say, and mean it, in spite of the skeptical look on her face.

"I was sure you were a gonner," she signs, and I couldn't agree more.

"That makes two of us. How long was I out for?"

"A few hours." But this time it's the Keeper guard who answers instead of Sneak.

"His name is Klaus," she signs with perhaps a little too much enthusiasm. "He went and found bandages for you. Can we keep him?"

I laugh and sign back. "He isn't a puppy, Sneak. You know how I feel about sightseers and tourists."

Sneak nods and her eyes drop to the bandages covering my stomach.

"I'll think about it," I reply out loud and catch Klaus looking on, like he doesn't have a clue what we're talking about. Only hearing one side of the conversation he probably doesn't. I peel away the corner of the bandage covering my abdomen and stop when I see something strange.

"What is it?" Sneak signs.

Ripping the bandage off completely, I reveal three Keeper slugs, lying against the flesh of my abdomen. The holes they tore through my skin are gone, along with any sign I'd even been shot in the first place.

Klaus sees this and his blue eyes keep flickering between me and what was once a gaping wound. "What are you?" he whispers.

"If I had a single USC for every time I've been asked that question, I'd be somewhere far, far away, I can promise you that."

I listen for Skuld, seeing if the crusty bastard's trying to knock around inside my head again, and settle down when I realize he isn't there. But then again, I don't feel any of the Zees and suddenly understand why. The poor sods in Sotercity have probably all been wiped out by that mob of pissy Grinders. The rest are likely too far out of range, which can only mean one thing: Skuld and his Zee army are moving on the capital. I jump up with a burst of renewed energy, tearing the remaining bandages from my shoulder and wrist. Rubbing the hardened flesh around the wounds makes it clear there isn't even a scar.

Then I see Klaus scanning me up and down; I feel a breeze and become acutely aware that I don't have a stitch of clothing on. Sneak hands me my clothes and puts a hand over his eyes. I wanna say that men are pigs, but I think even a pig wouldn't want anything to do with me, looking the way I do.

I'm nearly dressed when Sneak's fingers start fluttering through the air. "The ancient Keepers had tried to erase death."

She's talking about the documents we found, underneath the keep, back when we were racing to stop Skuld from mutating himself into a super Zee. She's referring to my wounds and how they've healed on their own. I can still recall, clear as day, the first Zee we came upon in the complex and how the flesh around his severed legs had slowly begun fusing together. But that must have taken several days and even then the changes were almost imperceptible. Whatever part of me was doing the healing, it was working faster than anything we'd seen before.

I sign to Sneak that it's time to go.

"Where?" she replies back.

"The capital. Where else?"

But she wasn't being dense. I can see she really wants to ask about Ret, Bron and the others, but stops herself. *That wasn't anything more than a fight between siblings,* she's probably thinking. *Happens all the time. Why not just tell them you're sorry and make up?* Sounds great in theory, doesn't it? But here's what she's forgetting: I tried to kill them. Doesn't matter that Skuld was the one pulling the strings. It happened twice and, frankly, they should have blown me away after the first time. Course I can't help feeling weighed down by the whole thing. Our little group of misfits was the only family Sneak's ever known and now it's been fractured in a way she may never be able to accept. Sure, the thought tears me up inside, but it

226

doesn't change the fact that Skuld's about to sack the capital, kill the Zee Queen and turn whatever's left of the world into his own private paradise. Which is to say, a hell on Earth.

Course, Klaus is standing there, blinking like a moron, probably trying to picture me naked again.

I gather my weapons and head for the door, thinking about how I can keep Skuld from sensing me as we approach. There is a chance that my temporary coma took me offline from Zee central just long enough for Skuld to assume I had bitten the big one. Sneak and Klaus are following me to the door and I can tell she wants to ask about the plan. I've always got one and usually the thing's half decent. There's a kernel of an idea, germinating in my head, but it's too early to tell if it has a hope in hell of working. Without the rest of our crew, I'm scared to admit that we don't stand a chance. I turn to the Keeper guard and say: "If you wanted an opportunity to head back to your family, this is it."

Klaus tries to straighten his nose and winces. "What family? I was an orphan, raised by Keepers. There's nothing in Sotercity now, besides streets filled with the dead."

He isn't the only orphan around. My parents were Grinders who drowned in the sewers beneath the city and Sneak never talks about the parents who gave her up.

Happy homes breed horrible Mercs. I might have just made that up, but I can't help seeing a pattern.

This time I turn to Sneak. "You wanted a new pet. Now you got one. Just remember, he's your responsibility."

Sneak taps her leg for Klaus to follow and, when he does, I want to burst out laughing. I would, too, if the thought of where we were heading wasn't tying my insides into knots.

77

Ret

"Ret, you sure this is the place?" Bron asks with a tinge of uncharacteristic doubt.

I turn to Dhal, who nods, and I have to admit, White Rock doesn't look at all like I thought it would. First off, it isn't white. It's more of a dusty gray, without a scrap of vegetation above or below. A twenty foot high steel door, recessed into the base of the mountain, appears to be the only way inside, but without Jinx and his wonderful bag of tricks, I'm not at all sure how we're gonna get inside. Not surprisingly, Bron doesn't look fazed in the least. We back away a good distance and he tilts his arm into the air, at forty five degrees, and lobs in a handful of grenades. We duck for cover behind a nearby boulder. A series of explosions and concussion waves hit us in quick succession. When the dust settles, I peek up and see the door riddled with dents and black powder splatter marks from the detonations but, even from our position, it's clear the barrier's been breached.

Bron winks at me. "Stick around awhile, Ret, and I'll teach you a thing or two."

"Hey Dhal," I say. "I'll pay you a thousand USC if you reattach those spatulas?"

The kid giggles and so does Bron, in a rare moment of self-deprecation.

Oleg's the only one who doesn't even crack a smile. His weathered features are still smeared with soot from the workshop fire. The loss of Azina and Sneak is a major setback and the old man's silence lets me know that's all he's been thinking about since it happened. I shoulder my shotgun as we approach the entrance to White Rock, trying desperately not to let it get me down. Truth be told, a large part of me is thankful I was tossed over that workbench and knocked unconscious because I don't think I could have shot Azina. I'd never whisper a word of that to anyone, especially Bron, but it's true. He only sees the Zee in her now. She's changed more in the last week than in all the time I've known her, there's no denying that, but I know the old Azina is still in there, lurking beneath all that hardened flesh. And I'd be willing to bet what's really stinging Bron is that she got the better of him. We know each other so well that the battle could have gone either way. If Azina hadn't dropped Bron with a shot to his nuts, she surely would have died.

We approach the entrance and find a gap where the metal is bent and Bron slides his fingers in and begins exerting force to pull the two ends apart. The strength in these new arms is something special. Back in the day, the big galoot woulda popped a vein trying to move something this heavy. Now, he makes short work of it. Soon there's enough space to enter and I catch a smug look on his face. I didn't think his overinflated ego could get any bigger. Clearly I was wrong.

The air inside is cool and smells of grease. A long corridor descends at a slight angle. It's wide enough for all of us to walk side by side. Air ducts and piping hug the walls like lengths of human entrails, stretched end to end.

"When did the Keepers build this place?" I ask.

"They didn't," Oleg says. "They found it, the way they find most everything. Prospectors. We believe it was a bunker, built by Dusters before the fall."

"So they could hide from Zees," Bron adds with disgust.

"Even before that," Oleg amends. "Back when the planet was governed by nations threatening to destroy each other with Atomic weapons. This isn't the only one in existence, only the closest to Sotercity."

"And the Keepers turned it into a hiding place for all the cutting edge technology they wanted to withhold from the bumbling masses."

Oleg doesn't look happy with my comment. "Technology that the masses weren't ready for," he says. "I'll be the first to admit that the Keepers have made mistakes but, without them, we'd all either be dead or living in caves."

"Yeah," Bron says. "Like White Rock."

Oleg's got a soft spot for the Keepers that may never go away. What's that famous Duster expression? You can't teach an old dog new tricks? It doesn't seem to matter to him that the Keepers were the ones responsible for starting this whole Zee mess in the first place. Giving the Keepers the respect they're due is just a bunch of hogwash, but there isn't any sense debating the point, especially here.

We come to an area where the hallway splits in two directions. Dhal's scratching his head, trying to remember which way to go, and the group looks to me. I freeze for a moment. These kinds of decisions were always made by Azina. I'm so used to following her into hell and back that the notion of choosing feels like a monumental task.

"I guess we'll go right."

"You guess?" Bron barks. "Is it right or left?"

"How the hell should I know? This whole thing was Dhal's idea."

The air inside is getting cooler and cooler, but I can see beads of sweat rolling down Dhal's cheeks. "Right," I say. "We go right."

Bron sighs and I can't help but feel like the world's most incompetent leader. I know none of them could do any better, but the thought doesn't do much to settle my nerves. We head right and enter a room big enough to contain two entire districts of Sotercity, one on top of another. Weak lighting spills out of brass fixtures strung along the walls, casting thick shadows along the floor and making the ceiling look like a starless night sky.

But, as impressive as all this is, it's nothing compared to the two copper figures up against the far wall, surrounded by scaffolding. They're nearly twice the height of Goliath, but not nearly as sleek looking.

A voice in the distance tells us to halt. That's when we first become aware that the room isn't empty at all. Men in white lab coats, swallowed in the enormity of the chamber, are perched over tables, working on bits of wires and metal piping.

Whoever the guard is, he's coming toward us from an entrance at the far end, his weapon at the ready. Bron walks ahead, waving an arm. "Don't mind us, we're just here to take these," he shouts, pointing at the prototypes. A shot rings out and ricochets off Bron's arm. The big guy turns around with a look of disbelief. "That stupid sonofabitch tried to shoot me."

So much for Bron's attempts at diplomacy.

The shot sends the men in white coats running for safety. An alarm sounds, echoing through the colossal chamber. Before us. the floor is dotted with rows of tables and shelves, packed with cogs and gears and every tool an engineer could want. From across the massive hall, I catch the sound of stomping boots and men barking orders. Dhal had said this place would be heavily guarded, but he also said these guys had been cut off from the rest of the world. As far as they know, things topside haven't changed one bit.

We scurry for safety right as a hail of bullets fills the air. Sparks explode all around us. A ricochet whizzes past my face and disappears into the darkness. They aren't just trying to kill us, they're trying to keep us pinned down, so they can finish us up close and personal. Dhal's lying on the ground with his head between his hands. Oleg's down beside him, not fairing much better.

My shotgun is all I have and the men blasting away at us are far beyond its effective range. I fire a few rounds in the air to keep their heads down, but it's starting to look like we're sitting ducks.

Bron's got his back against the table beside me. The look on his face tells me he's about to raise hell.

"We have to talk to them," I shout over the whizzing bullets.

"I tried and they nearly took my new arm off." He cradles it like an injured cat.

A round clangs against a piece of metal pipe lying on the table and sends it spinning into the back of Bron's head. It makes a wet sound as it connects and Bron touches the back of his skull, his fingers running over the lump that's starting to form.

"That's it, if you're not gonna do something Ret, I will." He pulls back the bolts on each arm, stands, and opens up with an ear shattering roar of fire. The new shells Dhal gave him might be smaller, but they're louder and far more destructive than anything the big man had before. Tracers go stinging off into the distance. One round splinters a work table, another catches two soldiers lined up and cuts their bodies in two. Tools and bits of metal go flying into the air. If their heads weren't down before, they are now. Perhaps just to drive the point home, Bron's right arm jerks as he lobs a handful of grenades. I plug my fingers into my ears as they go off. The shockwave from the blasts hits a second later, like five slaps across the back of the head. I peek over the upturned table to see a cloud of swirling dust and debris where the soldiers had stood.

"No one needs to get hurt," Bron says, although I'm not quite sure he understands there may not be anyone

232

alive over there to hear him anymore. The shooting has stopped completely. I'm up on my feet now, shotgun pointing into the shadows where those initial shots had come from. I'm about to wave us forward when I feel a jolt of pain fire through every nerve ending in my body. I hear Bron cry out beside me, before both of us collapse to the ground. It feels like the time I decided to go toe to toe with a Merc named Gor, a six foot seven bruiser who smelled of turnips and got a kick out of picking on anyone he thought he could beat. I won't lie and say I beat Gor, but the feeling I had when I woke up was a lot like this.

A group of soldiers surrounds us and I see exactly how they did it. Distracted us with a feigned attack while the bulk of them circled around from behind. Smart. I'm still on the ground, getting a great view of their boots, when I'm yanked to my feet. My jaw feels like it's been wired shut. Even Bron's a mess and it takes five men to lift him.

Their commander looks like one mean sonofabitch. He's glaring at me through a pair of ink black eyes, his face a moonscape of scars and craters only partially masked by a dark, wiry beard that reaches down to his chest. The men on either side of him all have beards, and what surprises me most is none of them look anything like Keepers. Oleg's beside me, with his red robes and shortly cropped white hair, looking just as stunned. The contrast couldn't be any clearer. Compared to this motley crew, Keepers aren't much more than a bunch of clean cut librarians.

Two of the men are holding strange looking rifles I've never seen before. They send out some kind of electrical pulse, like the stun guns Dusters used on one another. Which is another unlikely feature for a group this rough around the edges, until I realize why. They wanted to

233

capture us alive for one simple reason. The dead don't talk.

All four of us are led past the gleaming bronze Titans, standing to attention on our right. Scattered around are the men Bron killed, or at least what's left of them. A few bearded faces stare up at us with unmoving eyes as we hurry through.

The commander salutes the corpses as we go by. "They died a good death," he says in a gruff, but reverent tone.

The comment seems to resonate with Bron. A thousand years ago, these two would have been sailing Viking warships up rivers, sacking anyone and anything in their way. I guess Oleg isn't the only one who knows his history.

We're brought to the mouth of the chamber where a row of chairs has been set up, all bolted to the ground. The guards bind us to the seats with heavy rope. No doubt this is where they intend to question us, one fingernail at a time, to find out why we've come. I knew it was a bad idea for Bron to open fire. Killing their comrades won't have made this any easier.

A dirty looking man with a heavy limp and a dusty beard says: "This here's Commander Tind. He hates liars and scoundrels and, above all, he hates Mercs. In a minute, he's gonna ask you a few simple questions and, for your own sakes, I hope you answer 'em truthfully."

I'll never let it show on my face, but the fear's starting to settle in for the first time. Not just fear that we're all about to die horrible deaths, or that Skuld is about to turn the world into a Zee playground. But fear that we failed to do anything about it. I can't help but wish that Azina were here. She's was the only one who knows a goddamn thing about diplomacy. Oleg's too cranky. Bron's too blunt and my sarcasm will more likely get us killed than anything.

Commander Tind folds his hands behind his back and stands before us, glaring with noticeable contempt. "You've broken into a top secret Keeper facility and killed my men. Tell me why I shouldn't just slit all your throats and throw your bodies into the pits."

A visible knot catches in Oleg's throat and he swallows it down, hard, with an audible gulp. He may be an old sonofabitch, but he's certainly not in a hurry to die. What I'm really worried about is Bron and that big ass mouth of his. There's a smile on the oaf's face and I just know he's about to make things worse. I'm about to cut him off when I hear someone else speak and it takes me a second for the voice to register.

"We've come for the Titans," Dhal says, his teenage voice quivering with fear.

Dhal's answer produces a burst of wild laughter from Commander Tind's men. "And for what purpose?" he asks and right there I get a sense of what we're up against. These guys aren't just trigger happy. They're completely out of the loop. Oleg had mentioned they were largely cut off from the rest of the world, but now I know he wasn't exaggerating. I'm about to feed him a whopper of a story when inspiration suddenly strikes. "We need them to kill Prior Skuld."

That stops Commander Tind dead right in his tracks. The laughing behind him stops too and now he's leaning in my direction. "Well, that was easy," he said and turned to the limper with the dusty beard. "Slit their throats and throw their bodies down the pits."

Men with knives come toward us. Commander Tind's walking away when I shout after him. "You do that and you sign a death warrant for everyone in the ten territories."

Tind takes three more steps before halting. The men with the knives are almost on us, I can see the murderous glint in their eyes. They can't wait to teach us a lesson for killing their friends.

"Death warrant?" he asks, a single eyebrow raised.

"Tell your men to stand down," I shout. "Stand down and I'll tell you."

Tind nods at them and the men with the knives pause. "You've got ten seconds and this better be good."

I take a deep breath, feeling the stale, musty air rush into my lungs. "Skuld turned himself into some kind of super Zee and awoke all the Hives. Sotercity's in ruins. Now he's heading to destroy the capital."

It's impossible to tell from here if Tind believes me or not. Dusty beard's right there beside him, pulling his thumb across his throat and you don't need to know sign language to see where he stands. Tind seems to be mulling the story over. Not that I can blame him. It would be a hard thing for anyone to believe, especially if you've spent most of your life locked away from the world.

The Commander steps forward. "We're sending a runner to Sotercity to verify your story. If you're lying, we'll discover it soon enough."

But that's where Tind is wrong. They'll discover the truth all right but, by then, it might be too late.

-78-

Azina

Slipping out of Sotercity is proving to be tougher than we thought. The gates are closed tight and I can see some of the survivors manning the walls are armed with Keeper rifles. Grinders are forbidden from owning weapons, another means of preventing the masses from getting too uppity I think, but with so many bodies lying around, guns and ammo aren't hard to come by. We catch sight of another armed group heading for the keep and I can only assume they've given themselves the undignified job of clearing out what's left of the Zees.

"Krantz' hideout," Sneak signs.

She may have a point. The same route we used to enter the city before this mess started could get us out. Although I recall our hasty departure and the horde that was clawing after us. Chances were good they'd have followed Skuld's orders and left the city with the other shitbags. Only one way to find out.

We come to a narrow street with shops on our left. I recognize a grocers market as the place where Bron helped a group of frightened people seek shelter. Only now the metal shutter is open; I hope they were smart enough to wait out the carnage. A peek inside reveals that same upper class woman with the silk pajamas and the soft white skin. Except much of that skin's been chewed off. But she isn't the only one. Looks like the whole lot of them were killed at once.

"Idiots," I murmur. "All they needed to do was keep the door shut."

237

Klaus hears me talking to myself and his expression makes it clear he isn't sure why I'd concern myself with a bunch of strangers, and maybe he's right.

One of my earliest memories from childhood is collecting stray cats. Seemed whenever I'd go out to play, I'd always come home with some malnourished fur ball in tow. I still recall returning from a game of Keepers and Monsters, a kitten with a broken leg limping after me. And no matter how much I begged, my father wouldn't budge. We didn't have enough to feed another hungry mouth. That's when he took my weeping face into his callused hands and said: "You have a gentle heart, Azina. But you can't save the world."

The words still ring in my ears when we reach the manhole cover and the trash container Bron pulled over it. Doesn't take more than a quick shove to move it out of place. As always, Sneak is the first one in. Klaus and I aren't far behind. There's hardly a stitch of light down here, but I can see just fine. Klaus' got his hands out in front of him like a blind man, while Sneak seems to be faring a little better. She doesn't need to see in order to slit you from ear to ear.

We pass what's left of Krantz' man, Vasser, lying on the floor like a half eaten meal. And that's exactly what he looks like. His arms are little more than bones. Seems the Zees worked on him for a while after we locked them in here.

Soon we come to the pile of Zee corpses. A few of them are still alive and Sneak finishes them for good. I stay back and out of the way. I've been trying to keep a low profile and the last thing I wanna do is let Skuld know where I am. Part of that process goes further than staying out of sight from Zees, though. I need to stay off of Zee central, which is a double edged sword, since it's the only way of knowing for sure what part of the ten territories Skuld is in the process of ravaging.

238

The smell of human waste greets us as we make our way from Krantz' hideout into the sewers. There's a light up ahead. It's faint, but I know it means freedom. Freedom from the paranoid Grinders who are currently running Sotercity, now that all semblance of order has broken down. Then I sense Skuld and it feels like he's reaching out, looking for me. It isn't more than a tingle at the back of my neck, but I know he's searching and that our only chance of getting close, perhaps the only chance of keeping the people I love safe, is by making him think I'm dead.

Ret

We've been strapped to these chairs for well over three hours without any sign of Tind or that runner he sent off to check on Sotercity. I'm sure if Azina were with us, the commander would have taken one look at her and known we are telling the truth. Course, he might have blown her away on account of her looking like a Zee but, either way, we wouldn't be waiting around wasting time. The two barrel-chested men Tind left to watch us look about as friendly as a pair of cut throats. They're playing a dice game, over by the entrance, glancing back every few minutes, almost looking for an excuse to end us for good.

Bron sits beside Oleg, his arms tied with heavy ropes, knuckles pointed at his chest. If he wants to fire those 20mm guns, his own body will be the first thing they tear a hole through.

Beside me, Dhal is asleep, snoring quietly, his head resting against the heavy ropes keeping us in place. The naïve little punk actually thinks Tind is gonna free us when his man finds Sotercity clogged with dead bodies. For all we know, he's just as likely to pin this mess on us. I nudge the kid with my foot. He stirs, but doesn't wake. I try it again, with a similar result. That's when I stomp on his foot and see his eyes pop open. "Ow, what'd you do that for?"

The guards are looking over now and I bob my head like I'm dreaming some crazy dream that's got me stomping feet and lashing about. They watch me for a moment, chuckle at what a 'tard I am and then return to their dice. I find a similar expression on Dhal's face, one I'm embarrassed to say I saw from others the time I accidentally ate a wild mushroom. It probably nearly killed me, but the ride was fun as hell.

Dhal still looks pissed that I woke him up when I say, "Think you can get yourself out of these ropes?"

The fear on his face is immediate. "Are you crazy, Ret? If those guys see me gone they'll eat me for breakfast."

"They're not gonna eat you,' I whisper back. "They'll kill you, no doubt about that, but I can guarantee you won't be eaten.'

The kid doesn't look impressed. "What do you want me to do?" he asks with the kind of skepticism that usually precedes a no. "Get outta these ropes and go beat them up?"

"What's going on?" It's Bron. He's at the far end, stuck beside Oleg, feeling left out.

"Nothing," I whisper back, hoping it'll shut him up.

Bron's still asking questions as I begin telling Dhal what I have in mind. "Once you work those ropes free, you think you'll be able to get one of the Titans up and running?"

"Oh, geez, that's hard to say. I mean, the power core has to be removed and reinstalled all without the guards finding out…"

"Just make sure when you fire that tin can up, they don't start attacking us."

"I never said I'd go."

"Yes, you did."

Dhal swallows hard. "I did?"

I nod. "Don't worry, if anything happens we've got your back."

The kid is still skeptical and I can't say I blame him one bit. Tied to these chairs, the rest of us are about as useful as a bunch of newborns.

Dhal starts wiggling and writhing. "Thata boy," I say. "I'll cough if the guards start to turn around."

My reasons for making Dhal do this wasn't 'cause he's the only one who can get those oversized garbage bins working again. By far he has the slightest build and the best chances of working himself free. One of the guards begins to glance over and I pretend to clear my throat. But Dhal's not stopping. He's making good progress and not paying attention. I cough a bit louder and this time he freezes. The guard's still glaring at us when his partner throws the dice and shouts gleefully. A second later, both of them are focused on the game again.

When I turn back to give Dhal the all clear, he's gone and so is his chair. I turn to look behind me and see what the smart little bugger has done. He's slid his chair back behind mine and lined up the legs so the next time those guards turn around, they won't immediately see an empty chair. Course, something about the sight before them will look different, but hopefully they won't quite be able to put their fingers on it. My next concern is the tools Dhal's gonna need to get the job done. Already, I can hear a tiny clank here and there and I just know he's gotta hurry before these two gambling addicts figure out what we're up to. Slowly I turn my head, so as not to draw any unwanted attention, and catch sight of Dhal climbing the scaffolding around the largest of the two machines, with something that looks like a breadbox in his arms. He's about to insert the power core. I'm not certain, but that's my best guess. I turn back and at once my heart leaps into my throat. Dusty Beard's just entered the room and both of the guards are standing at attention. He's giving them shit over something, playing dice maybe, dereliction of duty, the usual riot act petty men use as their stock and trade.

A metal door slams behind us and there isn't a chance in hell those assholes didn't hear that. Dusty Beard is scanning through the dimly lit chamber for the source of the noise, then his eyes pass over us and stop in the space where Dhal was sitting.

He charges forward growling. "The boy, where is he?"

Behind us, almost in answer, comes the sound of compressed air and spinning gears. We all turn at once to see one of the bronze behemoths raise its arms and tear the scaffolding away as though it were cobwebs. The machine's eyes glow a bright yellow and Dusty Beard's just standing there, with this jaw hanging open. The guards nearby are wearing the same dumb expressions.

Without a moment to lose, I begin working free from my ropes. Dusty sees me and pulls out a knife from a sheath on his belt. I'm sure he's gonna stick all of us before we can escape and, judging by that gleam in his eye, he intends to start with me.

The knife in Dusty Beard's hand is ten inches long with a serrated edge. The kind that hurts like hell going in and tears you apart coming out. I haven't a clue where Dhal is now, after all that scaffolding came crashing down, but I can hear the joints of his machine squealing and the ground rumbling with every giant step it takes. Looks like Dusty's estimating how much time it'll take to kill me. Probably figures the job won't be hard, since half of me is still tied to the chair. Ten yards behind him, those two guards aren't sure whether to stay and help their man commit murder or hi-tail it out and save themselves from becoming turds under the Titan's shoe. Dusty's about two feet away, and making ready to stick me straight in the chest, when I straight kick his knee. Even over the screaming whine of the Titan's approaching footfalls, I catch the sound of his joint bending back on itself and snapping in two. He stumbles forward and I stomp his face, sending him sprawling back in agony. His beard is still dusty, except for the imprint of where my boot connected with his jaw.

I slide under the loosened ropes, snatch the knife from his limp hand and begin cutting Bron's ropes. They tied so many, it looks like an anaconda's coiled around him. I'm not even halfway done when he flexes his arms and the remaining coils fall away. The machine passes us as Bron stands and the sight of a twenty foot, brass giant sends the guards scurrying to safety.

We untie the others and the Titan stops at the mouth of the ramp leading up to the main entrance. Time is in seriously short supply, but we can't just leave without Dhal. He's the only one who knows how to work this thing. But, more importantly, this place'll be crawling with hundreds of those bearded White Rock Keeper guards and there's no telling what they'll do to the kid once they get their hands on him.

Oleg and Bron are staring in awe at the machine's glowing yellow eyes. I start racing toward the collapsed scaffolding and already I hear the sound of boots charging toward us, men shouting orders and weapons being readied.

The Titan lets out a metallic shout and it stops me dead in my tracks. I turn to see the top of its head peel back and a tiny figure stand up. It's Dhal. He didn't just start the thing, he's driving it and, judging by the smile on his face, having one hell of a time in the process. The hatch slams shut and Dhal begins steering the machine up the ramp. The others are close behind and so am I. A moment later, we're through the front doors. There isn't any sign of those White Rock guards, but Commander Tind's surely gonna be mad as hell when he hears what we've done. My only regret is that we only came away with one of those metallic beasts. Somehow, I'm not quite sure it'll be enough.

-80-

Azina

It feels like we've been following this old road forever. Highways, the Dusters called them, and, like long spindly fingers, they once stretched into every nook of the country. At least that was what Oleg told us, during one of his particularly boring historical sermons. More amazing were the mechanical boxes on inflatable wheels that used to clog the streets of million-man cities. That sort of transportation certainly would have served us well on our long trek from Sotercity. Back when Oleg first spoke of the old world highways, Bron's initial impulse had been to doubt what the old man was saying, although even he couldn't explain the not infrequent rusted hulk, rotting away on the side of every major thoroughfare. That the Keeper elite had outlawed any form of motorized locomotion was grounds enough for a rebellion in my view. Not that people knew what they were missing. Technology was the Keeper's currency and the carrot and stick they used to exert control. Only they could issue the necessary licences for engineers to work bits of metal into cogs, springs and gears. Master Lund was a member of an exceptionally tiny group. A group that a snotty nosed Dhal was likely excluded from, given he didn't have a license of his own. But the truth was, those Keeper sonsabitches were sitting on more than one technology that could revolutionize the world. I'd seen it with my own eyes and I'm not just talking about Bron's arms. Course those were a marvel and Bron's father had to pull the kind of strings only the very wealthy can afford to grasp to get them. Machines like Goliath seemed to be the next stage, kept underground and hidden away from the masses. Control the technology and you control the people. That was how Oleg had explained the Keepers' position. What use would a horseless wagon be to a Grinder anyway; they didn't have the time or the means to go off sightseeing or traipsing off on long trips. Besides, there wasn't much to see, not in the empty, mostly desolate space between cities. Didn't matter if you were a Grinder, Prospector, Trader or a Merc. In the Keepers' eyes, you were little more than a brainless child.

Klaus is beside me, still staring on with those bright, bulging eyes like he's never set foot outside of Sotercity his entire life. Though that may not be too far off. Bron said it perfectly before: Sotercity was a trash heap. Even as a Keeper, if you were unlucky enough to be born there, you could kiss your chances of advancement goodbye. Yet another reason I became a Merc. I don't take orders so well. A commander expecting a salute is just as likely to get a pair of brass knuckles in the face.

I hate to admit it, but I can almost sympathize with Prior Skuld's frustration. He'd been locked on the lowest rung of the totem pole and now he was gonna burn to ashes the very apparatus that imprisoned him. The logic itself melded perfectly with those Grinders you sometimes read about, who kill their co-workers with a socket wrench because their supervisor passed them up for a promotion. Men like Oleg used fancy Duster terms like sociopathic, although I'm more partial to what the old timers used to call people willing to sacrifice the life of thousands: bat-shit crazy.

"This'll be my first time in the capital," Klaus says. "Do you think we'll get to meet the Patriarch?"

Oh, boy, this one's worse than a newborn. "We're not on vacation, in case you haven't noticed." There's a distinct note of disgust in my voice and Klaus looks almost wounded by the comment, but I don't have time to bother with hurt feelings. It's questions like that that are making me more certain he won't be able to handle seeing the ocean of Zees I'm sure are surging before the capital's walls.

We veer off the highway and onto a well worn footpath which leads to Attica's main gates. The path that's cut through the forest is wide enough for an entire battalion of Wardens to travel ten abreast with ease. Still, beyond that, the damp ground beneath the trees on either side has been trampled by what Sneak and I can only guess was a swarm of Zees. Hundreds of years ago, swaths similar to this were cut through the countryside by massive herds of what Dusters called Buffalo. The Keepers taught us how settlers moving west would peg them off from smoke belching trains and nearly drove the species to extinction. Now we're the ones on the verge of extinction.

Sneak's on point, up ahead, and raises her hand in the air, curling it into a fist. I stop and crouch and need to tug at Klaus' Keeper robe before he does the same.

Sneak's signing back. "You should see this."

Except I don't need to, 'cause I know exactly what's there. In spite of Skuld's attempts to block my abilities to tap into Hive central and gain control of the horde he's assembled, tiny bits of code are always bleeding through, like a slow leak on a sealed jar. Klaus and I inch ahead anyway, although I'm growing more and more certain of what I'm about to see. The terror on his face when he witnesses the shocking mass of Zee flesh in the valley below, rushing through the city gates like a single dark organism, makes one thing perfectly clear. We're too late. They're already inside.

Klaus' whimpers draw my attention away from the trails of smoke rising from Attica and the unbelievable carnage surely taking place there, to the young Keeper. I might not be able to reach Klaus' mind the way I can

247

with a Zee, but I can sure as hell see he wishes he'd never left the bowels of that Keeper archive in the first place. Burying your head in the sand is what the Dusters used to say, and that's just what Klaus wishes he could do. Although, somewhere in there, he must know it's far too late for any of that. The fingers of his hand are cupped over his lips, holding in a scream. Even his eyes begin watering, like he's about to cry, and I slap him across the face.

"Man up."

The shock he's in dulls the pain, but he looks over at me all the same and to a passerby, the sight would almost be comical. A Keeper being slapped in the face by a Zee.

A burst of Zee code hits me with sudden force. A group of them are nearby, feeding. Tearing flesh from a recent kill is the closest thing they know to joy and they're beaming with it. But I'm starting to realize that the hunger they feel never goes away; no matter how much they eat, the stabbing pain of starvation is always tearing at their insides.

I reach out to meld with their minds and feel an invisible barrier keeping me at bay. I can't get through to them, not with Skuld and the Queen so close. I'm still not strong enough to overpower them and I can hear Oleg's words running through my head in a loop.

What remains to be seen is how she will fare when she enters Skuld's effective zone of control. Who are the Zees likely to follow?

And it makes sense. I mean, if the broadcast from every Hive leader was competing with that of the Queen, the Zees would be left in a mass of confusion.

Sneaks throws a rock at my feet to get my attention. There's a slope to our right, where the ground begins to roll down into a slight depression. Sneak's at the edge of it, pointing. We head to her and see the Zees I was feeling a moment before. It isn't a large group. Ten, maybe twelve of them, but they're munching on a corpse dressed in a short purple tunic and tights. "The Patriarch's personal messenger," Sneak signs and neither of us need to get any closer to see that she's right. Behind the body, recessed into a large rock, is a door that's slightly ajar.

"Looks like the poor bastard took an underground passage," I say, "and got nailed as soon as he popped out."

"It's like they were waiting for him," Klaus says in a conspiratorial whisper.

"More like shit luck," I reply. "Whatever message he was supposed to send is as dead as he is."

A fate I'm growing more and more certain awaits us all. Most people don't need a reason to live, just a reason not to die. For a while now, my team's been that reason for me and now, with them gone, that reason is Sneak. I haven't a clue how she'll manage when I'm not around anymore. The thought of her tied to another Trader's cart makes the blood in my veins boil with rage. And then there's Ret. I've tried so hard not to think about him and the others. What I wouldn't give to reach out with my mind, the way I can with these Zees, if for no other reason than to make sure he's okay.

Sneak is in the middle of asking what I think we should do and suddenly stops. The Zees have stopped ripping the poor messenger apart and they're now looking in our direction, eyes glowing, bits of flesh dripping from their blood soaked mouths. The Zee closest to us hisses and springs to his feet, stumbling into a full run. The others aren't far behind and they're heading straight for us.

Sneak's confused 'cause we haven't made a sound, but it isn't sound that's drawing them. The thought of Ret and the others pulled my focus away from staying off Zee central. I couldn't have let it slip for more than a fraction of a second, but it was enough for them to detect

249

my presence. Skuld's standing instructions are no doubt to kill us all on sight. I turn and see Klaus. The horror on his face makes it clear he's about to tear off but I grab his arm.

"If you run, you're dead," I say and I can tell he isn't sure whether I mean he'll get it from the Zees or from me and I'm happy to keep it that way.

The Zees are on us in matter of seconds. We opt for blades. Sneak's crouched low, a dagger ready in each hand, when they scramble over the rise, hissing. She spins and slices through the brain cavity of the first two. The light in their eyes flickers before they collapse to the ground.

Klaus has his standard issue Keeper rifle and he's riddling their bodies with bullets, but nothing's happening.

"In the head," I shout over the chaos, just as three Zees lunge at me. I bring the Katana straight down and feel only the slightest resistance as the blade glides through the creature's skull and upper torso. The second one gets a push kick to the chest while I finish the third with a thrust through the eye socket. The second regains its footing, but by then it's too late and his head rolls off his body before he knows what hit him. Klaus is now firing three round bursts and manages to drop two of them.

Sneak and I finish the last of them and I can't help but wonder how easily this woulda gone down if I'd been able to control them with thoughts instead of steel. There must be a way around it. A way to use at least some of Skuld's Zees against him.

Glancing over at Klaus, the young Keeper looks like he's just dropped a load in his shorts. His chest rises and falls with short, spastic breaths.

Sneak wipes the gore off her blades and sheaths them.

250

"You've never killed before, have you?" I ask him.

He shakes his head, his eyes scanning the bodies piled around us like fish at an open market. "No."

Sneak smiles and pats one of his quivering hands. 'Good job' is what that pat means and Klaus lets out a dry laugh that sounds more like a raspy cough.

I can't help but laugh myself. She has a weak spot for the dopey ones.

We're heading toward the underground passage to Attica and the desiccated body of the messenger lying before it when I catch hold of the faint glimmer of Zee code.

"We need to hurry," I say.

"What is it?" Klaus asks with alarm.

I point through a screen of foliage that overlooks the valley below. The two of them rush at once to look and all I hear is: "Newton save us!"

It's Klaus, of course, and if he hadn't crapped his pants before, he's surely doing it now. I should have realized before, but with that pocket of Zees charging at us I was more than a little distracted. We weren't able to kill them quick enough, not before they could send out a signal to the others that we were here. And the sight that Sneak and Klaus are marvelling at? It's a huge mass of Zees, reeling away from the city walls like an undulating flock of birds, heading straight for us. Worse than that, the fastest ones are almost here.

Ret

A series of rolling hills surround Attica on all sides. We approach from the south and no sooner crest the smallest peak than we catch sight of a city being overrun. An ocean of Zees swarm the walls, pouring through the capital's main gate. Skuld must have ordered his fastest Zees to rush in before there was time to swing shut the massive doors. Even from up here, the sounds of chaos and death are clear. Smoke begins to rise from a dozen or so places. The tiny pop of automatic weapons fire in the distance is the most striking sound. Surely Keepers stationed on the walls are pouring fire into the black mass below them, knowing all the while that their families are being slaughtered or turned into monsters and there isn't a thing they can do about it. Beside me, Oleg, has that skeptical look on his face again, like he's just realized going down there is suicide. But not everyone's feeling the same way. There's a fire in Bron's eyes, and it's clear enough that he can't wait to get into the thick of things. The sound of squealing metal draws my attention to Dhal, seated in the hollowed out head of the Titan, clutching the controls of the massive robot with glee. Along the way, the kid told us that removing the pilot from the machine's cockpit was a major innovation which allowed Goliath to autonomously follow a set of simple instructions. The Titan was, in many ways, just as leathal, except it required a human pushing pedals and yanking levers. Even the metal sheeting around the head rolls back over the driver on a set of hinges to keep him secure. But it's hot as hell in there, Dhal tells us. To which Bron replies: "I can just see us opening that hatch and finding nothing but a bunch of soaking rags."

It's the belching black smoke that makes subtlety and breathing difficult, though the Titan more than makes up for any of those deficiencies. Sure it isn't packing any weaponry. What it lacks in firepower, it more than makes up for in brute force. I'm sure it'll cut through Zees like a hot stone on a sheet of ice.

"The Patriarch has a secret passageway somewhere around here," Oleg says.

Azina used to get mighty frustrated with the old guy when he'd start up like this. Oleg's always looking for a way around the tough jobs, although the swarming mass down there is making me wonder if he might just have a point.

"Assaulting the city head on with that many Zees around is just plain stupid," I say and I can tell right away that Bron disagrees. The main reason's 'cause he's itching to use his new toys, but that doesn't mean he's got to put the rest of us into needless peril.

Dhal's still perched in the driver's seat of that bronze behemoth when he leans over. "I'm not sure what this secret passage looks like, but if it sure as heck better have a high ceiling or I ain't getting through the door."

He's got a point and whatever light of hope that'd started glowing in Oleg's eyes, is quickly doused.

I turn to the old man. "If Skuld reaches the Queen first, what happens then?"

Oleg clears his throat. "He kills her, presumably. In a worst case scenario, he manages to absorb her powers. If that occurs, I suggest we head north and find a cave where we can shelter and pray to all the gods he won't send his minions to find us."

Bron's checking the spring loaded grappling hook on his arm when he lets out an ominous laugh. "I'd sooner let those things tear me apart than live in some cave like a frightened animal."

Dhal agrees. "So what do we do, Ret?"

Now everyone's looking at me, but giving the order that effectively hands them a death sentence isn't nearly as easy as it looks. The truth, however, is that there aren't many options open to us, except to go forward. We all know it, even if stopping Skuld is a long shot. Grow a pair, Azina liked to say, and truer words have never been spoken.

I'm about to speak when we see something astonishing. A colossal chunk of the Zees surrounding the city peel away and begin charging up a nearby hill. Looks like they're after something, or someone. But it must be someone important. Someone worth killing at all costs.

Azina?

"What do you make of it?" Oleg says and he'd be happy to stand around for the next week, analysing the crap out of the situation, but I know exactly what this means.

"It's our lucky day. Everyone gear up."

Oleg looks down at the pistol in his hand like I'm talking to him. I finish loading the last few shells into the drum magazine of my automatic shotgun, click it into place and pull the slide. Bron's making some final adjustments to the sights on his 20mm guns.

I glance down at a city in its death throes and can't help wishing Azina and Sneak were here with us.

•••

Skuld

Azina's heading into the city. The Zees I have pursuing her through the Patriarch's underground

254

passage tell me so, their Zee code running back and forth behind my eyes. But she'll never reach us in time. Already my army is ransacking the city as the rest of us make our way toward Newton's Grand Temple and ever closer to the Queen, locked beneath that holy place in a stupefied slumber. Activating all the Hives began the process of stirring her awake. It didn't take long for that to become apparent, although her powers, even in her weakened state, made it all the more necessary to dispatch her as soon as possible.

A third horde is currently after the Patriarch, who's surely hold up inside the main keep. Every city has one and it's considered a final line of defence, once the walls are breached. He's a silly, predictable man and I'll enjoy tearing his eyeballs from his face, but not before I relish in the horror and surprise when he sees what I've become. Not that he'll understand my true magnificence, nor the irony that I'm the pinnacle of what our Keeper ancestors attempted to create, two centuries ago. Surely they never imagined we would look like monsters. Surely they never recognized our full potential.

Plak and the other councillors from Sotercity are by my side as we enter Newton's Temple. It's cool and spacious, with incredibly high ceilings, decorated with images of planets and stars. Behind the altar, a shaft of natural light illuminates a solitary apple tree.

A detachment of Wardens spill out from the cloisters and begin firing right away. I wave the Zees forward, watching through each of their eyes at once. And I can't help but think of Newton again, since this is the closest to a god any man has ever been, and the feeling is pure intoxication. On they charge, scrambling over pews and up the aisles. The Wardens fill the air with lead, but these men have never fought Zees before and their bullets riddle their bodies, ignoring the heads. The first Zee to reach their lines is a woman, dressed in a baker's apron,

255

and the mere act of shifting my awareness toward her lets me see her entire history laid out before me. Two bright children and a husband she loved dearly. All of them working hard in the family bread shop in Sotercity. One step up from a Grinder, with dreams of a bright future. She was the first to turn, when that sorry excuse for a city was invaded, and at once she attacked her husband. And when he was dead, she finished off the children. But she had traded one family for another. A much larger family. One which would never disappoint or try to hurt her.

She leaps through the air and lands on a terrified Warden who's scrambling to reload. She tears a mouthful of flesh from his face and keeps gnashing with insatiable hunger. The man beside them shouts and brings the butt of his rifle down on her head and opens her skull. She stops moving at once, but right behind her are hundreds more, just like her.

Bodies pile up around them and a young Warden lieutenant sounds the retreat, except it's too late for that now and the wave of Zees are on them before they can turn their backs to flee.

Directly beneath the temple are the catacombs, which contain the bodies of the first Keepers. But it's what lies under those dried and porous bones that really interests me. As powerful as I've become, I can feel the Queen's mind, pulling at my own, delicate fingers snaking through my thoughts like the electrified wires in one of engineer Lund's creations. The feeling is strange and somehow euphoric, and there isn't any doubt that when I tear her limb from limb, that feeling will fade and be gone forever.

But I must strike soon, before she's able to emerge completely from her sleep. Otherwise, all these Zees, held so tightly within my grasp, will shift their allegiance at once and visit upon me everything I'd planned for the Queen and more.

256

Off the South Transept is a gate over a set of stone steps. A handful of infected Wardens rise and join us, their flesh now brown, their eyes glowing faintly. I approach the gate, grab the bars and rip them from the wall with as much ease as tearing a page from a child's book. Down we descend, through the catacombs, past bones cloaked in dusty red robes, staring back from nooks carved into the hard stone wall.

Some of the corpses get snagged in the flood of rushing Zees and tumble to the ground. At one time, I might have seen this as a desecration. Today, it's nothing more than poetic justice. Our ancestors' eternal rest is being undone by the very creatures they created. The very creatures that will help them do away with the old world and rebuild a new one in their own image.

At last we arrive before a dirt wall with a steel door, dull now with the passage of time. The sight reminds me of when the scholars from the old world discovered the tombs of the ancient pharaohs. Those too were set in limestone. It's only the metal door that kills the otherwise perfect illusion. The ancient Keeper records from the archive made it clear enough that the Queen's resting place would be sealed and impenetrable. It was a door built without a key because the ancestors couldn't imagine ever needing to open it and, even now, standing before it, I can feel the Queen's influence growing stronger. I draw my eyes closed and concentrate on sending out a proper signal. The Zees around me are standing perfectly still, some are turning back and forth as though two competing signals are wrestling for their attention. The doubt is what is causing the problem. The door looks so impenetrable I can't imagine how to get past it and in that gap of leadership, the Zees turn to the next best thing. But then everything becomes clear. Why go through it when you can go around? With my brainwave, the Zees begin digging, scraping their nails

257

along the walls like a pack of moles, burrowing a new home. Soon the flesh on their digits strips away, revealing bone, and now we're really making progress. The Zees who can't dig ferry the rock dust back and out of the way. Some, with arms reduced to little more than radial bones, make way for their undamaged brethren. This same routine continues for close to an hour before the wall around the thick steel door is completely excavated. With a moan it begins to teeter and then, in a single motion, comes crashing to the ground, flattening a dozen unsuspecting Zees and filling the passageway with thick, choking clouds of dust.

I wave Plak forward. "Are you ready to make history?"

-82-

Ret

The sound of thundering footsteps and grating metal joints echo around us as Dhal leads the charge. He's strapped into that twenty foot, smoke belching monster and, even behind the protective metal visor, I can still hear him whooping and hollering with joy. The fool thinks he's invulnerable. The rest of us struggle to keep up. With all those Zee chasing something in the surrounding hills, we might just make it into the city before they return. We make first contact with a few Zee outliers at about the same time we reach the foot of the hill. They barely have a chance to hiss before Dhal plows into them. A red burst of blood and bone explodes off the machine's legs. At a full run, Bron lobs a handful of grenades ahead of us to clear a path. He's timed each detonation to trigger a half dozen feet in the air, tearing gaping holes in their ranks. Some of them are beginning to notice our assault and turn to face us. That's when Bron plants his feet and unleashes a hail of fire. The explosive shells rip into them. Arms and legs are sent spinning in mid-air.

We're approaching the gate when a pack surges in at us from the side.

"Contact right," I yell. The Zees are less than a dozen feet away when I open up with my automatic shotgun. One Zee out front, who looks like a Grinder from Sotercity, has his head blown clear off. The rest of him keeps running for three more steps before crashing to the ground.

Now Bron's got one arm pointing right, laying down a hail of destructive fire, his explosive shells penetrating five or six Zees deep before detonating. The carnage is awe inspiring. The sheer look of exhilaration on Bron's face tells me he agrees. On our left, another group of Zees comes charging in at us. Oleg pops away with his pistol and I'd be surprised if he hit a single one. I swing left and engage them. I've already used a quarter of the ammo in my drum magazine and I'm doing my best to make every shot count. The last thing anyone wants is to be in the middle of a reload when a pack of Zees reaches your lines.

The dead and dying are piled at our feet, but these aren't just Zees. These are the citizens of the capital, caught in the crushing wave of snapping jaws. Already some have changed into creatures themselves and joined ranks with the Zees. On the walls, a handful of Keepers are still firing down into the streets when they're attacked by a group of Zees, rushing along the battlements, hissing, their eyes glowing white hot.

Before me, Dhal is taking out dozens of them at a time with giant sweeps of his arm. Others he's crushing under the heels of his metallic feet. I see one Zee jump on him and begin scaling his back. Then another and, soon after that, a third. It's almost as if they know Dhal's in there. Swinging the shotgun around, I blast them off, but I see more of them coming.

"We need to get out of here," I shout. "Before we're overrun."

Dhal's still pounding away, oblivious to the six Zees climbing up the Titan's back. That's when I spot a Hive leader and realize their organized behavior isn't just by random chance. This guy's big, his skin red with black patches. That can only mean he isn't just one of Skuld's sergeants. This guy's something more and he's marshalling all of his resources to take us out.

260

I level my shotgun and blast a few rounds but the bastard doesn't do anything more than smile. He isn't stupid, that much is certain. He knows I don't have the range. Although I know someone who does. I tap Bron's right side and he swings around.

"Hive leader, on the roof of that food depot," I shout over the hail of fire. "Two o'clock."

Bron growls and lobs three grenades in his direction. The explosions send up a cloud of concrete dust and debris and, when it settles, the Hive leader is gone. Splattered on the roof tiles I hope, although I'm certainly not counting on it.

It's only when I glance behind us that I realize the least of our troubles. That horde of Zees in the hills is coming back and our only hope is to close the city gates before they reach us.

83

Skuld

Slowly the air clears and a room begins to take shape, a room human eyes would find too dark to see, but seeing without light is one of many benefits to being a Zee. We're in a wing of the old prison. A battered sign on the wall in the old language advises: 'No warning shots fired.'

A signal from Krall informs me that a handful of mercenaries, accompanied by one of Goliath's predecessors, have breached the main city gate. I direct him to pull together all surrounding forces to annihilate them. But the truth is I can't be bothered to care. Not when I'm so close.

The walls are dripping with a strange viscosity. I run my fingers along a section ringing the doorway and see a flash of the Queen's face burst before my eyes. Her features are grotesque, without a shred of the person she once was. The mix of her unique human personality and even rarer genetics merged to produce Zee royalty, no accelerators required. But in the process, her body had morphed into something unspeakable, never meant to be seen. And that's the point running through the nerve endings throughout my body as we make our way into her chamber. If that viscosity confirms anything, it's that she's in here, somewhere. The fibre of her being is woven into these very walls and the closer we draw, the more intensely I can feel her presence. Plak and the other councillors feel it too, but the thought of meeting her isn't nearly as exciting for them.

This was the place where the ancient Keeper documents describe her last stand. The place she was finally cornered and sealed away. Solitary confinement was what they called this wing. How fitting. The air inside is humid and thick. If I still had pores on my body, they'd be open and producing buckets of sweat.

But why hadn't she been killed? I've often wondered the same thing myself and the truth is beginning to reveal itself. Perhaps they didn't think they could defeat her. Perhaps her ability to tap into Zee central itself had begun a mutation of sorts. One that allowed her a foothold into the human brain. An explanation that seemed to make sense, given that every squad sent in to finish her seemed to suddenly turn on each other. Not unlike the way Azina was made to turn on her fellow mercenaries. A small mountain of dusty bones, piled in the corner, offer silent evidence that the reports were correct. That is all that remains of those brave troopers who never returned. And when they sealed her in, they assumed it would be forever. This was a prison, after all, and she was precisely where she belonged.

A pair of invisible hands are running through the stringy remains of my hair and the feeling sends shivers down my spine. A feeling charged with equal parts sexual energy and menace. She can't possibly know I've come here to kill her, to absorb her power and assume her place at the top of the pecking order. But how can a hand or a foot keep a secret? We're all connected, in more than just the vague way human beings are connected. I double my efforts to shield my intentions. She must be convinced I've come to liberate her.

Rotting cell block doors on either side of us, all coated with that same dark crust. The realization sinks in almost at once. This is not dirt, it's her skin, shed in tiny particles over the centuries, wafting through subtle currents of stale air until they came to rest on… everything.

263

The rows of cell doors come to an end and I know she isn't in any of them. There is only a wall before me, caked black, like the rest of her inky prison, but I can feel her now, crawling through every inch of my body. The Zees are behind me, many of them twitching. One walks into a cell door and keeps trying to move forward, oblivious to the impediment blocking his way.

The wall at the end of the cell block is the darkest of them all and, even with my ability to see through the darkness, it's hard to draw any shape from the blackness. Then I see it. A pair of rubies, embedded in the wall, a sea of white surrounding blood red pupils. A cracking sound follows and bits of the wall begin to crumble and fall to the floor. The first to break free is an arm, then a leg. Finally, the Queen tears the rest of herself from the chitinous cocoon, where she's slumbered for decades and, catching sight of her now for the first time, I see how hideous she really is. The flesh over her face and body is webbed has hardened into some kind of armor. A honeycomb of curved bones protrude from her shoulder blades. She's also taller than I imagined and my head tilts back to take in a full view of her. She lifts a hand to her lips, draws in a full breath and blows a vile wind into my face. Suddenly, all thought of killing her begins to fade, like a distant ship slipping over the horizon. In fact, she doesn't appear nearly as ghastly looking as she did a moment ago. A small voice in my head keeps trying to tell me I'm being fooled by what those doddering Keeper scientists call pheromones. A powerful scent so common in the animal and insect kingdoms.

And those thoughts no sooner form than I feel Zee hands grasping my arms and legs. I glance down in disbelief, only to see that not a single one of them is twitching anymore. They're in sync with the Zee signal, only it isn't the one coming from me. I try to shrug them off, but their grip is like iron.

Plak is beginning to hyperventilate and turns to flee but the Zees descend on him and the other councillors without mercy. His shrieks of terror and agony go on until they're muffled by the sheer number of Zees crowding his body, tearing it apart.

The Zee hands pull my struggling body to the ground, splaying my arms and legs as though in preparation for some bizarre ritual.

Or a sacrifice.

More hands, tearing at my robe. She means to gut me and I struggle all the more, but it isn't any use. I'm nude from the waist down and here she comes, her hardened skin and red glowing eyes. It's only when she straddles me and lowers her pelvis onto mine that I have a solid inkling what's about to happen. She's using me to mate and suddenly it's all so clear. No sooner had I mutated and joined Zee central, she became aware of who I was and how useful I could be. Despite appearances, there isn't an ounce of pleasure in what she's doing and I try in vain to buck her off. It isn't long before she has exactly what she wanted all along. The Zees are still holding me tight when her scaly hands cup my face.

"Together," I say pleadingly, "we could rule the ten territories for the rest of time."

Her head tilts to one side. She's trying to make sense of the comment, but there isn't an ounce of humanity left in her. The sound of snapping bone and tearing flesh comes a second later. I catch sight of my headless body, lying below me, robes that were once white, now torn and stained with dark blood. The pain is excruciating, but a Zee can lose his head and still live, I know that much. She props what's left of me above the crowd of Zees and already there's a bulge in her belly and movement there. But maybe she's had it in her all along, only waiting for the appropriate fertilizer to come along. The Zees before us are slowly rocking back and forth. She isn't just their leader, she's their creator, their God. I watch as the glow from their eyes begins to fill the room. Then, with shocking speed, she crushes my skull between her hands and blackness descends.

84

Azina

Our feet scrape along the dirty passageway floor. Sneak is in the lead, blades drawn, her arms pumping furiously. Behind her is Klaus, robe flowing behind him, bleeding off enough fear the hissing Zees charging after us can almost certainly smell it in the air. And mostly that's all we hear behind us, hissing; the light from their eyes bouncing off the passage walls. The messenger's body kept the door from closing and I could already see the first group of Zees cresting the hill and beginning to reach for us when I gave up trying to shut the door and broke into a full run. There's so many of them there isn't any use laying down a barrage of fire behind us. Especially not with my puny repeater. If we had Bron's heavy guns it might be another matter altogether, but the last time we were face to face, he tried to burn mine off with his flame thrower.

Dim light up ahead and my heart begins to swell. Even though I'm technically a Zee, I know they wouldn't hesitate to tear me to shreds. Sure, they might not normally attack their own kind, but when orders from headquarters demand it, Zees will follow the top dog every time. In a way, it's their greatest strength though it might also be their greatest weakness.

A signal barrels through over Zee central that nearly stops me in my tracks. It's so shocking I can hardly believe.

Skuld is dead.

That's when I realize the Queen isn't nearly as weakened as we thought. Playing possum, was what the Dusters used to call it. The details are still rather fuzzy, but I'm sure Skuld's incredible arrogance probably played some part in his demise.

The light in the distance is drawing closer, but so too are the Zees. My attempts to seep into their minds still isn't working and surely won't, as long as her grip on them continues to grow stronger. But that isn't the only bit of Zee news I manage to pluck from the airwaves. The Queen is pregnant and suddenly the pieces begin to fall into place. His drive to reach the Queen wasn't only Skuld's idea. No doubt his resolve was solidified the minute he mutated himself into what he thought was the biggest, baddest Hive leader on the block. But there's always a bigger fish and it's beginning to look like the Queen played him from the start. Played him in order to break her free but, more importantly, used him to mate. And when she was done, she ended the relationship in the way insects have a tendency to end things: by killing and eating the unsuspecting partner. But as bits of code trickle in, it's becoming clear the Queen isn't just pregnant, she's about to give birth, and I'm afraid to think of what monstrosity is about to emerge.

-85-

At last we reach the light. It's a doorway, but the Zees are nearly on top of us and Klaus is alternating between cursing his gods for abandoning him and begging them for forgiveness and deliverance. I swing my repeater around and empty the entire magazine. I'm not trying to kill them, just slow them down and hope the ones who fall will trip up the others. Sneak tries the handle, without any luck, and then begins pounding on the door with the heel of her boot. Klaus brings his Keeper rifle around and doesn't take his finger off the trigger until it clicks empty. There isn't enough time to swap magazines, but it doesn't matter. A final blow by Sneak and the narrow corridor floods with light. We charge onto an open-ceilinged catwalk. Below us, the streets are packed with Zees pushing forward. They're heading toward the front gate. The sound of gunfire roars just beyond view. A few remaining Keepers in a last stand? Then my ears perk up with the thundering boom of Bron's 20mm cannons and I see Sneak's expression register the familiar sound too. But the Zees are still behind us. At the other end of the catwalk is another door. The lip of the roof lies a paltry three feet above that and I'm sure if we can get up there, the Zees won't be able to follow. Sneak glances back and I sign, telling her the plan.

She hops as she reaches the door, one foot on the handle, the other along the frame and in a second she's up. She makes it look so easy Klaus takes a leap and smashes his face against the wall, landing in a heap. I don't have a choice but to pop in another magazine and lay down some fire. I'm aiming for their legs now, since gimps don't run nearly as fast. Sneak's got her hand hanging over the top edge and she's waving it emphatically to say, 'all you gotta do is reach out and hold on.'

The Zees are fifteen feet away. Bullets to the legs hobbled the first few, but they are simply knocked over and trampled by the ones behind them. So much for brotherly love. When I turn around, Klaus is nearly up, his feet struggling to find purchase on the slippery wall. Sneak's face is red, but it isn't just from the effort. She's worried this buffoon's lack of coordination might have sealed my fate. A second later he's up and I break into a full run, repeater and Katana slung over my back. I'll have one shot, otherwise I'll have to turn and fight, or jump down and take my chances in the sea of Zee flesh below.

The leap I take isn't nearly as solid as I hoped it would be. My footing is all wrong and the horde hissing behind me isn't making things easier. Sneak reaches out a hand and our fingers barely connect. The Zees are right below me, reaching for my feet and legs and I'm kicking back at them with enough force to send a few tumbling to the ground. One of those bastards grabs a hold of my pants and starts yanking with everything he's got. Poor Sneak jerks forward and nearly comes tumbling over the edge. Now Klaus' got her by the waist and they're playing tug of war, with me as the rope. More hands reach out and it's obvious that if I don't break free, these leathery pricks are gonna do to me what they did to the Hive leader. I free my right hand, draw my Katana and bring it down in an arc behind me. Five severed arms and hands tumble to the ground. The sixth doesn't fall 'cause the muscles in the stubborn bastard's fist are still clenched tight. I toss the Katana onto the roof and swing up with Sneak's help. Klaus is staring at that hand like it means to go for his throat. Sneak signs me with one hand: "Doesn't get much closer than that." She pries the fingers open and tosses the hand over the edge. Klaus is white as

270

a cotton tunic and his own hands have started shaking. I keep forgetting how new all of this is for him. Although it hasn't been more than a handful of days since we came upon that underground complex, it feels like years have passed.

That's when Sneak taps my arm and points. The Zees on the causeway below us aren't giving up as easily as I'd hoped they would. The edge of the roof is only five or six feet above their heads and those pricks are crawling on top of one another, like ants, to get at us.

-86-

More firing and I remember now why I was in such a hurry to get up here in the first place. Ret, Bron, Oleg, and maybe even Dhal. They aren't far away and, judging by the swarm down below and the frantic sound of the gunfire, they're in trouble. A cable runs from our building to the next one over. The kinda thing residents use to send messages back and forth.

"This way," I shout and we grab hold and begin shimmying across, hanging upside down like one of those sacrificial deer paraded through the streets before the Summer Solstice. We're dangling in mid air between the two buildings, certain death swarming below us, when the Zees scurry onto the roof and come straight for us. The first actually makes it two full strides onto the cable before losing his footing and toppling to the ground below. Wave after wave follow and the result is almost the same every time. Mostly 'cause the average Zee is as dumb as a pile of rocks. They spot a target and, more often than not, charge at it in a straight line. It's only when there's a Hive leader directing them do they begin to act with a moderate amount of intelligence. That's the reason there isn't a chance in hell of them catching us. They're too stupid to mimic what we're doing. But that isn't what's making me worried. Each of those twits that goes tumbling off the cable is making it bounce and vibrate just a little bit more and, as we draw closer to the center, it's becoming harder to hold on. And yet on they come, in a relentless stream, salivating for a chance to sink their bacteria-soaked teeth into our flesh. That's when I notice the spot where the cable is anchored to the building. Bits of concrete are being chipped away with every bounce. This sucker isn't going to hold much longer. I tilt my head back and catch sight of Klaus, holding onto the cable with everything he's got, a terrified and determined grimace on his face. You toss a hungry pack of Zees a juicy morsel like that and you'll be lucky to find anything left. They'll even eat the bones, when they're hungry enough.

I'm about to tell them to keep moving when I hear a loud twang and it doesn't take a Keeper's smarts to tell the cable's just snapped off the building. Wind buffets my ears as we glide through the air. One of the few books to survive the fall was about a half-man half-monkey, who would swing from tree to tree using vines and this is exactly the thought going through my head as the edge of the building quickly approaches. I'm in the middle of a rather graphic curse word when we hit. Sneak manages to swing her legs out front to absorb most of the impact. So have I, but the sound of the wind being knocked out of Klaus' lungs tells me he wasn't so lucky. His body falls past me a second later and I swing out to grab hold of him, but don't manage to snag more than the tail end of his Keeper robe. The mass of Zees below aren't more than a few feet away; their heads tilting up, along with their reaching hands, as though the gods decided to dangle some delicious treat before them. I can hear Klaus coughing and I'm not sure how much longer I can hold him.

"Try and grab the cable, will you?"

Slowly, his hands close around it as he rights himself. I keep hold of his Keeper robe until the burning in my forearm becomes unbearable. I'm trying to give him time to catch his breath because we're heading for the roof as soon as he can move. Sneak's nearly there already, waving us on. She races to the other side to survey the situation and reappears a moment later, fingers signing so fast I can barely keep up. The others are there, Bron, Ret, Oleg and a giant Goliath machine, and the Zees are closing in from all sides. But it's worse than that. A bad ass Hive leader's directing the troops and he's called back part of the chunk that had originally peeled away to chase us through the passageway. They're about to head through the main gates and when they do, our friends will be overrun for sure.

We struggle to the roof and I pull myself over, my arms burning something fierce. This new Zee body of mine might have tremendous new strength, but it doesn't have a whole lot of endurance. With Skuld gone, I might have a chance of tapping into Zee central, even if only momentarily, to help even the battle, but none of that'll be possible unless we can take out this Hive leader.

Klaus is perched over a water tower coughing up blood.

"Can you move?" I ask and wonder if the young Keeper's about to kick the bucket right here on this very roof.

He shakes his head. "I need a minute."

"We don't have that kinda time."

Sneak and I move to the edge and peer over. She's using her eyes to scan the rooftops to find the Hive leader that's causing all the problems. But I don't need eyes to spot him. I can feel the bastard, moving amongst his Zee soldiers. For a moment I can even see through his eyes. He's watching as the bronze colored machine drives its fists into the ground, crushing a dozen zees in the process and that's when I realize not only is Dhal with them, he's driving that thing. The angle is all weird, but seeing things from the Hive leader's perspective helps me pinpoint his location. He's on the ground, surging forward with his men. The Zees outside the city gates are getting closer. Suicide mission or not, I know it's now or never.

There's another cable at my feet which leads to the corner of the next building. If I can kick off at just the right angle, I may have a chance of getting close enough to make a difference. Sneak watches my eyes trace back and forth and knows exactly what I'm thinking. She darts across the cable like a fearless acrobat and even I'm impressed with her agility. As soon as she's on the other side, I dangle from the wire with one hand and use the Katana in my other to hack it free. It takes three full chops before it cuts loose and my feet kick off at the very last second. A blur of speed and the ground races up to meet me, then the cable grows taut and I'm sailing less than a foot above the crowd of Zees. Landing will be the tricky part and when I let go I can feel my legs cycling wildly in mid air. I probably look like a human windmill, until my boots make contact with the first Zees skull and from there I go sprawling to the ground, knocking dozens of them down as I go.

A quick glance at my hand reveals the Katana isn't there anymore and now the Zees are starting to scramble back to their feet; I'm about to be lunch when I notice one of the poor wretches has a sword protruding from this side of his head. I lunge forward and slide the blade out, swinging it wide enough to kill another three before bringing it to my side. From there it's a mad hack and slash toward the Hive leader, who's sure as hell aware of my little stunt by now. The blade sweeps back and forth, cutting down several Zees at once, but there's always more to take their place. Already I can tell he's drawing his drones toward me, so focused on taking me out he doesn't notice the little girl drop down behind him. A glint of sun winks off her twin blades as she goes to work. Watching her move in the chaos around me, I see she isn't just a killer or an assassin. Sneak is an artist and watching her deliver precise, almost surgical death makes the hardened skin on my arms crawl with gooseflesh. The Hive leader barely has time to turn before a line opens across his throat and a thick stream of blood begins pumping from the wound. Sneak learned a thing or two from her encounter with the first Hive leader. Never underestimate your opponent. But more importantly, don't leave them an opening. Her next strike goes up through the bottom of his chin and into the brain. The light in his eyes dulls and goes out before he hits the ground.

This was the gap in leadership I was hoping for. If I can splice into Zee central and pirate the Hive leader's signal, before the Queen can tell he's down, we might have a chance of saving Ret and the others.

Sneak fights her way to me and works to fend them off as my eyes close and I see a burst Zee code streak past my closed eyes. My feet lift off the ground and I'm hovering about a foot in the air, arms splayed out, and suddenly every Zee around us stops dead. They're staring at me, their faces filled with unwavering adoration, their eyes glowing as brightly as the windows in Newton's Temple. I'm watching all of this through the thousands of Zees surrounding us. Sneak, poised in case they decide to attack. Bron, Ret and the others not quite sure what's going on. Only Dhal, locked inside his metal cocoon, high above the others, has any idea what's afoot. Then, in unison, the Zees drop to the ground, not in death, but in admiration. They're bowing before me. Now the others are truly in shock. I feel myself weakening and know I won't be able to hold this for long. By now, the Queen surely knows what I'm up to and is doing her damned best to slither into my head and cut my signal off, but I can tell she's having trouble. Her body is weakened and in terrible pain. I can feel every nerve in her body screaming as if they were my own. And then I realize why. The Queen is giving birth. And no sooner does that thought run through my brain then I feel a burst of light and everything goes black.

-88-

I open my eyes to find a crowd standing around me. I blink hard, wondering if they're Zees, preparing to eat the Queen's imposter. My eyes focus and I see Ret kneeling down beside me. Next to him is Dhal.

"Did you manage to close the city gates?" I ask and judging by the look on Ret's face it's clear they didn't.

"We barely had enough time to scoop you up and make it into this warehouse."

The building we're in is filled with electronic parts, scavenged by Prospectors from each corner of the ten territories. From here they're destined for White Rock, but something tells me this shipment won't ever make it. I lift my head to see Sneak and Klaus standing a few feet away.

"How did he get here?" I ask, motioning to Klaus in surprise.

"He found his way onto the roof and we heard him banging to be let inside."

A voice I know all too well pipes up from a pocket of shadow behind us. "Yeah, the little Keeper didn't find Bron's arms so funny this time, let me tell you."

Bron's talking in the third person, which is a good sign, but the strain I detect in his voice makes it clear enough he's still not sure about having me around. No doubt Ret must have settled his nerves after I'd saved their hides.

I get to my feet and dust myself off. Bron comes into the light. His arms and chest are splattered with Zee blood. In fact, all of them are and it becomes clear just how close a call it was. Bron isn't about to thank me for saving them and I can't entirely blame him. It wasn't long ago that I nearly killed them all, even Ret. But the situation's changed and I have to let them know.

"Skuld is dead," I say.

"What?" It's Oleg, off to the side and sitting on a make-shift stool, probably trying to figure out what he wants on his tombstone. "Did you see him die?" he asks.

"No," I reply. "Not exactly."

"Then how can you be sure?"

"He entered the Queen's chamber, that much I know. But it didn't go down the way he expected it to."

"She killed him." Dhal says, with clear disappointment. Skuld murdered Master Lund, the only father the boy had ever really known, and the kid wanted nothing more than to even the score. But revenge is a nasty little cycle that feeds on itself.

The sound of Zees pounding on the warehouse doors hits me for the first time. They've got the place barricaded, although it's clear by the way that sheet metal's bulging under the pressure, that it's not going to hold for long.

"When you took control of those Zees," Oleg says. "I was quite sure Skuld and the Queen were both dead."

"I wish that were so."

"Can you do that again?" he asks.

"I doubt it. She did something at the end that knocked me out of Zee central. Some sort of burst wave."

"Sounds like a mental EMP," Dhal says matter of factly.

Bron spits in disgust. "A what?"

"Electro magnetic pulse," Dhal replies.

"If only there was a way to block her signal," Ret adds. "The way Skuld was doing to you."

"That's not a terrible idea." Oleg says and turns to Dhal. "Think you can whip something together from the junk that's lying around?"

279

Dhal picks up what looks to me like a metal box covered in tiny switches. "Maybe, but I'll need some time, and even then the AOE wouldn't be larger than about ten meters."

Dhal sees Klaus scratching his head.

"Oh, yeah, sorry I forgot. Area of effect. It denotes the radius..."

Those Zees are still outside banging louder than ever and all I can think of is how much I wish Dhal would quite blabbing and start building. He's worse than Oleg, if that's even possible.

"If this thing works," the kid says, "it'll block anything within ten meters from sending or receiving Zee signals."

"Effectively neutralizing the Queen's ability to control her troops."

"For as long as it works, they won't be her Zees anymore," I say. "They'll be mine."

"Great! Then just send them in to kill her," Bron says.

"She can't," Oleg replies. "Once they enter the area of effect, as Dhal calls it, they'll be effectively cut off from all direction and go dormant. Likewise, if the device stops working, the Zees will once again be hers."

Ret looks about as frustrated as I feel. "Azina, can't you send out an order for the Zees to kill themselves?"

I shake my head. "I can make them step off a rooftop, but an all-out order to commit suicide just won't work. The sense of self-preservation must still be strong, even in Zees."

Bron smacks his metallic fist into his palm with a clang. "Damn shitbags."

Suddenly I'm hit with a burst of Zee code that's chock full of bad news. "Looks like we've got bigger problems."

The chatter in the room dies down and all I can hear is the sound of Zees hissing outside, trying their damnedest to break down our barricade. "The Queen," I say. "She's given birth."

89

Perhaps against my better judgement, I spill the beans about what happened to Skuld, that the Queen turned the crusty old bastard into some kind of love slave before twisting his head off.

Dhal's splicing a set of red and green wires with effortless skill. "That old gal doesn't waste any time, does she?"

The sound of crashing metal rings in our ears and we look over to see the weakened barricade has given way and Zees are streaming in. Dhal looks up from his work on the jamming device with panic in his eyes. He's probably wondering if there's enough time to hop back into the Titan, but I can already see there isn't. Klaus is the first one firing and the young Keeper hits three headshots in a row. All that manages to do is ignite Bron's competitive streak. The big man plants his feet and opens up. The first Zee to eat a 20mm shell is a palace guard, recently turned. These guys are the Patriarch's last line of defense, sworn to lay down their lives to protect him. If they've been infected, there's little hope the crusty old bastard is still in one piece. Soon, everyone but Dhal is firing, although even as he tinkers feverishly on his device, he must know we can't keep this up forever. Bron's heavy guns have managed to push them back to the entrance and now he's firing straight through, lobbing the occasional grenade. Bits and pieces of Zee guts fill the air in all directions. I'm about to tell Dhal to forget the jammer, that we're hi-tailing it out of here, when we hear the sound of a battle horn. We hold our fire. Even the Zees have stopped charging in. A second later there's a second horn blast, followed closely by a third.

"The hell is going on?" Ret asks, staring up into the darkened warehouse rafters as though trying to peer through the very walls.

"Keeper battle horns," Oleg exclaims in a reverent hush and all of us stare, dumbfounded.

"They haven't sounded since the Zee wars, over two hundred years ago."

"What does it mean?" Klaus asks.

"It means the Keepers are launching a counter attack."

90

The Zees aren't trying to get into the warehouse at all anymore and it doesn't take a genius to figure out why. Sneak, Ret and I scale a ladder to the roof, leaving Dhal to finish his jammer and the others to watch over him. Heat from the mid-afternoon sun warms my darkened flesh. Sneak rushes to the edge. From there she can see over the wall and she waves us over in a hurry. I'm not nearly prepared for what I see when I get there. A savage battle is raging outside the capital. On one side are a veritable ocean of Zees, rushing relentlessly forward. On the other is what looks like Keepers, from every corner of the ten territories. Impressive a sight as that is, it isn't the carnage below that shocks me. It's the strange machines the Keepers are fighting with. Mechanical pods on two bent legs, operated by men firing heavy machine guns. Others look like metallic elephants, sweeping aside dozens of Zees at once with their massive trunks. Ret's beside me, watching all this through a set of binoculars.

"Commander Tind," he says, as though the name's supposed to mean something. Doesn't take long for him to catch the blank expressions on our faces.

He points to a figure, barking out orders, staying cool in the heat of battle. Tind motions to a machine that looks a lot like the one Dhal was using in the courtyard earlier and sends it into a pack of approaching Zees. Even from a distance, the commander's presence is impressive, but already it's becoming clear that none of it will make a lick of difference, since he's outnumbered fifty to one. Machines or no machines, they won't stand a chance.

"We've got to help them," Ret cries. "Attack the Zees from behind and relieve the pressure on Tind's center line."

Even Sneak's shaking her head at what a bad idea it is and she's right.

"The only chance any of us have," I tell him, "is if we can get close enough to the Queen to use Dhal's jamming gizmo."

Ret isn't convinced. "But that's assuming he's able to build it in time or that it even works."

"And if we rush out there like fools," I shoot back. "We doom the human race to extinction." The full weight of my statement hits me as I watch Ret's gaze reel back to the battle below. What hits me isn't so much the extinction part, but more about including myself as a member of the human race. I'm not human anymore. The minute I was bitten, in the bowels of that underground shopping complex, I became something distinctly unhuman. If the Zees were about building up their own society instead of tearing down the ones around them, then I'd be the first to fight for co-existence. But, the truth is, they're an infestation and they need to be wiped off the face of the Earth.

Just then, Bron pokes his head through the hatch, showing off his discolored teeth and I know Dhal's got something he thinks is gonna work. I don't get a more than a single step toward him when something in the sky streaks overhead, casting a long, eerie shadow over us. A low flying bird is my first thought, but it's far too big and the wingspan… Bron must have seen it too 'cause he scrambles up and bolts in our direction.

"What kind of a bird was that?" His ears catch the sounds of men and monster below us, tearing each other apart, wild gunfire, and for the first time he sees what's underway. But the strange machines, smashing handfuls of Zees at a time, hardly seem to faze him. That giant bird is back overhead and now I can see it isn't an animal. It's the Queen's new son.

91

The realization hits us all at once and Bron's cannons stab the air and fill it with lead. The creature folds its wings and dives directly at us and I understand I'm witnessing the birth of a new breed of Zee. As if they weren't formidable enough already. Now there isn't any question; the Queen must be stopped or she'll continue to pump out these flying killing machines. He's in my head right away, scrambling my thoughts and trying to bring me to his will. He's a tough son of a bitch, especially given he's been around for all of ten minutes. In a flash I see the birth. The Queen, squatting over a trench dug in the ground, a tear splitting open between her legs and a set of claws sliding through. With almost practiced ease, its fingers grip the edges of the orifice and pull the rest of itself out. Her insides are being torn apart, but she knows she'll heal. She also knows Prior Skuld has provided her with everything she needs to fertilize thousands of flying monsters. But this is her first born and she gives it a name: Volg. To the Keepers they were Volgorath. Was the choice of name a display of irony, the final threads of the Queen's fading humanity?

The flash vision ends with just enough time to see Volg spread his wings at the last second and swing his legs out before him. Bron barely has enough time to react before Volg's clawed feet connect with his chest, throwing him back a dozen feet. The last I see of Bron is his body flying over the edge. Ret's right there with his shotgun and nearly gets a shot off before the flying Zee flicks it from his grasp like a child's toy. He's about to skewer him, right before our eyes, unless I can do something quick. The Katana is out with a flick of my wrist and cutting through the air a second later. But no

287

sooner does the move materialize in my brain than he can see it too. The bones along the edges of his wings are hard as steel and he parries each and every one of my attacks. Ret's got his boomstick again but can't get a clear shot. That doesn't stop Sneak from jumping in, head first. All I see are blurs of motion and sparks as the two of them face off. She's small and easily underestimated, but her clearest advantage is that he can't read her mind. That's when I see a hand grab the edge of the rooftop. It's Bron; in an unheard of display of quick thinking, he used his grappling hook to keep from falling to a certain death. The steel cable's still coiling back into his arm when he charges Volg at a full run, the veins in his neck, nearly bursting with rage. The blades in his palms eject and now he's twirling them viciously before him. Bron's almost on top of Volg when the Zee prince parries one of Sneak's overhand strikes and spins his body, sweeping Bron's legs out from under him. I throw everything I've got against him, knowing I don't have a chance of breaking through. But even he has his weaknesses and when he overextends, in an attempt to bring the sharpened point at the end of his wings down on Sneak's head, she's ready for him and slashes him across the face, opening his left eye like a ripe grape. He recoils at once and flaps his wings, hitting her with a burst of air that sends her skidding back. Two more thrusts and he's back in the air, trying to escape to a place where he can heal up. Ret's shotgun is bucking in his arms as he tries in vain to bring him down. I'm about to swing my repeater out when I catch sight of the grappling hook from Bron's arm cut through the air and bury itself in the thigh muscle of Volg's leg.

"I got myself a big one," Bron shouts and for a moment he looks like one of those old pictures of fishermen on the high seas. I can hear a whirring sound as the grappling hook starts to reel him in. But the flying

288

Zee isn't gonna go down without a fight and he flaps his wings, dragging Bron toward the edge of the roof. I grab hold of the big man at once, all of us do, and we're trying to prevent him from falling to his death for real this time.

"Cut the line," I shout.

But Bron's pretending not to hear me. The stubborn bastard is on a suicide mission and I know nothing I say will change his mind. He's even firing his 20mm and I see a handful of tracers whiz by Volg as he tries desperately to escape. One round goes clear through his right shoulder and suddenly the wing on that side stops flapping.

That's when Bron rotates his wrist twice, getting a good solid hold on the steel wire, and yanks it with everything he's got. Volg is jerked back like a faltering kite being pulled from the sky. Bron's pulled so hard the creature's about to come crashing into him, but that's exactly what the big man wants and when it happens, both of Bron's twelve inch blades are waiting for him. The first tears a six inch gash in the creature's chest and the second goes clean through its skull. The light in Volg's eyes, fixed firmly on Bron, begins to fade at once. The blades retract and the Zee slumps to the ground.

"This isn't Bron's day to die," the big man says.

He might be right, but the day isn't over yet.

92

Back in the warehouse, Dhal's tongue is sticking out as he puts the finishing touches on his jamming device. Ret's bent over, leaning on one knee, trying to catch his breath. Bron, on the other hand, has got his chest puffed out and I'm sure he's about to launch into a bad fish catching joke.

Across from me, Oleg's handing bits of metal panelling to Dhal, staring on rather helplessly. Engineering isn't the old man's area of expertise and the control freak in him is having a hard time dealing with it. And I can't entirely blame him, either. Last we saw, those Keepers outside were slowly being flanked by a fresh group of Zees from the south and it won't be long before the human army is completely surrounded and destroyed.

Bron makes his way to the now mangled warehouse barricade and peers out. A quick hand signal reveals no Zees in sight. Not that it's much of a surprise. The Queen's pulling all available resources in order to wipe Commander Tind's troops from the battlefield.

A few agonizing minutes later, Dhal looks up with a beaming smile and that goofy look of his tells me one thing.

The jammer is ready.

There's a second, smaller device in his hand with a faded red button on top. The whole thing looks cobbled together from bits of junk, which shouldn't be a surprise since that's exactly how it was made.

Bron hardly looks impressed. "Couldn't you just turn all this crap into a big bomb and blow her Zee ass away?"

"If I had more time, I prolly could," Dhal replies and even I can tell that isn't just his teenage arrogance talking.

He raises the device in the air. "This button activates the jammer," he explains.

I point to a similar looking button on the jammer itself.

"If you wanna get that close, be my guest, but I think our only shot of making this work is to toss it in and jam her remotely."

The corner of Ret's mouth twitches in a show of doubt. "But we still need to find someone dumb enough to walk right up to her."

Bron's metal hand is in the air, volunteering before Ret even finishes. Not a bit surprising, but I know that's not gonna work.

"We need your heavy guns to keep the Zees off of us," I tell him. "It'll have to be someone else."

I can see that Ret's about to step up, in spite of his 'dumb' comment from before, when Dhal beats him to it. "I can use the Titan to get closer than anyone. When that metal cockpit is closed and sealed, nothing can touch me. Once it's in place, I'll activate it from inside."

He turns to me. "After that, the rest is up to you, Azina."

Yeah, no shit it is. "Check your weapons," I bark. "I don't want anyone running dry or jamming when we're in the thick of it." There's a mounting weight creeping over my shoulders, in part because I'm still not entirely sure what to do in the narrow window of time the Zee's are under my control. When I find myself in difficult situations, I've always preferred to think on my feet. Never have been much of a planner, but now the future of mankind is hanging in the balance, all I can hope is that I won't choke.

93

We arrive before Newton's Temple not long after, the sounds of gunfire echoing in the distance. It's a good sign because it means Tind's men are still alive. Dhal's just ahead of us, driving that colossal smoke belching machine. He's got the remote with him in the cockpit. The jammer is nestled in the machine's left hand. Predictably, Klaus and Oleg look as pale as a bucket of goat's milk. Next to me stands Bron and the dense muscles in his jaw keep flexing in anticipation. In a strange way, I can't help but think that he was born for this very moment. And maybe, in some other reality, the one where Oleg's pensive gods sit around contemplating new ways to make the lives of mortal men hell, this has all been foretold.

A thought which is suddenly dashed by the sound of a thunderous crash as Dhal brings one of the machine's giant fists down on the temple archway. The entrance wasn't nearly large enough for him to pass through and the look of utter horror on Oleg's face is almost comical.

"That's sacrilege," he mutters.

I slap the old man's back with a firm hand. "We're just getting started."

With a kick from one of the Titan's bronzed feet, the double entrance doors shatter into thousands of splinters. There's silence and murky darkness inside for nearly a full second before we hear hissing and see the glow of hundreds of Zees eyes, as they sprint out toward us.

If there was any doubt before that the Queen was inside, it's gone now.

The attacking Zees barely reach the light before Bron opens fire. The concussions are so loud I feel my eardrums threatening to burst. One round rips through five Zees before it detonates, plastering brains in all directions. I still feel that sting when a Zee dies, but right now Oleg's got a different kind of pain on his face. This is the holiest place in all of the ten territories and there's no ifs, ands or buts. We're about to rip it apart.

One Zee, wearing a tattered wedding dress, manages to get a few yards from Klaus before I land two rounds in her face and one in her brain box. She falls at once, skidding along the ground, her lips coming to rest against Klaus' Keeper boots. He glances back.

"Nice shot."

"Go for the head," I remind him.

Truth be told, the failure wasn't his alone. Sneak doesn't use guns, only blades, and it's her job to take care of any Zees that manage to breach our perimeter. She slices her blade clean through the neck of a shrieking Zee who used to be the temple's high priest and then spin kicks the severed head back through the temple archway. But this isn't Sneak trying to showboat. That's her funny little way of telling me she got the message, that it won't happen again.

The flood of Zees slackens and, with squeaks and groans, Dhal begins maneuvering his metallic beast inside. A pile of dead and wounded Zees clutter the entrance and Dhal steams ahead anyway, squishing many of them into a bloody pulp.

The minute we enter I realize the word temple doesn't do the place justice. It's absolutely immense, webbed in deep shadow. Then I catch a glimpse of something in the distance I know Oleg's gonna hate. The Queen has set up her little nursery over the main altar.

The ceiling seems to reach up forever and that's when a blur of movement overhead catches my attention and I know it isn't any of that fancy artwork of Newton and falling apples that's done it. The Queen's given birth to another Zee and, with that epiphany, something else becomes obvious. She's lured us into a trap.

There's a card game that's popular in the entertainment district of Sotercity called Occam's Razor, where players try and bluff their way to victory. Hold your cards close to your chest and feign weakness. Cocky opponents are the easiest to beat. The Queen may not know a damn thing about Occam's Razor, but she'd make one hell of a player.

Letting me see exactly where she was, setting herself over the altar, out in the open, exposed and, best of all, leading us to believe she'd only given birth to a single flying Zee. Although it doesn't take more than scanning the high temple ceiling and the shadows flitting above us to see how foolish we were. I'm struck a second later by a blast from Zee central. Yet another thing she'd held in reserve and I feel like my head's about to come apart at the seams. That's when I feel my right arm about to reach for the Katana on my back and I use everything I've got to hold it in place and block her out. It's clear enough what she's after. She wants me to cut down my own people, just as Skuld tried to have me do back in Sotercity.

My hands are pushing against each of my temples, trying to quell the storm in my head. And, through it all, I become dimly aware of two things. The first is Bron, glancing my way with a dark concern settling over his face, like he knew this was going to happen and maybe he should blow me to bits before I have another freak out. The second has to do with the flying Zees, circling overhead. The air fills with the sound of hissing and I realize at once they're diving down on us.

Ret shouts and everyone fires into the air frantically. All except for me and Dhal. The kid and that machine of his are grinding forward, metal gears whining, smoke belching from the exhaust pipe behind his cockpit, chunks of marble floor churning up with each colossal step. We're about halfway to the altar, Dhal's proxy clutching the jamming device, and it seems like nothing can stop him. Tracers from Bron's cannons light up the temple, suddenly illuminating the real target of their assault. The flying Zees aren't coming for us, at least not yet. They're after Dhal.

Bron cuts one of them right out of the air and it tumbles into a row of pews with a violent shudder. I'm still struggling to push the Queen out of my head when I see three of those things land on Dhal's bronze shoulders and use their razor sharp claws to slash at exposed cogs and hoses. His free hand reaches back and grabs hold of one of them, before it can squirm away, and crushes it into a meaty stew.

Barely a second later, two more crash into Bron and send him sailing through the air. He hits a mural, depicting Newton's childhood, shattering it to pieces. They land and now they're moving toward him, claws glinting in the dim light. Bron isn't moving and I'm not sure I can make it there in time to help him. I'm running, but the Queen's still slamming around inside my head; every step is a gargantuan effort. The first to reach him raises its hand to strike and immediately bursts into flames. Bron's used his flame thrower and pivots to let the other one have a taste but, before he's able to, the Zee lands a crushing blow to his arm, denting the nozzle and rendering it useless. The blades pop out of Bron's arms at once, but I can already tell he's woozy from whacking his head against the wall. A set of claws rake across his chest, leaving deep horizontal gashes. As he looks down and sees it, for the first time I can tell he's worried. The big oaf's never seen his own blood in battle before.

Still fresh, the flying Zee lunges forward to sink its teeth into Bron's neck. The big man barely manages to avoid the attack, but I know he's nearly done for. The others have their own problems to worry about and I'm growing more convinced that the Queen's little plan has worked perfectly. I'm ten feet away from the struggle going on between Bron and the flying Zee when I see it retract its arm for the killing blow. The anger building up within me is just enough to drown out the Zee code buzzing through my brain. There's a broken pew between us and I leap over it, Katana in hand, with the clear knowledge I've only got one chance to keep Bron from being skewered. The Katana slices through the Zee's elbow and the arm splits in two, dark Zee blood pumping from the wound. It turns, incredulous, and that's when I spin, the blade whispering just below its chin, and I watch as its head rolls to the ground. But if there's one thing I've learned about Zees, it's that there's only one real way to kill them. A final thrust into the brain cavity puts its lights out forever.

I rush to Bron at once. He's bleeding badly and Ret's too far away to be much help, tearing a flying Zee in half with his automatic shotgun. Behind us is a wooden statue of Newton, complete with white flowing robe. I can only imagine the kind of palpitations Oleg will have when he sees what I'm about to do, but right now there isn't much choice. I slice a wide strip off Newton's robe, turning it into what the Dusters used to call a miniskirt. The piece I cut wraps neatly around Bron's wide chest and should stop some of the bleeding. I'm just starting to feel hopeful when I spot Dhal's giant machine, teetering with over a half dozen winged Zees ripping at it. They haven't managed to pry the cockpit open, but they don't need to. Sparks are bursting from the machine's giant back and shoulders. They've inflicted crippling damage and I gasp as I see it wobble and then collapse, face-first. The jammer skitters from its open fingers and I don't know if Dhal is still alive, but one thing isn't in doubt: the device won't be close enough to the Queen to jam her signal.

-95-

My heart drops when I see Ret sling the shotgun over his back and break into a run. He's about to do something foolish. He's gonna grab the jammer and run it into range before activating it by hand. I start to scream out for him to stop when I see him reach out to snag Klaus's robe, just as a flying Zee crashes into him. Ret sails through the air, arms and legs kicking wildly, before colliding with a stone pillar. He sinks to the floor, leaving a trail of blood running down the white stone. I rush to his side, suddenly aware it was Klaus he was trying to stop from running in, knowing it's a certain death sentence.

"Bron," I shout, pointing to Klaus. "Covering fire!"

Ret's eyes are closed and he looks dead. But there isn't even time to find out for sure.

Those things are still tearing at Dhal's cockpit as Klaus rushes past them. One of then reaches for him, right as a shell from Bron's 20mms cuts his arm in two. Now all of us are firing with everything we have, in a vain attempt to clear a path for Klaus. He reaches the box and nearly trips, pulling it to his chest. He's maybe thirty yards from the Queen now and she's sitting behind her protective shell, working hard to pump out those flying Zees. Even from here I can tell she sees him and the message over Zee central is loud and clear.

STOP HIM!

The Zees on Dhal's machine take to the air in pursuit. Bron and the rest of us unload with everything we've got, shooting down two more. And that's when our luck runs out. I'm in the middle of fishing out a fresh magazine for my repeater and Sneak's locked in a heated battle with one of those bastards who circled back to take out Oleg.

299

A big, nasty looking Zee touches down, right in Klaus' path, and gets one of Bron's searing shells in the face, spraying the young Keeper with black gore as he runs by. Tracers cut through the air, trying to intercept one that's diving in too quickly. Bron cuts him down and the creature crashes into the center aisle, knocking Klaus to the ground. I wanna run toward him, but I know I'll never get there in time. A second later, the Keeper's back on his feet and limping. His robe is torn and, even from here, I can see the trail of blood behind him. Then I catch another signal coming from the Queen and a swarm of regular Zees comes rushing out from behind the altar. She's kept a reserve force, as a last resort, and even as we continue pouring lead into their ranks, I see we're not going to get them all. It's hard to tell how close Klaus gets before the Zees take him down. He's on the floor, face down, and I can hear him screaming as the Zees tear the flesh from his lips. I wanna reach out and end his suffering, but it's over in a matter of seconds. For a moment the temple is silent, except for the sound of Bron's heavy breathing and another noise I can't quite make out at first. It's coming from the mound of Zees ravaging Klaus' corpse and it sounds like... beeping. The Queen's code that's been bouncing around inside my head suddenly stops and I realize what's happened. Klaus must have activated the jammer, right as he was taken down. If we want any chance of stopping the Queen it's now or never.

I know already that ordering the Zees to commit suicide won't work. That survivalist instinct is buried deep within, a carryover from their long lost humanity that was never completely extinguished. And if one could nail down a single prime directive, which has guided humanity throughout the ages, it would be this: kill or be killed. No, I won't try and order the Zees to bash their own brains out. They won't intentionally harm

300

themselves. But being one of them, there's something else I do know about Zees. Something they proved when they tore the Hive leader to shreds, a violent remnant from the human code developed, as Oleg says, over thousands of years. The perfect willingness to kill one another.

I feel my eyes begin to glow bright as I lift nearly a foot off the ground. I'm syncing with the totality of Zee central and suddenly an incredible feeling of oneness washes over me. The Zees are an extension of my physical body. I see what they see. Feel what they feel and they are engaged in a battle outside the city walls and are about to win. Commander Tind and his army have been reduced to a small fraction of men and machines, trapped on a tiny outcropping, experiencing what they can only assume are the final moments of their lives. That's when I form the signal and blast it out in all directions simultaneously. The compliance is immediate. Only the Zees within the jammer's range remain oblivious. In the blink of an eye, Zees everywhere begin attacking one another. Gnashing with teeth and hands. Ripping each other apart. Commander Tind's men stand, in stunned silence, as this swarming army of Zees, that moments before was on the verge of wiping them out, has now turned on one another. It doesn't take more than a few moments for the battlefield to become a lake of dark Zee blood and I can't help but feel a hint of sadness as I feel the last of them wink out.

Soon, Dhal's device begins to sputter and the Queen once again regains control, although the extent of her army has been reduced to the handful of Zees who remained in the cone of silence. It doesn't take more than a few seconds to blow them away and then we approach the altar. Bron, walking slowly and looking pale. Ret limping beside him, helped along by Sneak. He's alive, but clutching his side like more than one of his ribs have

301

been snapped in two. Then comes Dhal, free from his metallic cockpit. Beside me is Oleg and all of us stand before the hardened shell the Queen has wrapped around herself. Only her face is exposed; a hideously insectile thing, that doesn't contain an ounce of the humanity she once possessed. Although the look of defeat on her face does make me wonder.

I glance over at Klaus' mangled body and then back to the Queen.

"Fast or slow?" I ask her and the answer she gives doesn't surprise me one bit.

-96-

6 Months Later

Ret's leaning coolly on the end of his shovel, watching a bank of white puffy clouds roll in. This soil isn't going to till itself. That's what I'm thinking, Sneak beside me, dripping with sweat in the noonday sun. If you'd told me before all this I'd hang up my repeater and trade it in for a shovel and a farm, outside of Sotercity, I probably would have kicked your teeth in. I guess I never thought of myself as the settling down, domestic type.

Then I catch sight of what Ret's really looking at. It isn't the clouds overhead. It's a cloud of dust, approaching from a distance. I can't help but wonder if it's a horde of Zees. Not that I can sense them anymore, least not after they started the reversal treatments.

It isn't long before the dust cloud gets close enough for us to make out what's creating it. Fast, experimental contraptions, on three wheels, called Trikes. There are two of them and I have a feeling I know who's on board.

Bron and Dhal tear up the dirt path, leading to our farmhouse, and come skidding to a stop. The big guy probably still has a scar where those claws tore his chest open, although I couldn't say for sure since he's decked out in a fancy purple uniform. He's been made head of the new Patriarch's personal security team and I'm sure he's come by just to gloat.

Dhal stands, cupping his ass like it's about to fall off.

Sneak's fingers dance through the air and I pass her message along to Dhal. "The outhouse is around back, if you need it."

Dhal laughs and so does Bron. "It's these damn wheels," Bron says, wiping a layer of grime from his

303

brow. "They're so hard, I probably can't have kids anymore."

"Then there's hope for the human race," Ret fires without missing a beat.

"I found a fascinating document in the archives," Dhal cuts in, ignoring the light-hearted spirit of the moment, "about how Dusters once covered the metal rims of their vehicles with pockets of air."

"That is fascinating," I say. Then to Bron. "I guess the kid's really taken to his new job then."

Dhal squares his shoulders. "Coordinating the Prospectors and releasing the hoarded technology held at White Rock is no small job."

"I hope Oleg's nomination as Patriarch hasn't gone to the old bastard's head."

Sneak sends me a quick sign to ease up a little. Maybe she's right.

"Oleg might be the best Patriarch we've ever had," Dhal says, beaming. "I mean, his first act was to open the technological vaults for everyone. No more secrets."

For once, even Ret doesn't look skeptical.

I feel Bron's eyes running up the length of my arm. Glancing down, I see what he's looking at. Olive skin. I realize I haven't seen the big oaf since the service for Klaus, Krantz, and Master Lund… but more importantly since my treatments began. The contraption underneath Sotercity was still there and, with a bit of tinkering, it didn't take long to make it do what I'd been after all along. Reverse my condition and get the old Azina back.

"How many more treatments?" Bron asks.

"One," I say, spotting a dark patch under my bicep I hadn't noticed before. "Maybe two." I don't tell them of course, but there are still some residual elements I'll be sad to see disappear. Night vision, for one, can be mighty handy on your way to that outhouse in the middle of the night. Oleg asked if I could sense any other Hives before

304

they began the treatments and I told him I couldn't. But, either way, if another group of unfortunate souls ever stumble upon one again, the policy is simple enough. Keep it sealed.

It was around then that Oleg did his best to explain why some of the infected had become Hive leaders and others were reduced to simple drones. The reason had something to do with a FOXO gene, responsible for longevity. A gene which feverishly repairs damaged cells and strengthens a person's immune system. Perhaps it's one of the reasons some people can spend their entire lives in the entertainment district, performing all sorts of debaucherous acts, and still live to see 90.

"How long will it take you to get ready?" Bron asks.

"Ready? For what?"

"Oleg's prepared a banquet in your honor. He's got a whole speech prepared."

"Oh, why does that not surprise me?"

Ret's smiling. He knows mingling with a group of stiff upper crust Keepers is the last thing I wanna do.

The two trikes catch my eye. "I hope you don't plan on taking us on those things."

Sneak nudges me again.

"Come now, Azina," Bron says, cupping my shoulders with his cold metallic hands. "It'll be fun. I hear Dehlia's making her famous chicken dish." The big oaf's eyes light up and for a moment he looks like an oversized child.

Ret's nodding with gentle approval. Even Sneak's wearing a wide grin. I can tell she's anxious to feel the wind in her hair and I know now, without a doubt, that that sense of family and belonging I've always sought might have been with me all along.

Thanks for reading Hive: The Complete Collection!

For more post-apocalyptic action, check out Primal
Shift Vol 1 & 2!